FOUL PLAY ON WORDS

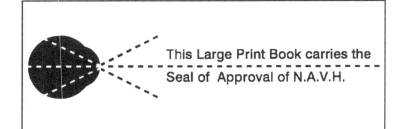

This Large Print Book carries the
Seal of Approval of N.A.V.H.

A MYSTERY WRITER'S MYSTERY

FOUL PLAY ON WORDS

BECKY CLARK

THORNDIKE PRESS

A part of Gale, a Cengage Company

Farmington Hills, Mich • San Francisco • New York • Waterville, Maine
Meriden, Conn • Mason, Ohio • Chicago

LIBRARY OF CONGRESS CIP DATA ON FILE.
CATALOGUING IN PUBLICATION FOR THIS BOOK
IS AVAILABLE FROM THE LIBRARY OF CONGRESS

ISBN-13: 978-1-4328-6280-0 (hardcover alk. paper)

Published in 2019 by arrangement with Midnight Ink, an imprint of Llewellyn Publications, Woodbury, MN 55125-2989 USA

Printed in the United States of America
1 2 3 4 5 6 7 23 22 21 20 19

A 12007 292704

For writers everywhere,
even ones like Garth.

ONE

Waiting for someone to pick you up at the airport is like being forced to be eight years old again. Waiting at the curb for the school bus. Waiting in the corridor shoulder-to-shoulder with your line buddy until everyone in class has puffed out their cheeks, holding invisible "Quiet Bubbles" in their mouths until it's acceptably hush-hush-hallway enough to march out to recess. Waiting for your mom to rescue you much too late from a disastrous birthday party, like when she forces you to go to Tommy Ryan's, that annoying hair-puller. She promised I'd have fun once I got there.

Why do parents lie like that? Did she really need two hours' peace that desperately? If she'd only leveled with me that she needed a break from my incessant chatter, I'd have gladly sat quietly in a dim room mentally thinking up rhymes for my teacher, Mrs. McRucker's, name. That always amused my eight-year-old self.

My thirty-year-old self wasn't as easily appeased.

Again, I edged out from under the shelter of the overhang to peer down the roadway, hurrying back when rain began dripping off the tip of my nose.

"Where is she?" I spoke to myself, even though several people also waited nearby. Perhaps like me they were waiting for someone — parent, spouse, pal, clown car — to swoop in and pick them up at the Portland airport. Behind me, the terminal. In front of me, past the large concrete overhang, soft Oregon rain. To my left, bored or anxious or annoyed passengers, resigned or worried or irritated that their designated rides hadn't shown up yet. To my right, the MAX light-rail train loading passengers for the trip to the Portland city center or other travel hubs. I'd already watched seven trains on the two tracks come and go. But still no Viv.

Despite my exasperation at having to wait for her, I couldn't help but smile when I thought about hanging out with her again. I hadn't seen Viv in a few years, but we'd had some glorious adventures in the past. Sharing hotel rooms at writers' conferences like two teenagers at a slumber party, sitting on

8

panels, teaching workshops together, and going on that book tour. Oy, that book tour. Our first books were published within three weeks of each other, so we'd organized a tour together through eight states stretching from my home in Colorado to hers in Oregon, hitting every major city as well as many podunk towns in between.

Our publisher didn't foot the bill for our book tour. Viv and I paid for everything out of our miniscule advances, so after every signing event, she talked our way into free meals, drinks, or hotel rooms along our route. After a while, I couldn't remember what was the truth about us and what was the fictional embellishment she wrapped us in. Regardless, we seemed like the two most interesting women in the world. So what if it wasn't completely accurate? At least it was entertaining, especially for us.

If I felt uncomfortable when she got too outlandish, Viv convinced me that it was what people came to hear. We were obligated to give them their money's worth. When I reminded her we spoke for free, she said, "If they only met boring old us, they'd be disappointed. At least now they have awesome stories to tell at parties about the time they got to hang out with those two crazy writers."

9

I laughed out loud. Did anyone actually remember any of her tall tales?

A man standing nearby smiled at me, then spoke with a British accent. "I shall go barmy if I have to wait much longer, but it seems you bloody well don't mind waiting to be picked up." He gestured toward the terminal. "I heard a bloke inside say there was a tie-up on the motorway."

"Actually, I'm thinking about turning around and flying right back to Denver. Or at least going back in for a grilled cheese sandwich. With bacon." I eyed the terminal doors behind us.

"Don't like Portland?"

"I love Portland. But I'm here to speak at a writers' conference, and I'm nervous. I've been on panels before, and taught workshops, but my friend Viv, who's the organizer, wants me to give the keynote speech at the banquet on Saturday."

"Are you an author?"

I nodded and thrust out my hand. "Charlemagne Russo. Charlee. I write mysteries. But I'll bet you've never heard of me."

He shook my hand and quirked his mouth apologetically. "I'm Sir Richard Headley. Sorry. I don't read mysteries."

"Ooh, I'm in the presence of royalty." I gave a demure little bend of the knee, making him laugh.

"Nah, not really. Just pretending. Call me Ricky." The posh British accent was gone, replaced by a flat Midwestern one. "I'm from Nebraska. Practicing my accents. I was in the Russian Politburo on the way here."

I raised my eyebrows at him, hoping there was more explanation coming.

"I travel a lot — I'm a motivational speaker — and believe you me, every single person on this planet pretends to be something they're not and feels like a fraud. And some of them actually are."

"Like me."

"I'm sure you're not."

"Are you here to . . . motivationally speak?"

He shook his head. "Friend's wedding. Haven't seen him in years. Not really sure why I agreed. The things we do for friends."

"Indeed. I'm even using my own hotel points and I flew in early because flights on Wednesday were cheaper." I peered hopefully at the cars coming down the passenger pick-up lane, but they all stopped for other travelers. "I should have called a cab or taken the MAX, though."

"Same here. I'm supposed to be taken for a tuxedo fitting, but I don't know where. Otherwise I'd be in a cab." Ricky glanced at

11

his phone, then dropped it back in his pocket. "So, tell me. What does one do at a writers' conference? Surely you don't sit around and write."

"Well, sometimes, depending on the workshop you're in. It's a group of writers, I think about three hundred this weekend. All different skill levels and all genres, although some conferences focus on just mystery or romance or sci-fi or whatever. It starts Friday afternoon with pitch appointments —"

"Pitch appointments?"

"Writers looking for literary agents or publishers can get short meetings with them to see if there's interest in whatever story they're working on. The agents ask for a few chapters or the whole manuscript, and then the writer can spend the rest of the conference giddy with relief. Or they might get the brush-off and decide never to write another word as long as they live. Never, ever, ever."

Ricky smiled and showed his dimples. "You seem to have some experience with that."

"Yep. If you've never wanted to quit writing, you've probably never shown your work to anyone."

"Is that all that happens over the weekend?

People either get manic or depressed?"

"Nope. That's just the fun part." I smiled, hoping to get him to show those dimples again, and was rewarded. "There are also critiques of pages you submit —"

"More heartbreak —"

"Lots more. But there are also workshops about all kinds of writing-related topics, and you get to meet other writers, some of whom are famous —"

"Like you."

"No. Famous ones. I'm midlist. Nobody knows me."

"I think you're selling yourself short. You were asked to give a keynote speech at the banquet of a weekend conference. I've never been to one of these things, but I suspect that's where they put the most famous of their faculty."

I wrinkled my nose. "I told you, the organizer of this conference is a friend of mine. She couldn't get anyone else."

Ricky sighed at me like my father would have. "Tell me about your speech."

I made a noise in my throat. "It's called Seven Things I Know About Writing."

"And they are . . . ?"

My mind blanked. I squinched my eyes but that didn't help, so I pulled the notes out of my messenger bag. I flipped and shuffled pages, all strike-throughs and scribbles, trying to identify any of the seven things.

Ricky held out his hand. "Can I see?"

I offered the pages. They shook gently as I held them out, which surprised me a little. My tremor hadn't bothered me very much in the few weeks since I'd found out what really happened to my dad. I'd had the tremor for years, since his funeral, but maybe I could soon be free of it.

"You may need to Lysol your eyeballs after you read this," I said.

He was holding the opposite end of the pages. "I'll take my chances."

I finally let go, and he pursed his lips while he skimmed the pages. "This is good." He pulled a pen from his shirt pocket. He cocked his head at me. "May I?"

I had no idea what he wanted to do, but he certainly couldn't hurt that mess any worse than I already had.

He went back to the first page and circled single words. Then he turned to the blank back of the last page, flipping back and forth through the text as he wrote a list. When he finished, he stepped closer to me and pointed at the list with his pen. "These are the keywords for your seven main points. Now I just need to —"

into the front. After he hooked his seat belt, he gave me a wave and disappeared into rainy Portland.

"That right there was fate," I muttered to myself. A professional speaker to help me figure out my keynote speech? I must have done a good deed in a past life. Or I owed the Universe one. Either way, I was happy to comply.

I reviewed the ACHIEVE acronym and tried to memorize the corresponding keywords. I could type them into my phone and use that for my notes. The idea of my nerves magnifying my tremor and making the pages quake like an aspen tree in the wind during my speech made me a bit queasy. I'd forgotten to ask Viv if I'd have a podium to rest my papers on. But this would be better anyway; I could use my phone with the acronym and the keywords showing. Uh oh. What if I forgot to charge my phone? When that had happened a few weeks ago, I'd almost gotten myself killed. Since then I'd been trying to keep at least 65 percent power, but who knew what would happen this weekend when I was out of my routine.

Curious, I pulled out my phone: 48 percent. Darn it. Better to memorize.

I had only reviewed keywords up to the C

in ACHIEVE when Viv screamed up to the curb in her Toyota.

"Finally!"

She popped the trunk from her seat but didn't get out of the car to help or to hug. I lifted my rolling carry-on into it and slammed it shut, hurrying to avoid any more of the misty weather. My bangs were already plastered to my forehead, and I knew that when I shook out my braid later, after it dried, I'd have kinky hair that would make a witch proud.

I slipped into the passenger seat, dropping my messenger bag at my feet. "Hi. Did you get stuck in that accident —"

Viv roared away from the curb before I even got my seat belt buckled.

"Charlee, my daughter's been kidnapped."

Two

I clawed at my seat belt, trying to buckle it as I absorbed Viv's words. "Kidnapped? Hanna? Why? How? When?"

Viv didn't answer. Her head swiveled at the heavy airport traffic as she tried a breakneck merge. I felt everything rushing too fast — the traffic, the Toyota, the MAX train on the tracks parallel to us, my thoughts. It was too soon after Melinda's murder for me to be involved in chaos again. First with my agent, and now my friend? I want to write about crimes, not be involved in them.

"Did you call the cops?"

"No, they said they'd kill her if I got the cops involved."

"You have to let the police handle this, Viv." It was excellent advice, even though it wasn't what I did when Melinda was murdered.

"No. I shouldn't even have told you."

Viv continued to drive like Mario Andretti, swiveling her head and agitating her blond bob like it was a washing machine. While I wanted answers to so many questions, I didn't trust her to talk and maintain control of the car at this speed. It wasn't too long before traffic stalled in front of us and she was forced to slow to a crawl. She beat a fist on the steering wheel and spewed a litany of expletives I'd never heard strung together in quite such a manner.

"Okay. Now talk to me. Tell me exactly what happened."

Viv turned my way and I saw her dark lip liner but no lipstick. Like she'd gotten interrupted while putting on her face for the day. "I got a phone call this morning and someone said they had Hanna and not to call the cops or they'd kill her."

"But why?"

Viv inserted her car into the fast lane and earned an angry honk from the car behind us.

"Why Hanna?" I repeated.

"I don't know."

"When did you last see her? Did you have a fight?"

"No, nothing like that. We had a game night a couple weeks ago. She beat me at Scrabble. Everything seemed . . . fine."

"Why did you pause? What aren't you saying?"

"Things have been . . . challenging with Hanna the last few years, but I thought we'd turned a corner. Maybe I was wrong." Viv changed lanes too fast and with barely enough room.

With my eyes squinched tight, I asked, "Have you called her? Gone by her house?"

"Of course I did. She's not answering her phone and her car isn't at her apartment." Viv took her eyes off the traffic and stared at me. "Charlee, I need your help."

"I can't do anything!" My voice pitched up two octaves. It was well documented that my sleuthing skills only worked in fiction, not real life. I'd just asked all the questions I could think of and no answers had clicked in my brain like you see on cop dramas. "I don't want anything to do with this. I'm way out of my depth here. Take the next exit back to the airport." I glanced over my right shoulder to see if she could change lanes. Pulling out my phone, I said, "I'll call my brother Lance. He's a Denver cop. He'll know —"

Viv leaned across and knocked the phone to the floor. "No! No cops. I'm sorry I said anything." She kept one eye on traffic and the other on me groping around for my

21

phone. When I came up with it, she stared fiercely until I shut it off and dropped it back into my bag.

She groaned but calmed the teensiest bit, the fierceness replaced by concern. "You solved your agent's murder. I need your help. I don't know what's happening. I can't call the cops. Hanna is an adult — twenty-five years old — and she doesn't even live with me. There's nothing the cops can do since there's no evidence of a crime. You should know that. I'm not even sure it's true — maybe it's a bad prank. It was a cryptic phone call from a blocked number." She glanced at traffic beginning to move again, then back to me. "I told you, Hanna and I have a . . . difficult relationship these days. But I need to find her. I can't risk anything happening to her. You have to help me. I'm begging you, Charlee."

I thought back to all the help Viv had given me with my career over the years. She'd taken me under her wing at that conference, introduced me to Melinda, who became my agent soon afterward. I'd always suspected Viv had pulled some strings and went out on a limb to get Melinda to agree to represent me. She was perhaps the spark that had ignited my career all those years ago.

It broke my heart, but I said, "You know I'd do anything for you, but there's nothing I can do about this." I couldn't look at her.

"Yes, there is. The kidnappers don't know you, so you can skulk around and help me find out what's going on. They're probably following me, watching my movements. I just know it." Viv sped up, passing cars by narrow margins and finally shooting off at an exit into the city.

Prickles formed on the back of my neck. "If they're following you, they've already seen me. Besides, skulking around isn't a big part of my skill set." I glanced at the cars around us. Nobody looked kidnapper-ish. I didn't want to tell her that my investigation into Melinda's murder hadn't gone very well and I was likely to get Hanna killed in the process. "I can't, Viv. Call the cops. That's their job."

She didn't say another word until we'd skidded up under the circular portico at the Pacific Portland Hotel ten nerve-wracking minutes later. She popped the trunk but didn't move from her seat, staring straight ahead. "Fine. If you're not going to help me find Hanna, at least help me with the conference."

"The conference? You didn't cancel the conference? You have to."

She snapped her head toward me. "I can't. It's too late. It starts in two days. I can't afford to cancel this late." She fluttered one hand at me, indicating I should get out. "Be there for me, since I can't."

I collected my messenger bag from the floor, slid out of my seat, and stepped to the concrete. Holding open the door, I leaned in to try and talk sense into her, but I saw her pleading eyes and that pathetic lip line. "Fine. You concentrate on Hanna and I'll help with the conference."

Viv expelled a big breath. "I can't thank you enough."

Before I could ask about the specifics of what she needed me to do, she said, "Oh, and all my main volunteers got food poisoning, but I made some calls and think I got some others. And whatever you do, don't tell anyone about Hanna. Especially not Jack, the concierge. They're friends."

She zoomed away, only to back up ten seconds later with her trunk bobbing.

I grabbed my suitcase and slammed the trunk. "Call me as soon as you —" She was gone before I straightened. The things we do for friends, indeed.

I don't know how long I stood in the middle of the lobby of the Pacific Portland Hotel. I still held the handle of my rolling suitcase, and my messenger bag was wadded up under my arm. My unfocused eyes gazed all the way across the lobby, through the floor-to-ceiling windows and past the patio area where I assumed the pool and hot tub lived. I wished a nice soak in the Jacuzzi could make all this disappear.

Someone touched my elbow. "Ma'am? Ma'am, are you okay?"

I blinked at the twenty-something man studying me with concern. His brown hair tousled with expert care, he looked like he belonged in a boy band. He wore a name tag that read *Giacomo, Concierge.*

"Can I help you?"

Glancing behind me toward the front door, then past Giacomo toward the registration desk, I assessed my options. Hightail it back to Denver or check into the hotel, the chaos, the drama, the trouble?

"Ma'am?"

The concern in his voice shook me awake. "I'm checking in."

"Very good." He flashed his perfect boy band smile filled with perfect boy band teeth. He reached for the handle of my suitcase, which, as I knew it would, rattled in his hand, threatening to fall off. His smile disappeared but immediately returned as he

25

got a practiced grip on the bag and pivoted me toward the registration desk. As we crossed the lobby, he said, "I'm Jack. Let me know if you need anything. I'm almost always here. If you don't see me, the front desk will page me, or if it's not urgent, feel free to leave a note on my desk." He gestured to a small desk on our right, between the registration desk and the wide hallway near some conference rooms.

I pointed at his name tag. "Jack?"

He leaned toward me conspiratorially. "I get better tips as Giacomo."

Clearly this boy knew who had money and who didn't, but I was grateful for his help and chose to ignore his unintended, I'm sure, insult.

He hovered while I checked in, then took the key from the front desk clerk and led me toward the elevators, pulling my suitcase behind him. The wheels twisted and threatened to overturn the bag, but he simply righted it without missing a step.

"You're a true professional," I said.

He flashed that wide grin at me. "I do my best."

"I'm not a big tipper, though."

"My tip is to see you happy, Ms. Russo."

"Wow. Let me reiterate. Even when you say stuff like that, I'm still not a big tipper.

And call me Charlee."

He laughed and pushed the elevator button to the eighth floor. As we waited, I watched a gawky young man in a white shirt and paisley tie sitting alone in the lobby, scrolling on his phone. He glanced up at me and quickly buried his nose back in his device.

My paranoia was on heightened alert. Was he doing something like cyberstalking a celebrity on Instagram, or was he involved in a kidnapping? Whatever it was, he looked guilty. Across the lobby, the bartender chatted jovially with a couple of middle-aged guys sitting at the restaurant bar. While I kept an eye on the guy on his phone, I heard one of the guys at the bar say, "Trailblazers were the whup. Denver was the ass. I think the Nuggets showed up for cheerleader practice." The other two men howled with laughter.

"Basketball game last night," Jack explained.

"I figured." I tore my eyes from the guy on the phone and glanced up at the elevator lights. "I'm from Denver."

"Basketball fan?"

"Nope. Football. But my boyfriend watches the Nuggets sometimes."

The elevator doors opened and we stepped

aside to let a couple off. Jack shook the man's hand, greeted them both by name, and wished them a great afternoon. We rode up and got off at the eighth floor, and I followed him to my room. He unlocked the door and made a big show of handing me the key. He ushered me in and then followed, dragging my suitcase. He lifted it up onto a luggage rack next to one of those big rolling luggage carts, both of which had a home in an alcove near the door.

"Let me show you around."

The room was a tastefully decorated suite, but not huge, and I was fairly certain I could find my way around it.

I dropped my messenger bag on the loveseat. "Yep, looks like a junior suite." Bedroom, bathroom, tiny living room, inadequate lighting, cootie-covered remote.

Jack saw me looking at the large armoire and stepped efficiently toward it. He opened the cabinet doors. "TV," which filled the entire space. Then, pointing below and to the right, "Mini-fridge." Pointed to the left, "Minibar. Snacks, libations, and such." He closed both cabinets, but the left one slowly drifted open again. Jack pivoted back toward the loveseat and pointed behind it. He twirled one arm above his head. "Free Wi-Fi, and you have a private balcony. Best view of the grounds from here. Word of advice, though. If you go out there, don't pull the sliding door all the way closed. Sometimes they stick and you'd be stuck in the rain until housekeeping comes."

I crossed the living room and took in the view from the sliding door. "Hmm. Rain." I glanced at the rectangular balcony and saw that the far corner had a small dry patch protected from the weather, but no chair. As if reading my mind, Jack said, "The furniture is bolted down. We get complaints from guests all the time about wanting to drag a chair to a dry spot, but we've had a couple of incidents."

"Do tell."

Jack leaned in conspiratorially. "Couple had a fight one time and the guy locked his wife on the balcony to get her to calm down —"

"Sure. That always works."

"She said she started tossing chairs off to summon help."

"Did it work?"

"Yep. Summoned help from police, three fire stations, the local news, and forty-eight psychologists here for a symposium."

"On-the-job training." Eight floors below, I saw the pool and hot tub. Trees and shrubs surrounded the hot tub, rendering it very secluded. "Probably won't be out there much."

Jack grinned. "The sun might come out while you're here."

"Really?"

"Maybe. How long are you staying?"

"Just until Sunday."

"Oh. Then no. But if you were staying until August . . ." He moved toward the hallway door.

I did too, walking past the desk and stopping at the armoire to close the left cabinet door. Again, it drifted open.

A worried look crossed his face. "Let me get maintenance up here to fix that for you."

I waved him away. "Don't bother. I won't be up here much anyway. I'm on the faculty for the writers' conference downstairs."

"Well, then you don't have to worry about tipping." He flashed that perfect smile. "The Stumptown Writers' Conference takes very good care of us, and we in turn take very good care of their faculty. They're the biggest annual conference we have here." He put his hand to the side of his mouth and in an animated stage whisper said, "Minibar is on the house for faculty." He pointed to the open door of the armoire. "It's beckoning."

"Sweet." I tugged the door of the minibar and saw plenty of tiny booze and snacks.

"Want anything?"

"Nah, I'm good." Jack opened the door to the hallway. "The meeting rooms are in the area behind my desk in the lobby. The conference workroom is the Clackamas Room. Everything's easy to find down there. The rooms all go in a big square." He stepped into the hall. "And remember, if there's anything I can do for you, anything at all, please don't hesitate to ask." He pulled the door shut behind him.

If they took such good care of the Stumptown Writers' Conference faculty, why didn't he already know I was one? It made me wonder if Jack was being truthful when he said there was no charge for the minibar items. Getting back at me for telling him I wasn't a big tipper?

I flipped the security lock across the door and scavenged in the minibar, grabbing the first quick food I came to. I poured eight-dollar roasted almonds into my mouth while I walked into the bedroom, but found them hard to swallow when I wondered if Hanna was hungry, wherever she was. I stopped mid-chew and mid-step when I heard my doorknob rattle. Tiptoeing back toward the door, I made sure I had indeed flipped the security bolt. I heard the noise again but didn't see the knob rattle. I crept forward to the peephole in time to see a woman emerge from an alcove with a bucket full of ice.

Great. Paper-thin walls *and* near the ice machine. I listened to her explain to someone about her travails in filling the container. "I had to push that darn button like a thousand times!"

I sat at the end of the bed, chewing and searching for my phone. The distraction of Jack's tour and Ice Bucket Lady disappeared and my anxiety about Viv and Hanna returned full-force. I finished the almonds, then called my brother. I knew Viv didn't want me to tell anyone, especially the police, but Lance didn't count. He was my brother before he was the police, and he never steered me wrong.

"Hey, Space Case. What's up?"

Lance's childhood nickname for me calmed me a bit, making me think things could be normal again. "Something weird happened." I explained as best I could given my limited information about Hanna's kidnapping.

My brother let out a long whistle. "How do you get yourself into these messes?"

"I didn't do anything. I got off an airplane and stepped in it."

"Well, your friend is right that it's useless going to the Portland cops. They can't do anything."

"Can't or won't?"

"Both. There's no evidence or proof of a crime. Tell me again what the alleged kidnapper said on the phone."

"I don't really know. I wasn't there when she got the call."

"And the girl is an adult?"

"Yes. Viv said she's twenty-five."

"And she doesn't live at home."

"No."

"Was there a ransom demand?"

"Viv didn't mention one." I paused. "She also said it might have been a prank." I began to feel silly. Was I overreacting?

"All you can do is get some evidence of foul play." I heard the skepticism in Lance's voice. "And then if you're lucky, you can involve the police."

"Could the police trace the phone call?"

"Doubt it. Certainly not if she won't tell them about it."

"That's what I was afraid you'd say."

"Were you also afraid I'd tell you to stay out of it? This sounds like a squabble between a mom and a daughter. Are they on the outs? What do you know about them?"

"I've never met Hanna. Viv said their relationship isn't always that great, but she

33

didn't elaborate."

"All the more reason to butt out. Family issues can get ugly. Gotta go." Lance hung up.

I hadn't even dropped my phone from my ear before my text ringtone played. *And be careful, butthead,* he wrote. Then he sent a poop emoji.

I texted back. *You're a butthead.* And added kissy lips.

No. You are. He punctuated it with two poops this time.

Oddly, buttheads and poop made me feel better.

I remained at the end of the bed, playing with the crinkly plastic packaging from the almonds. What kind of life did Viv and Hanna lead, where they'd be involved in a kidnapping? Why was their relationship difficult? And how difficult could it be if they played board games together?

Was it an elaborate prank, like Viv had mentioned? I thought back to our book tour. All the tall tales. All the fake stories she'd told about us. All the pretending to be who we weren't.

On reflection, maybe Drama Queen Viv wasn't completely credible.

I used my phone to search online, typing "How to stage a kidnapping." The first result was an article titled "Arranging Your Own Kidnapping for Fun and Profit." The gist was that adrenaline junkies can arrange for customizable abductions for a fee.

Had Viv and Hanna gotten bored with playing Scrabble on game night?

THREE

After reading several pages of results from my internet search, each more horrifying than the last, I called Viv. She answered on the first ring. "Is it possible that Hanna staged this herself?"

"What? Why would you say that?"

"Apparently it's a thing people do. They pay a couple thousand dollars for someone to kidnap them."

After a moment, Viv spoke precisely, distinct spaces between each word. "First, Hanna would never do that to me. Second, she doesn't have money to spend like that. And third, it's simply ridiculous!" The last three words came out less precise, all as one word and a little screechy.

"Viv, I'm sorry. I didn't mean to upset you."

I heard her take a deep breath. "I thought you weren't going to help me find Hanna."

Ugh. I was making everything worse. I felt

foolish for suggesting Hanna would hire a kidnapper. I apologized again. Clearly I was ill-equipped to help her anyway. I should have learned my lesson after Melinda's murder. I'm not an investigator. I'm a writer who knows fiction is so much easier than real life. But I could do one thing. "I'll take care of the conference, like I said. You find Hanna."

She disconnected without a goodbye.

I washed my face and hung up the outfit I planned to wear for my keynote speech — assuming Viv really wasn't going to cancel things and the conference would proceed as planned. I grabbed a five-dollar package of neon-orange peanut butter crackers from the minibar and ate them while I stood in the only dry area of my balcony, making sure not to close the door behind me, just in case.

The grounds of the Pacific Portland Hotel were lovely. Rose gardens strategically placed for optimum viewing. Benches available to take advantage of on both sunny and cloudy days. The perfect number of trees and shrubs for seclusion yet still offering an open feel to the patio and pool areas. I stared out, trying to think of something — anything — to do to help Viv. Other than reporting this to the police, which Viv had made me promise not to do under any circumstances, I came up woefully empty.

The pool was crystal clear, with only the tiniest ripples from the soft rain. I spotted a couple behind one of the shrubs, perhaps employees sneaking away for a furtive make-out session in the drizzle. Must be true love if neither of them cared about drippy clothes. As I stared, though, I saw they were not standing close enough to embrace. In fact, body language made it seem as if they were having a spat. She stood her ground, all feline grace and confidence. I assumed she was teeming with confidence, anyway, because not every woman can get away with a patterned African-motif headwrap over blue scrubs and sneakers. He appeared to be holding his own too, although at one point he ran an exasperated hand through the long hair flopping across his brow.

I finished my crackers and stepped back inside, locking the door behind me, glad that Ozzi and I never argued. Well, almost never. There was that one time recently when we accused each other of being homicidal maniacs.

I checked my teeth, dug the visible orange-colored globs from them, and headed down the hallway to the elevator. Back to reality. I wished my biggest problem was a tiff with my boyfriend.

Whether Hanna's kidnapping was real or not, Viv clearly was caught up in some sort of drama, so I figured I should just focus on helping the other volunteers put on the conference. I have a great affinity for writers' conferences and hanging out with other writers; no reason to deny that experience to anyone. If the Stumptown Writers' Conference was like others I'd been to, there would be a bunch of first-timers just realizing they wanted to be writers, come to explore what that might mean. It was the first step, maybe even a life-changing experience for some. But only if the conference went forward.

I took the elevator to the lobby and glanced out the large windows. Still raining. So different from Colorado thunderstorms, which come and go so quickly. I crossed to the area where Jack had said the conference rooms were: behind his concierge desk and past a wide hallway running east and west. Out of view behind the registration desk was another hallway running north and south. I took that one, glancing at the signs for each room as I passed. Columbia. Mount Hood. Deschutes. The Clackamas Room was at the end, but I noticed the hallway continued to the right just past it.

The rest of the conference rooms must be on the other side, like Jack had said, making the big square. It probably created a huge ballroom when all the accordion doors between them were open. Conference hotels were predictable in their uniformity, and in their choice of unfortunately designed carpet.

The workroom was unlocked. I stepped in and saw six-foot tables around the perimeter, many of which were stacked high with boxes of office supplies, plastic file cases, bags and boxes of snacks, and a tower of shrink-wrapped cases of water bottles. In the center of the room were two tables pushed together with four chairs evenly spaced on one side, like an island in the middle of an ocean of debris. Two people sat side-by-side at one of them, doing absolutely nothing — a distinguished-looking older man and a smiling black-haired woman about my age, who jumped up and grinned wide when she saw me.

"Hi! I'm Lily Matsuo! And this is Orville Baxter! Are you one of the new volunteers?" She spoke with such energy, her wispy bangs bounced.

"Um, I guess. I'm Charlemagne Russo."

Lily squealed. "You're one of our keynote speakers! And you're teaching this weekend!

I hope I get to go hear you! I'm so happy to meet you, Ms. Russo!"

Her enthusiasm was the opposite of contagious. I felt my energy level cut in half. Was she perhaps sucking out my life force? "Relax, and please call me Charlee."

"I'm sorry. I get so darn excited." Lily hurried back to where she'd been sitting, not taking the direct route. Halfway there she paused, then willed her feet to start again, slower.

"She's a little dynamo," Orville said, patting Lily's back as she sat down. He smiled up at me with a tiny mouth. He looked a bit like a cartoon mouse.

"Are you still in trouble for your agent's murder? Has that all been taken care of? Did you just get here? Have you checked in? Do you need water? Are you hungry?" Lily gestured toward a large carton on a table near me that was brimming with individual packages of cookies, crackers, and granola bars. "Sorry."

I had hoped not to talk about my agent's murder this weekend, assuming, wrongly it seemed, that it wasn't common knowledge. Or that if it was common knowledge, at least people would have all the facts and know that Melinda's killer had indeed been caught. I took the easy way out and pre-

41

tended I hadn't heard. I plucked a granola bar from the pile. As I opened it, I looked at Orville and stage-whispered, "Is she always like this?"

"Yup."

Lily giggled and bounced in her seat. "My husband says that when he met me, he had to triple his nap quotient."

"I get that," I said with a smile. "You're what I think is called a *people person.*" I bit into the granola bar, dropping oat crumbs everywhere.

"Yes!" Lily clapped her hands.

"Well, stop it. It's exhausting."

Her face fell.

"Oh my gosh. Lily, I'm sorry. I was just joking."

She grinned at me and clapped some more. "I know! Me too!"

"This is going to be an interesting weekend," I said.

"I know!"

I wanted to give Lily a chance to settle down, if that was possible, so I ate the granola bar while I pushed aside a few boxes and bags, making room to perch myself on the edge of the table across from their island. Lily held out her hand for my empty wrapper and I dropped it into her palm. "Thanks, Mom."

She giggled.

"So, Orville," I asked. "You're one of the volunteers for the conference?"

"I am."

I eyed the empty table in front of them. "And what is it you're doing?"

"At the moment? Nothing. We're waiting for instructions."

Lily nodded emphatically.

I glanced around the room, mentally noting a dozen tasks they could be accomplishing. "Have you two ever been to a writers' conference before?"

"Yes, of course!" Lily said. "I've been to this one three times, and to a children's conference twice. I write for kids."

"Of course you do." She might as well have informed me that water was wet.

"And Orville's been here longer than me," she added while I rooted through the box of snacks near me, scoring a package of Oreos.

As I fished a cookie out, I asked Orville, "And what is it you write?"

"Medical thrillers."

"Ooh, are you a doctor?" I bit the Oreo in half, then popped both halves into my mouth. It seemed more demure than cramming the whole thing in at once. But it wasn't.

"No. Retired engineer. I'm more of a

computer guy. Kinda techie. Branching out."

A computer guy writing a medical thriller. It could certainly happen, but the advice we always heard as writers was *write what you know*. That's easiest, of course, but many gripping page-turners have been written by authors who twisted that advice into *write what you want to know*. Done right, that's what allows a computer guy to write medical thrillers. "Done right" being the operative phrase. Research is tricky. You need enough to make the reader believe you know what you're talking about, but not give them a huge info dump that makes them want to fake their own death so as not to have to finish your book. I'd be interested to see which kind of writer Orville was.

"But neither of you have volunteered behind the scenes at a conference before?"

They both shook their heads.

"And nobody told you what needed to be done?"

Lily glanced around the room as if looking to see one of the nobodies to whom I'd referred. Orville frowned, as if he'd just that moment realized volunteers might actually work in the workroom we sat in.

"Are *all* of the main volunteers down with food poisoning?"

44

"Yes, that's what Viv said when she called me." Lily pointed at a large whiteboard mounted on the wall. On it were eight or ten names and phone numbers with a line through each. At the bottom were Lily and Orville's names and phone numbers, as well as *Clement!ne Sm!th* and her phone number. I laughed at the exclamation marks and assumed Lily added them.

"How in the world did everyone get food poisoning? At the tasting for the meals?" I finished the Oreos. Again, Lily held out her hand for my wrapper.

"No, that was way last week." Lily dropped the wrapper in a nearby trash can. "If it was that, everyone would be better by now."

"They probably had a final meeting with food served," Orville said.

Lily snapped her fingers. "I bet you're right." She beamed at him like he'd won a gold medal at the Volunteer Olympics.

"Well, at least that's the only major problem. We can handle that." It was the best rallying cry I could summon right then.

I saw Lily and Orville exchange a look. "What? Is there something else?" I asked.

Lily's arm shot up like she had the correct answer in school. Which she probably did. A lot. "Nothing major. Just a little glitch we heard about with the online registration."

45

"Computer glitch? Sounds right up your alley, Orville." I tipped my head at Lily. "Lucky we have a computer geek here, eh?"

She beamed at him again and nodded hard.

"Can you show me the website?" I asked him.

"I don't have a computer. Do you?"

"No, I didn't bring mine down. It's still up in my room."

"I have one." Lily dragged a laptop case from the floor by her feet up to the tabletop. She pulled it out, tapped some keys, and slid it toward Orville.

He pulled it closer and adjusted his glasses while looking up and down at the screen. He hovered one finger over the keyboard. "I just touch that one?" he asked Lily. She nodded. Then he asked, "And how do I . . . interweb?"

"Wait," I said. "You don't have a computer with you . . . or you don't have one at all?" Hadn't he called himself a computer guy? A techie?

"I worked mostly with spreadsheets," he said, not answering my question.

Lily pulled the computer back toward her and tapped more keys. Finally she turned the screen around so we could all see the website that was set up for people to register and pay for the conference. Filling the screen in big red letters loomed the words, "Website down for unscheduled maintenance. Try back in an hour."

I relaxed. "Just an hour. Must not be a big deal."

"It's been on there since yesterday," Lily said. "But probably!"

I thought for a minute. "It's Wednesday afternoon. Most everyone is already signed up by now anyway, since the conference starts on Friday, so our only real problem is the loss of our main volunteers."

"True!" Lily grinned. "Except for the double-booking!"

I narrowed my eyes at her. "The what now?"

"The hotel double-booked the conference rooms," she explained.

"There's a bunch of people expecting to share the conference meeting space with us?"

Lily laughed. "Don't be silly. Half of them are dogs! They double-booked a dog show!"

The Oreos backed up into my throat. Without a word I opened a shrink-wrapped package of water bottles and took a swig from one, wishing it was vodka. I set it down, then walked to the whiteboard and reluctantly wrote my name and cell number under Clementine's. Then I copied Lily's and Orville's numbers into the contact list in my phone. I added Clementine's without the exclamation marks. This was going to be an interesting weekend. I pushed up my sleeves, glad I'd agreed to help Viv. There was no way she could handle things here and also take care of her problem with Hanna.

I took a deep breath. "Orville, you need to call the registration website people. Lily, you need to get some more volunteers here. I'll go talk to the front desk about whether we have to make our coats glossy for judging or if we need to teach dogs to write."

FOUR

I braced myself with both hands on the reception desk and felt my neck and shoulders tense. "So" — I glanced at the clerk's name tag — "Bernice. What's this I hear about the Stumptown Writers' Conference having to share space with a dog show this weekend?"

I expected the smile to slide right off her face and land somewhere in Guatemala, but it did the exact opposite. Got bigger and faker. She was a true hospitality industry professional.

She gave a dainty, Southern belle flip of her wrist. "That just dills my pickles! That is not what's going on. Who told you that? Whoever it was has entirely misunderstood the situation."

"Oh good." I felt the tension leave my neck. "What exactly is the situation, then?"

"There's no situation" — this time she flipped both wrists — "at all."

I cut my eyes at her but continued to grip the marble countertop.

The corners of the huge fake smile twitched.

"Aha! I knew it. What's going on?"

"Nothing. It's nothing. Nothing at all. Really. Nothing."

"Nothing?" I used my mother's glare on her. It had always worked to make me confess.

She assessed my determination, but when I didn't flinch, she wrinkled her nose as if smelling a whiff of bad hospitality. Or maybe now her pickles were extremely dilled. She looked both ways before leaning in close to me. "Just the teensiest little something. Hardly anything."

"Would you please tell me already?" I felt my neck and shoulders tighten up again, this time worse. It's been my experience that when someone goes to this much trouble to tell you everything is hunky-dory, it's probably not.

"We double-booked the conference rooms this weekend."

"So, exactly the situation I asked you about a minute ago."

"Yes, but you made it sound so . . . so —"

"Like a situation?"

"Yes. No. Here's the thing. Whoever

booked the dog show input the wrong date. We expected they would be here *next* year on this weekend. But it was *this* year. Isn't that silly?"

"Not the word I'd use. My real question is, what are you doing about it? Am I going to have a doggie beauty pageant in the middle of my workshop about how to write dialogue?"

Bernice's face lit up. "It's actually not a regular dog show like what you're thinking. It's an agility competition."

My mouth dropped open. "That's even worse. Are you telling me we're going to have dogs jumping through hoops and spinning plates while we're trying to learn the ten elements of a good plot?"

She flipped that wrist again. "You're thinking of, like, a Vegas thing or the old Ed Sullivan show. This is different."

I wanted to grab her by her navy blue blazer and shake out all the information she was withholding from me. I wanted to see it scattered across her marble reception desk so I could piece it together myself. But I didn't. Instead, I took a deep, cleansing breath like my yoga instructor taught. I held it for a count of five, then released it for a count of five.

"I don't get to Vegas much. But now I'd

51

really love to hear what you plan to do about this fiasco."

Again with the wrist and the Hospitality Smile. "Pshaw. It's not a fiasco! I'm making some calls." As if to illustrate how she'd go about this Herculean task, she picked up the hotel phone and waved it at me. "We'll get it all taken care of. You won't notice a thing. It's completely under control."

I released my grip on the smooth marble counter and flexed my hands to get the feeling back. "Are you sure?"

"Absolutely. Completely under control. Completely."

I didn't believe her, but there wasn't much I could do about it. "How 'bout if I check back with you later and you can tell me about those phone calls?"

"That would be super. Super duper!" She used her Hospitality Smile on me, flashing every single one of her teeth.

I was not fooled.

I crossed the lobby and sank into a soft upholstered armchair, trying to decide how much to worry about the agility dogs. The lobby was calm and quiet. A few people nursed drinks across the room, two at the restaurant bar and three at a high-top table in the corner. The young man in the white shirt and paisley tie I'd seen earlier still sat nearby. This time, instead of his phone, he had a newspaper open in front of his face, reminding me of a spy in an old Cold War movie. He kind of creeped me out. Who just sits around a hotel lobby? Besides me, that is.

Jack the concierge crossed the room carrying a plastic bag the size of ten pounds of flour. When he got to the large glass table in the center of the lobby, he stopped and poured some of the contents into small bowls. Perhaps peanuts for the bar. It reminded me I needed to talk to someone about the food for the conference.

I walked over to him. He acknowledged my presence with a smile but concentrated on his task. I glanced at the label on the bag. *Canidae Organic Bakery.*

"Hey, Ms. Russo. Everything okay?"

"Ask me again later. And please call me Charlee. I'm not that much older than you."

He finished filling a bowl, then pushed it toward me as he filled another. It was some kind of trail mix, not peanuts, so I scooped up a handful in my palm before plucking out a nice-sized nugget and popping it in my mouth. As I chewed I pointed at the label. "Yum. Latin for hotel snacks?"

Jack frowned slightly and I noticed the miniature scoops near the bowls. This wasn't my first party foul and certainly wouldn't be my last. Same with ice tongs. I never remembered to use them. Just dug my hand into the ice bucket to extract what I needed. "Oops. Sorry. Too hungry, I guess."

He kept working but asked, "Can I help you with anything?"

How nice of him to gloss over my faux pas with the trail mix. "Actually, yes. I need to talk to the catering manager about food for the conference. Can you point me toward her office?"

"I can do better than that. I can point right at her." He settled the bag of trail mix on the table before pointing at a woman hurrying toward the exit carrying a large box. He called out "Roz!" and motioned her to come over.

She didn't break stride. "I'm in a hurry, Giacomo. Can it wait?"

Jack and I hurried toward her. As we crossed the lobby, he said, "Roz Zwolinski, this is Charlee Russo. She needs to talk to you about the food for the writers' conference this weekend."

As we neared, Roz fumbled with the flaps of her box. She positioned it away from us but didn't stop walking. Jack reached out to carry the box for her, but she jerked it away.

It seemed like a rude, unnecessary reaction to his helpful gesture and I disliked her immediately. From across the lobby she'd looked well put together, but up close I saw that her charcoal power suit was frayed at the cuffs and her gray roots were showing. She was a Suicide Blonde, dyed by her own hand.

"I just need a couple of minutes to make sure everything is okay for the conference. I understand many of the volunteers got food poisoning recently —"

Roz stopped abruptly. "Viv? Did Viv get food poisoning?"

"No, I don't think so —"

Her phone chirped and she bobbled the box as she checked the screen. Jack again offered to help her but she ignored him. She also ignored the call. She pocketed her phone and finally looked at me as though she saw me as a person, not simply an obstacle keeping her from exiting. "Who are you?"

"This is Charlee Russo, Roz," Jack patiently explained again. "She needs a couple of minutes for an update of the menu for the conference."

Roz waved Jack away, but he stayed by my side.

"Everything is fine for the conference. We

had the tasting last week with Viv and her volunteers and they signed off on everything." Roz hastened toward the exit again, calling over her shoulder, "Don't worry. It'll all work out. The chef and kitchen staff are good. It's not their first rodeo." Then she entered the revolving door and it spit her out on the other side.

I looked at Jack, who shrugged. "She's pretty busy," he said.

"Clearly. Can I talk to the chef?"

Jack pointed past the bar and to the right. "Kitchen's back there."

I followed his directions, passing the bar. I saw the same guy who'd been talking about basketball earlier still talking to the bartender. I made my way through the dining room, weaving through the tables, most of them empty at this time of the afternoon.

I pushed open the swinging doors, expecting to find dishes being washed and dinner prepped. Instead, six or eight employees in aprons sat or leaned on the stainless steel countertops. Nobody worked.

"Um . . . can I talk to the chef?"

"Nope," one said.

"He's not here," said another.

"He got fired," said a third.

Roz should have led with that. But it explained her rush. She had to go find a new chef, pronto. But telling me the chef and staff were good and it wasn't their first rodeo? That was some hard-core lying. She'd never even flinched, although she hadn't looked me in the eye while she said it.

"Did Roz fire him?"

I heard some indistinct mutterings — "probably" . . . "wouldn't doubt it" . . . "ruthless bitch" . . . "always gets her way" . . . "wanted him out."

Finally, a fresh-faced kid who looked like he belonged in middle school Earth Science rather than a hotel kitchen waved them to be quiet. "Who are you?" he asked me.

"My name is Charlee Russo and I'm helping with the writers' conference this weekend."

A voice popped up from the back. "One of the lucky ones who didn't get food poisoning, eh?"

"Roz probably poisoned them herself," a different voice said.

I swiveled toward the voice. "What makes you say that?"

The fresh-faced kid stepped toward me after giving the voice behind him a warning glance. "Don't mind them. We're all a little upset. Spouting off. Venting. We don't know anything. Just that Chef was supposed to be here for his shift, but he came an hour late, cleaned out his desk, and left. Didn't say anything except that he'd been fired. That's all we know." He glanced around the room. As a warning for them to be quiet? Not to air their employer's dirty laundry to the guests? Not to contradict him? I couldn't tell.

I didn't know what to think, but my curiosity had been piqued. Why hadn't Roz mentioned it? What was in that box? Did she get fired also? Was she cleaning out her desk?

I relaxed my clinched fists. None of my business. I needed to focus on my mission. "So what happens about the conference meals? How are you going to feed three hundred people all weekend without a chef?"

None of them had an answer for me.

I returned to my comfy chair in the lobby. No meals, no volunteers, and a dog show. This was shaping up to be a great conference. My stomach rumbled and I checked my watch. Three o'clock. No wonder I was starving. Or maybe all the snacks were rebelling. At any rate, I should eat real food. I headed toward the bar and slid into a stool away from the other patrons.

The bartender came right over, wiping his hands on a bar towel that he then flipped onto his shoulder. He placed a cardboard coaster with an unfamiliar logo in front of me. "What can I get you?"

"Can I get some healthy food here?"

"Hmm. Define healthy."

"Not Oreos or trail mix."

"I can probably find you something."

"Even without a chef?"

"Well, that does make it harder. How picky are you?"

"Not very."

The man I'd seen earlier swiveled toward me from his barstool several seats away. "I had a pretty good frozen pizza earlier."

"I bet they could fry a burger," the bartender said.

My stomach told me it was not interested in either of those choices. "Perhaps something more, um, gentle? Think anyone back there can slap together a turkey sandwich with lettuce and tomatoes? On sourdough?"

The bartender nodded. "I'm sure of it. And if not, maybe Jerry can call his mom to come help."

"I knew it. That kid should be in Earth Science class."

The bartender laughed. "Right? Apparently he's actually old enough to drink. I've seen his ID. You want mustard and mayo on that sandwich?"

"Just mustard."

"Anything to drink?"

I toyed with the cardboard coaster. A girl can't day-drink without a drink. "This Rogue stuff any good? I like ales, porters, stouts. Dark stuff."

"You're in luck. Let me get this order in since it might take them a while. Then I'll get you a Dead Guy Ale." The bartender walked away.

"You'll like the Dead Guy. Rogue brews lots of good beers. They're local. The Double Chocolate Stout is good too." The man lifted his glass. "This is the Voodoo Doughnut Mango Astronaut Ale."

"Seriously? That's a lot to unpack before I've had my Dead Guy, but I always try to drink locally, act globally." I studied the cardboard coaster. "You're local? I heard you trash talking the Nuggets earlier."

He stood up and I immediately regretted engaging him in conversation. I wasn't in the mood to get hit on. Just wanted to eat in peace.

He held out his hand. "Hi. I'm Brad Pitt."

I laughed out loud. As he moved closer to shake my hand, I saw he was at least twenty years older than me. Good-looking, but still, what a line. "That's hilarious. Girls fall for that?"

He slid into the stool next to me, placing his half-glass of beer in front of him. "I'll have you know that I was Brad Pitt before Brad Pitt was Brad Pitt." He pulled an Oregon driver's license from his wallet and handed it to me.

"Bradley Calvin Pitt, born June 14, 1963." I handed it back. "I have no idea how old the real Brad Pitt is."

"I just told you, I'm the real Brad Pitt. I got him beat by six months."

The bartender brought me a gorgeous, deep orange colored beer, then turned toward my companion. "Ready for another, Brad?"

"Are you kidding me?" I laughed. "You heard us talking."

The bartender looked confused, so Brad said, "She doesn't believe that's my real name."

"I saw his ID," the bartender told me.

"So did I. But I still don't believe him." I sipped my beer. A bit sweet. A bit fruity. Very mellow. Just what the doctor ordered.

"And I don't believe I'll have another. Still have work to do." The original Brad Pitt sipped his beer, then set it down and looked at me. "You won't hurt my feelings if you

61

tell me to shove off. I didn't mean to insinuate myself into your very late lunch."

I decided it might be nice to have a little light conversation before I had to return to problem-solving mode. Since Brad's driver's license said he lived in Portland, I assumed he was here either for the conference or the dog show, neither of which I wanted to discuss. "Nah. Stay and finish your beer. I could use some company. But just so you know, I don't want to talk about writing or dogs. And I have a boyfriend."

"Good to know. I won't waste my A material on you."

"You have A material? Did you get it from your namesake?"

"I told you, I'm older than him. And I notice you haven't told me your name yet."

"Oh, I'm sorry." I held out my hand. "Angelina. Angelina Jolie. Pleased to meet you."

"Very funny." He gently brushed my knuckles with his lips. *"Très gallant."*

"I need to step up my game for the beautiful Ms. Jolie. Wait." He paused and squinted at me. "Hey, you're not the actress."

"You found me out."

"You're much more beautiful than she is."

I felt myself turn red. It's so irritating to

blush. "Actually, I'm just a lowly author. My name is really Charlemagne Russo."

He stared at me. "Charlemagne dares mock Brad's name?"

"Yep. My friends call me Charlee. But get this, my boyfriend's name is Ozzi."

The bartender brought me a perfectly serviceable turkey sandwich on sourdough. They'd even remembered my plea for no mayo. Brad Pitt, the bartender, and I exchanged funny stories about funny names while I ate it. I found both of them charming and pleasant company. Again, just what the doctor ordered.

I finished my sandwich and beer, wiped my mouth, and asked for my check. The bartender told me I could sign it to my room, so I did, being careful not to let Brad Pitt see my room number. Girl can't be too careful. I handed the leather folder back to the bartender. "It was nice to meet you, Mr. Pitt, but I've got a date with some conference volunteers."

"Lucky. I haven't had a date in longer than I can remember. I have a roommate that cramps my style."

"Then it's good you're spending time at a hotel with a conference going on. Maybe you'll get lucky." I slid off the stool and collected my bag.

"Doubt it. I have a roommate here too. Also cramping my style."

"You didn't plan very well."

"I never had a room of my own." He gave a comical pout. "Until I bought a house. And then almost immediately my loser brother moved in and started cramping my style."

"With the ladies?"

"With everything. But how about you, Charlee?" He waggled his eyebrows at me. "Got a roommate here?"

"Just my invisible one, Ozzi."

He laughed. "I'll see you around."

"Maybe. Nice to meet you."

He waggled his fingers at me. "Love, peace, and bacon grease."

"Excuse me?"

"Nothing. Just a silly thing my brother always says."

I spread the fingers on my right hand two-and-two, like Mr. Spock. "May the grease be with you, then."

"Wow. Wrong on so many levels."

As I made my way back to the workroom, fortified by food, beer, and a little light flirting, I heard Jack's voice around the corner near the conference rooms. He was talking to a girl. I smiled, thinking they might be indulging in some light flirting of their own. But when I heard them mention Hanna's name, I skidded to a stop and hugged the wall where they couldn't see me. Bernice at the reception desk tugged the sleeves of her blazer, then returned to her computer.

The female voice said, "I don't care about that. Hanna's not getting her way this time."

My mind raced. They both knew Viv's daughter? Was that the same Hanna they were talking about? Did they know she'd been kidnapped? What didn't the voice care about? And what could the ominous *this time* mean?

By the time I'd focused myself to listen to more of their conversation, they'd moved on. I peeked around the corner, but they'd disappeared. I knew they hadn't come back toward the lobby, so I started down the hall. I took a veritable tour of Oregon while poking my head into each room: Columbia, Mount Hood, Deschutes, Clackamas. When I opened the door of the workroom, both Lily and Orville looked up expectantly and smiled at me. Lily started to speak, but I retreated and shut the door before she could engage me in a conversation, probably about more conference fiascoes. My search took precedence. I traced the path I presumed Jack and the girl had taken down the hallway, squaring the corner to the Tualatin, Multnomah, and Willamette rooms. All empty. Where had they gone?

As I resigned myself to return to the workroom without learning anything about the mystery girl or the conversation about Hanna, Jack casually emerged from the Willamette Room. Alone.

I jumped backward as my adrenaline spiked, and he immediately apologized for scaring me.

"I'm just surprised. I thought I saw you over there talking to a girl." I waved vaguely toward the lobby so he wouldn't think I'd been spying on him, but I kept my eyes on his face. I was rewarded with a slight narrowing of his eyes. He recovered almost immediately, and I knew that if I hadn't stared, I would have missed the flicker of whatever that was. Guilt? Wariness? Sneakiness?

He didn't respond, just moved toward his concierge desk.

I followed him. "I bet you have a lot of friends here at work."

"Not really. I try to keep my work life and personal life separate." Jack opened a drawer, then immediately shut it. Lined up the stapler with the phone. It seemed to me he was pretending to be busy.

"Have you worked here long?"

"A few years." He moved his pen next to his business card holder so that it made a perfect right angle.

He was clearly nervous, and I needed to figure out why. How were he and the girl and Hanna related?

"This conference has been held at this hotel for a long time. Do you know my friend Viv Lundquist, who organizes it?"

Jack looked up but immediately shifted his eyes from mine. "I've seen her around, I think."

"Do you know her daughter, Hanna? You guys are about the same age."

"No, I don't think so."

A guest at the reception desk waved a luggage claim ticket at him. Jack called, "Be right there, sir!" and then turned to me again. "Excuse me. I've got work to do."

I could have sworn I heard him whisper, "Thank God."

He plastered a big smile on his face and scurried toward the guest. He schmoozed him for a bit, asking about his day while taking his luggage claim check. In a few moments, Jack returned with two suitcases, which he deposited in front of the man. He held out the claim tickets in his hand, next to the tickets attached to the bags. The guest nodded in acknowledgment that he had the correct bags and reached into his wallet. As he handed Jack some bills, he said, "Thank you for your excellent service during my stay, Giacomo."

Jack pocketed the cash without looking at it. "It's been my delight, sir." He picked up the bags and motioned the guest toward the revolving door where a cab awaited.

I watched until the cab drove away, Jack waving from the portico. Why was he lying about knowing Hanna? Before she'd driven away, Viv had told me not to say anything to Jack about Hanna because they were friends. Was it possible Jack had something to do with her kidnapping? I vowed to keep an eye on him.

I turned abruptly and almost crashed into the man in the white shirt and paisley tie from the lobby. Up close, he looked even younger than I'd thought.

"Gosh, excuse me!" I said.

He turned without a word and practically ran in the opposite direction.

I don't usually have that effect on people, and he kind of gave me the willies. I had a flash of Viv begging me to skulk around and help her figure out what was going on. Maybe she'd asked him to skulk around too. I hurried after the man, intending to find out.

I felt and heard a squelch under my Keds. "Gross!" I lifted my foot and saw a big pile of dog poop with my footprint in the middle of it. The skulker got away from me, disappearing down a hallway.

"I'm so sorry!" A man hurried toward me waving a small plastic spatula. "Jean Louise!" A gorgeous black-and-tan German shepherd calmly walked toward him and he snapped a leash on her. She sat regally next to him, clearly unperturbed by her intestinal faux pas.

The man scooped the poop into an orange plastic bag he'd whipped out of his pocket.

I hadn't moved. My sneaker hovered at an angle six inches off the floor. Seriously? Dog poop?

"It's good luck, you know." The man handed me a canister of disinfectant wipes from the small backpack he wore.

I plucked out four and began to wipe my shoe, hopping to a nearby chair for balance. "It's good luck to step in dog poo? Says who?" I plopped down into the chair, trying to keep from touching anything gross.

"Me. And everyone else on the planet. Or maybe just those of us involved in dog shows." The man plucked a couple of wipes for his spatula. "I'm Scott and this miscreant is Scout. Jean Louise when she's in trouble." At her name, the dog lifted her face angelically at him.

I looked around for someplace to put the wipes I'd used. Scott offered his hand and I gladly gave them to him.

He spoke to his dog. "Tell the nice lady you're sorry."

Scout placed her head under my hand and raised up slightly so it looked as if it was my idea to pet her.

"Jean Louise. That's funny." I fell in love immediately, putting hands on either side of the dog's huge hairy face and forgetting all about my shoe. As I rubbed the fur on her face and neck, Scott untied my sneaker and pulled it off my foot.

He finished cleaning my shoe and the carpet, even pulling out a small carpet cleaner spray can. While he sprayed the area and white foam penetrated the spot, he apologized again. "We were headed out back, but I detoured to get a newspaper. Guess I took too long."

We both looked down at Scout, who wagged the top inch of her tail, clearly acknowledging her innocence in this situation.

"She's normally better at keeping her knees crossed, but I think she's a little nervous."

"She sure doesn't look nervous. She's gorgeous."

"Thanks. Well, maybe it's me that's nervous. We're competing in our first major agility competition in a couple of days." He handed back my shoe. "Good as new."

I crossed my ankle over my opposite knee and secured the sneaker on my foot. I stood and looked at Scott. "So, agility dogs. You guys are the ones they double-booked with our writing conference."

"Seems so." Scott held out the handle of Scout's leash. "Could I ask you to hang on to her for a minute while I go throw all this away and confess our sins to housekeeping?"

"Sure." I knew the man in the white shirt and paisley tie had disappeared, and Jack had long since left the portico out front so my surveillance of him and the mystery girl would have to wait anyway. Holding the leash, I walked Scout over toward the door to the patio and grass out back. Raining. "Sorry," I said to her. She leaned her big head against my thigh and we watched the rain until Scott returned.

"Thanks so much." He took the leash from me and the three of us watched the rain together.

"What's involved in an agility competi-

71

tion?" I asked.

"It's basically an obstacle course the dogs run."

"Do you tell them how to do it?"

"Kind of. We move through the course with them, but they have to do it."

"How does she know what to do?"

Scott let out a snort. "I'm not sure she does. It's my job to teach her all the tricks and obstacles, so if there's any failure, I'm sure it'll be all mine."

"Is every course the same?"

"No. The judge sets up the course and we won't see it until the day of competition. It'll have all the obstacles, but they're never put together quite the same way. One competition may have hurdles, weave poles, A-frame, tunnel, dog walk, pause table, teeter-totter, and then end with a tire jump. The next time, an entirely new judge sets it up completely differently. All the same elements are there, but switched up."

"Sounds complicated."

"It can be, but so far Scout has really taken to it. She seems to love the mental workout as much as the physical."

I thought about the double-booking. "And you have these competitions indoors?"

"Not very often. But the lady in charge of this competition is kind of a Nervous Nellie, so she likes to book an indoor arena in case the weather is bad."

"Hotel conference rooms are considered an indoor arena?"

"Only in a pinch. Usually they use horse arenas, like at a fairground, but apparently those are expensive to rent. And this is a fledgling organization without much money. If they charged the participants fees high enough to cover the rental cost, nobody would come. There's prize money, but not tall dough until you get to the bigger clubs and more prestigious events." Scott scritched Scout behind the ears. "But Nervous Nellie has an aunt or someone who got her a deal on this place. Too bad they got the date wrong. I heard a rumor that the hotel called around and found a high school gym for us in case we can't use a park or someplace outside. But not for the whole time. We still need to practice. At least Scout and I do."

"Maybe the rain will stop before the competition."

We watched the rain for a bit longer.

"I guess if it doesn't let up, we'll just have to practice in here." Scott glanced around the lobby.

"Ha! I'd love to see that." I rubbed the side of Scout's big head. "A lobby full of

German shepherds jumping hurdles."

"Oh, they're all different breeds."

"So Scout might square off against a pug?" I smiled, thinking about my upstairs neighbors' pug, Peter O'Drool.

"No, but I would pay to see that," Scott said. "The dogs compete in height groups, measured at the shoulder. Doesn't matter what breed, but each group is the same basic size. Then, of course, there's novice, intermediate, and master courses."

"You said there's prize money for this?"

"Yeah, but not much. And there are plenty of costs involved with the dogs. But professional handlers who consistently win can earn big bucks from the dog owners, who really just want the prestige of the title."

"Are you Scout's owner or handler?"

"Both. I want to do well enough to earn better sponsorships and breeding fees. So far, she's doing well, but we've added in the agility portion to the plain ol' dog shows to see if we can pad our bank account a bit more. She's already a pretty competitive show dog."

I was impressed and a bit jealous of Scout. I wondered if I could make a living jumping over and crawling under things and standing really still for judging. Scott ran a hand along Scout's coat. I smoothed my own hair.

"Wow. So much I didn't know about dog agility competitions."

"Probably because you have a more interesting life than I do."

"Doubt it. But I probably should get back to it. It was nice talking to you." I thumped Scout on her side. "And stepping in your good luck poop."

"Again, we're sorry about that, aren't we, Jean Louise?" Scott lowered his voice a bit when he said her name, reminding her of her faux pas and causing her ears to flatten.

As Jean Louise looked up at me with sorrowful brown eyes, I immediately forgave all the dogs in my orbit who'd ever barked while I was trying to sleep, all the dogs who'd chased me on my bike as a kid, and all the dogs — past, present, and future — who'd deposited poop in a place where I might step in it.

Scott tugged at Scout's leash. "And we need to figure out how to practice for our big day." They walked away, Scout's tail sweeping magnificently from side to side with each step. I was sure she'd do well in an agility competition.

Scott and Scout going off to practice reminded me I still needed to memorize my mnemonic device for my keynote speech at the banquet on Saturday. I found a comfortable seat in the lobby but felt a pang of guilt as I settled in, having forgotten briefly that there might not even be a banquet. That is, if Viv came to her senses and cancelled it, or worse, if something truly awful had happened to her daughter. Many attendees, and likely all of the volunteers, were friends of hers. Writers take care of their own, and if word got out, none of them would want to enjoy a conference under those circumstances.

I still couldn't quite wrap my brain around the kidnapping. Again I wondered, what kind of people know people who get kidnapped? I guess I'd have said the same thing three weeks earlier, about people knowing people who got murdered, and yet there I was, involved in a murder. And why Viv's daughter? She hadn't answered when I'd asked. Viv wasn't rich, and she wasn't powerful or from an important family, as far as I knew.

I felt another pang of guilt when the thought flitted through my brain, once more, that maybe this wasn't really a kidnapping at all — just the book tour all over again with Viv making up more and more outlandish lies. But instead of scoring some free dinners and hotel upgrades like on the tour, what would her motive be this time?

I hated that this theory was now lodged in my brain. Had I watched too many movies? Read too many books? Fiction was so much easier than real life. My head began to throb, so I slid the elastic from my braid and raked my fingers through my hair several times. As expected, my hair had dried kinky from the wet braid, but I didn't care how I looked. I finished my mini head massage and let my wild, witchy hair cascade down my back. I closed my eyes while rolling my neck and shoulders. I wasn't relaxed in any sense of the word, but it was as close as I was going to get for now. I re-braided my hair.

Real life awaited me in the conference workroom. As I crossed the lobby, giving a wide berth to the dark circle of carpet cleaner, I scanned the area for the man in the white shirt and paisley tie, but he hadn't returned. Neither had Jack. Since I couldn't talk to them at the moment, I tried to remember my mnemonic device and what the letters of ACHIEVE stood for as I walked back toward the Clackamas Room. I got stuck on the A. I knew "agility" wasn't correct, but it was all that came to mind. I gave up in disgust.

Jack came around the corner, chatting with Bernice and another employee. When they passed, only Bernice acknowledged me, with an automatic smile. I watched as they opened a door with a sign that said *Employees Only.*

If there wasn't a kidnapping, what did the conversation between Jack and the mystery girl mean? Why would they mention Hanna's name like that? It was a common enough name, but could it really have been a coincidence, given that my questions made Jack so nervous? Why had he lied about knowing her?

My steps slowed and finally stopped outside the Clackamas Room. I leaned against the wall opposite the closed work-room door.

The stories Viv had told me over the years about Hanna filled my head. Whether they were funny, sweet, or exasperating, she always spoke with lots of squishy love for her daughter. Maybe their relationship was in fact "complicated" for some reason at the moment, but how many mothers and daughters didn't have a relationship complicated in some way? My mom and I did, on occasion. That didn't mean anything.

I fished my phone from my bag, pulled up Facebook, and went to Viv's page. I scrolled through her photos. Most were of her and Hanna, smiling, arms around waists or shoulders, heads touching. They didn't look like they had any animosity between them, but everyone knows photos can lie.

I clicked out of Facebook and went to the saved photos in the "Favorites" album on my phone. There were a bunch of me and Viv at various conferences over the years. Viv had the same smile on her face in those photos as in the photos with Hanna, the one I used to see a lot but hadn't seen today.

I regretted that there were no photos from our book tour, but that had been before camera phones were so ubiquitous. Such an adventure that was. We were both so new and dazzled by the book business. Several weeks sharing motel rooms also made you share much of your life. At the time, I'd wondered if that was what it felt like to have a sister. A much older sister, but still.

Viv had shared stories of Hanna's teenage antics back then. Nothing she said had made me think she was anything but an excellent mother, despite the obvious financial difficulties of raising a kid on her own. Although, when the tour brought us to Portland and I stayed at Viv's house for a couple of days, why hadn't I met Hanna? I remembered joking about how neat and tidy everything was, no sign of a teen girl living there. Were they having more than just typical mother-daughter problems even back then?

I flushed with shame at my refusal to help Viv find Hanna, and at my persistent theory that one or both of them could have staged the kidnapping. But I still couldn't wrap my brain around it, because really? A kidnapping? Yet what if it was? How could I ever look Viv in the eye again? And still, even if Hanna had not been kidnapped, something very weird was going on. Something Viv needed help with. And if I could team up with the guy skulking around in the white shirt and paisley tie, so much the better.

I made a call. After the beep I said, "Viv. I'm in. I'll help you find Hanna."

FIVE

I didn't exactly know how I was going to help Viv find Hanna. And until I figured out how to investigate Jack and the girl, or otherwise brainstorm a plan, I still had to put on this conference.

As I pulled open the door to the Clackamas Room, I saw that Lily and Orville had been joined by another volunteer, who was also doing absolutely nothing. Lily jumped up when I entered and clapped the tips of her fingers together in front of her face. I wasn't sure I'd ever get used to her exuberance at seeing me. Even Peter O'Drool was more sedate — sedate like a Maori war dance — and it's kind of a dog's job to adore people.

"Charlee! Clementine is here! Clementine, this is Charlemagne Russo. Charlee's on the faculty, she's giving the keynote on Saturday, AND she's taking over for Viv."

"I'm not actually taking over. I was here

anyway, so I'm helping out since so many volunteers got sick. Hi, Clementine." I smiled at the young woman and dropped my bag on a table still covered with piles, boxes, and bags.

Clementine was sitting on another table with her legs crossed in front of her. She didn't smile back at me. Just tilted her head to the side as if studying an unusual human specimen.

While Lily chattered on about all the true-crime articles Clementine had written for magazines, Orville readjusted the Velcro on his sneakers by ripping the tabs over and over again until he was satisfied.

"— she interviewed this guy who lived in a tree house who —"

I studied Clementine's asymmetrical hairdo. Pure Portland hipster. She was outfitted in a large man's plaid flannel shirt belted over a white schoolgirl blouse with a black bow tie.

Lily prattled on. "And that great story you did about that girl who was killed at the Three Mouse Squeak rave!" She stared into the middle distance with a sudden frown on her face. "I forget how that one ended, though."

Clementine adjusted her rhinestone-studded cat-eye glasses before removing them altogether. I noticed they had no lenses.

"Oh, yeah! Now I remember! It was the drummer who did it," Lily said.

Clementine slid her glasses into a soft case made from Hello Kitty fabric. "Yes. He lost all credibility when he refused that Pabst."

Before I could ask what in the world that meant, Lily squealed with excitement. "And the grandmother who murdered all those door-to-door salesmen! You *have* to read her article about that!"

"You write true crime, huh?" I said. "That must be interesting."

Clementine unfurled her long legs and I saw that she also wore leggings with a frog pattern, pink leg warmers, and neon blue pointy-toed stilettos that matched the stripe in her hair. "Cute shoes." I flashed the grin that girls flash when we compliment one another on our shoes. I expected her to compliment my pink Keds with the rainbow laces, especially since she was mercifully unaware they'd been covered in dog poo until very recently. Plus, they were kinda hip.

But she didn't. All she said was "yes."

I didn't know if she was responding to my comment about her writing or her shoes. She didn't even flash a courtesy grin. In fact, she hadn't moved a facial muscle since I'd walked into the room. I vowed then and there to make it my life's mission to make her smile. Most people can smile, right? Even hipsters?

Lily suddenly shrieked, causing me to jump. "I just had the best idea! Clementine should write about your dad, Charlee!"

Every muscle in my body tensed. I stared at her. What was she insinuating? I balled my fists. I refused to ask what she meant, and I certainly wasn't going to get into an argument about my dead police officer dad. Besides, Clementine wrote true crime. Not related in any way to my dad. I was just going to pretend that Lily hadn't spoken.

Zen-like, I willed myself to relax and changed the subject completely by asking Clementine, "Have you volunteered for this conference before?"

"Affirmative."

"Oh, good. Lily, Orville, and I are all new to this. What needs to be done?"

"No idea."

"But I thought you said . . ." I left my question hanging, assuming she'd fill us in. She didn't. I tried again. "So, you've volunteered for Viv before?"

Clementine glanced from Lily to Orville to me before she sighed in an exaggerated manner, like she was on stage and had to play her emotions to the balcony. "I've tried to volunteer for years now. Viv is a real control freak. Does most everything herself. And what she doesn't do, she stage directs and micromanages."

"Oh. That sounds . . . unpleasant," I said.

"Not at all. I waited years before someone stepped aside so I could take their job." Clementine must have seen the confusion on my face because she sighed again. "It's a coveted position to be in the inner sanctum of volunteers. Perks without works. Food poisoning seems to be our way in." She indicated Lily and Orville.

Orville smiled vaguely. I wasn't sure he knew what was going on, but Lily nodded emphatically. "I'm so proud that Viv called me to help! Aren't you?" she asked Clementine.

Clementine maintained her mask of ennui, but I could tell she felt the same as Lily. "Meh. I just wish she were here. Viv makes a lot of people mad, but she solves problems. But I guess it probably sucks to have food poisoning."

I was still processing the statement that Viv made lots of people mad, so didn't think before I said, "Viv doesn't have food poisoning."

Ugh. Now I'd have to come up with some other reason why Viv wasn't at the conference. She didn't want me to mention the kidnapping but she didn't have food poisoning. Wait. Why didn't Viv have food poisoning if all of her key volunteers got it?

Lily rescued me by telling Clementine that Viv was probably busy with all of her other volunteer activities.

"What else does Viv volunteer for?" I asked, glad for the change of topic.

Lily ticked them off with her fingers. "Reads to the blind. Teaches Sunday school. Tutors at a middle school. And her nonprofit, of course."

Orville had returned to adjusting the Velcro on his shoes. Riiiiiip. Was this his first experience with the magic that was Velcro? Did he have OCD? Was he bored?

I tried to ignore another irritating riiiip. "Nonprofit?"

"I don't know much about it —" Lily began.

"It's called Strength in Numbers," Clementine said. "It teaches people to write fundraising appeals and how to organize letter-writing campaigns."

"For what?" I asked.

"All kinds of groups ask for their help. Neighborhood groups. People who don't want fracking. Parents fighting with the school board."

Orville piped up from his bent-over position. "Basically Little Guys trying to protect themselves from Big Guys."

I pulled a small notebook from my bag and jotted "Strength in Numbers" to remind myself to look it up online later. I'd never heard Viv mention it. Circling it with my pen, I noticed the acronym was SIN.

Relieved I hadn't had to make up a lie about why Viv was going to be absent from her own conference this weekend, I asked Orville how things were coming with the registration problem.

"Still broken." Riiiiip.

"What did they say about it? Is it a server problem? Software? Hardware? What?"

He sat up straight. "Didn't say."

"Wait. They didn't say or you didn't ask?"

"Yep." He motioned to Lily's closed laptop and she slid it toward him. He opened the lid and slid it back to her. "Where's that place . . . ?"

I felt my eyes bug. "You mean the website? The registration website?"

"I've got it right here." Lily clicked some keys and slid it back to Orville.

He looked at the screen, turned it so I could see, and then turned it back in front of himself. He hovered a finger over the keyboard and glanced at Lily for confirmation. When she nodded, he pressed a key and peered at the screen.

Lily grinned up at me. "Orville is a genius with computers. Before he retired he was an expert in Excel!"

"So I hear."

Orville kept his eyes on the laptop but nodded in acknowledgment of his accomplishment.

He clicked a couple more keys. "People have been emailing and saying they've been billed twice. And a few people who've registered in the last day or so are telling me they've been charged $3,999."

"Four thousand dollars?"

"Glad I got my fees comped," Clementine said.

"I am almost positive this conference does not cost four grand," I said.

Lily solemnly agreed.

"Can I see?" I asked Orville.

He slid the laptop toward me and I saw he was in the backroom administration area of the registration website, not the place where people would go to register for the conference. That he'd managed to get there was a good sign, I thought. I went to a different page, which showed the number of people who had registered, along with the money deposited directly into the Stumptown Writers' Conference online bank account.

I couldn't make sense of what I was seeing. Every time I looked at the number of registrants, it fluctuated wildly, like there was a chimpanzee spinning a number wheel. "This makes no sense," I said, scrolling through the pages. "There's gotta be something wrong on their end." I slid the computer back to Orville. "You have to call their tech support and figure this out. We need to know how many people are going to show up here on Friday and how much money we have. And if people have been overcharged, where is that money? Is it real money in the account or is it fake numbers on the screen?" I started to hyperventilate a bit. "You have to call them."

"Can't," Clementine said.

"Why no —"

She tapped the oversized pocket watch dangling from her belt. "After six. Closed."

"Tech support is usually twenty-four hours —"

"Nope." Orville squinted at the screen. "Eight a.m. until four p.m. Eastern time. I'll call tomorrow. Figure it out." He stretched and gathered his things. Lily and

Clementine did the same.

I wished I had his confidence. That left one day until the conference began. I looked around the room, knowing there was much to be done, but I didn't feel comfortable asking them to stay and work. Especially when I really had no idea what specifically needed to be accomplished. I'd been to many writers' conferences before, but I regretted not asking Viv for a list of the important things that needed to be done. Seemed like a no-brainer. You know. In retrospect.

I waved them out the door and let Lily hug me on her way out. When they were gone, I systematically worked my way around the room looking in each box and bag, finally determining that much of it was the swag that belonged in the tote that each attendee received upon checking in for the conference.

I cleared a table, then set up piles of the swag I'd found in the various boxes and bags — pens with the Stumptown Writers' Conference logo, small composition books for note-taking in the workshops, individually wrapped assorted hard candies and mints, bookmarks, and the conference brochure listing all the faculty and workshops.

Green reusable totes with the conference logo imprinted in white were stacked high at the end of a table. Placing my left arm through the handles of as many as would fit, I carried them to the table where I'd set out the swag. I shuffled around the table, one bag at a time, grabbing each item of swag and systematically, methodically, hypnotically dropping it in. In the corner of the room nearest the table, I stockpiled the loaded bags as neatly as possible, handles all pointing in one direction to make it easy to carry them out to the registration desk early Friday morning.

Shuffling around the table, I was bent at an angle that would make my chiropractor cringe. I could hear him now. "Charlee, you're over thirty now. Take care of yourself." But this job needed to be done. Filling ten bags hurt my back. Twenty more made me dizzy. And by fifty, I was ready to quit. This was going to be a long evening.

Just when I'd talked myself into a visit to the hotel bar, my phone rang.

"Viv! What's going on? Any news about Hanna?"

"No. But the message you left earlier said you were in? You're going to help find Hanna?"

Viv sounded exhausted, so instead of telling her about the conversation I'd overheard with Jack and the mystery girl and his denial that he knew Hanna, I simply said, "Yes. Whatever you need me to do." I'd tell her about Jack when I knew something concrete.

"Thanks, Charlee. I wish I knew what to do." She took a deep, shuddery breath and I knew she'd been crying. My heart broke for her.

Neither of us spoke for a few moments. Then Viv said wearily, "So, tell me about the conference prep. Everything okay?"

"Um . . . well, I found all the freebies and I'm putting them in the bags."

"By yourself? That'll take all night!"

"Nah, it's fine." I rolled my shoulders and neck. "It was late so I sent the volunteers home. They'll be here bright and early tomorrow to help fix the —" Oops. I hadn't intended to tell her about the problems we were having.

"What? Fix the what?"

"Ah, it's nothing."

"I don't believe you. Tell me." The exhaustion in her voice turned to panic.

"First, you have to promise to stay calm. We have everything under control."

"If you don't tell me right now, I'll —"

"Fine. There was this little problem with

double-booking of the conference rooms."

"Another conference was booked at the same time as ours?"

"Kind of . . . it's a dog agility competition."

"A what?"

"Dog agility. They jump over things and crawl through things —"

"In a hotel?"

"It's a long story. But the hotel is working on it." I should have checked on their progress earlier. "I'm sure we'll be able to cross that off our list tomorrow."

"Your list? You have a list of problems?"

"Not problems, exactly . . ." Oh, who was I kidding? We had problems and I decided to come clean with Viv. She couldn't help, but maybe she had ideas for me. "Okay, yes. We have problems. The dogs, for one. And the chef was fired."

"What? Why?"

"I don't know, but his staff seems . . . capable. And they're on it. He left his notes about the conference food."

"Oh, geez. Is that all?"

"I wish." I clamped a hand over my mouth.

"Tell me." Viv's voice was back to sounding exhausted.

"Computer glitch with the online registration provider. It's billing people twice when they register. Unless it charges them four grand."

Viv remained silent, taking in all the bad news, I assumed.

"Viv? You still there?"

"Charlee, I've gotta go. Thanks for taking care of everything."

Taking care of everything? She must have had a different definition than I did.

And she'd hung up before I could ask if she had hired the guy in the white shirt and paisley tie. I sent her a text, then pocketed my phone and moved back to the swag table. At least rote activity wouldn't tax my brain.

I reached for more tote bags, but a memory stopped me mid-air. When I did a beta read for Viv's most recent book, she'd told me that she needed my critique in a hurry so she could push the book through production to get the rest of her advance. Something about her screwing up her quarterly taxes and owing the IRS.

Viv had been quick to end our conversation after I told her about the registration money. I boomeranged to an impossible thought that I tried to tamp down, push away, ignore. But I couldn't.

Was the kidnapping just some elaborate

ruse to embezzle money from the conference? Was I being used?

SIX

After Viv's call, I talked myself back into a visit to the hotel bar. I made my way to the lobby, where I saw a commotion out of the corner of my eye. I expected it to involve one of the dogs and was surprised to see the guy in the white shirt and paisley tie grab Clementine's arm. I gaped as she shook him off and marched away from him. He followed her and I wondered about their relationship. They certainly didn't look friendly. I suddenly had the overwhelming sense that he had something to do with the kidnapping or whatever was going on. Which meant that Clementine did too.

I had a terrible thought that shook me to my core. Maybe he *was* the kidnapper. And maybe Clementine was in danger.

I hurried after them, no plan in mind other than finding them, or at least Clementine.

Racing around the hallway, I poked my

head in all the conference rooms. Unsuccessful, all I could think to do was travel the big square of conference rooms again, finally ending at the Clackamas Room. I opened the door again, poked my head in, and saw everything exactly as I had left it.

Not knowing where else to look, I closed the workroom door and turned in time to see the guy in the white shirt and paisley tie exiting a hidden hallway door. Alone. I hadn't noticed it before, even though I'd passed it several times. It was covered with the same wallpaper as the wall. The only thing that distinguished it from the wall was a practically invisible recessed handle, and even that was painted to match the wall.

I froze. What was behind that door? Did it lead to Hanna? Was Clementine now with her?

I knew I needed a plan, but had no time to think of a good one. So I settled for saying, "Hey. Are you here for the conference? One of the volunteers?" As if seeing it for the first time, I gestured to the hidden door. "Oh, where does that door go?"

He didn't respond, just cut his eyes both ways and scurried away like an enormous cockroach. As soon as he was out of sight, I yanked open the hidden door and immediately pulled it shut behind me.

As my eyes adjusted to the dim light dribbling from a bulb in a wire cage high on the wall, I checked my phone battery. After all the time I'd spent using it today, I was down to 33 percent. I deployed my flashlight app and waved my phone around the short hallway. Surely there was a light switch somewhere.

Maybe somewhere. But not here.

My eyes had adjusted a bit, so I shut down my phone to save the battery and tiptoed down the stairs, keeping one hand on the wall for safety. As I got to the bottom, I stopped and listened for any sound that might guide me toward Clementine. I turned to the left, because it seemed as good a choice as any. I made my way through the labyrinth of the hotel basement, stopping every so often to listen for something, anything, to make me feel more confident I might find her.

Suddenly a beam of light danced behind me. I watched in horror as it grew bigger. Whoever held that flashlight was coming closer.

I hurried forward, my left hand feeling the way ahead along the wall about waist-high. If there was a doorknob, I needed to find it, and fast.

I didn't even need to glance behind me to

see the light from the flashlight bounce around me. I was just beyond its reach, but not for much longer. I broke into a trot. Footsteps thudded behind me.

My thumb jammed into a doorknob and I cried out in surprise. I clamped my hand over my mouth and stumbled the few steps back to the door. I yanked it open and flung myself inside, closing it quickly and, I hoped, quietly behind me.

I leaned with my back to the closed door, listening for the footsteps and waiting impatiently for my eyes to adjust to the pitch black. I opened them as wide as I could, willing my pupils to speed into night vision mode. My heavy breathing sounded like a freight train and I took a deep breath and held it, hoping whoever was following me would pass right on by.

As I held my breath, I heard the footsteps stop outside. Light from a flashlight danced under the door at my feet.

SEVEN

I took a chance and turned on my flashlight app, quickly scanning the small room, taking care to steady my light high on the wall so it wouldn't bleed under the door. Stacks and stacks of boxes, all with bright white labels marked *Kitchen.* I clawed at one on the top of the stack nearest me, which was held closed not by tape but by the flaps of the box. I popped it open, only to find it empty. I tore open the box next to it. Also empty.

I glanced at the base of the door and saw the light growing dim, as if the person had moved down the hallway. They didn't know I was in here! I scurried across the room and opened another box.

Aha! This one was full of pots and pans. I dug out a wobbly-handled skillet, shoved my phone in my pocket, and waited behind the door. Relief flooded me as I watched and listened. The light and the footsteps faded to almost nothing. I slowly let out a breath, then sucked it in again as the light grew brighter and bolder under the door.

I clenched my fists around the handle of the skillet, planted my feet in a wide stance, and choked up on it like it was the bat my dad gave me when he taught me how to play baseball.

The doorknob turned slowly.

The door opened inch by agonizing inch.

I crouched down into my stance and bounced lightly, skillet up next to my ear.

Bring it.

Light blinded me and I swung wildly through the air. I swung again immediately and connected on the backswing.

The flashlight dropped. There was a thud that made my stomach lurch and I saw, illuminated in the eerie glow, a paisley tie rippled on the floor.

I scrabbled for the flashlight and shined it directly into the man's face. He raised one arm to cover his eyes. He crossed his chest with his other arm and rubbed the arm he was using to shield his eyes.

Simultaneously, I was relieved and dismayed that I hadn't conked him upside the head. Still shining his flashlight into his eyes, I grilled him like he was a Soviet spy. "Why are you here? Where is Clementine?

101

Is she down here somewhere? Where's Hanna? Are they together?"

He didn't respond. Just squinted with his arm across his face.

I took a threatening step toward him. "Well?"

Still no answer.

I thought I had the upper hand, but maybe I didn't. My arm holding the skillet began to tire. Both hands began to sweat and shake, part tremor, part fatigue. Keeping the light in his eyes, I sidled around him toward the door, knowing I could make a run for it if I had to.

As I took a step, my foot jammed into a stack of boxes. The surprise jolted me and I lost my balance. I dropped the skillet and it crashed to the floor next to his head. I jumped back as he rolled into the doorway and stood up, blocking any escape I thought I had.

I managed to keep hold of his flashlight and continued to shine it in his eyes. The skillet was at his feet, and I expected him to grab it and come up swinging. Instead, he kicked it behind him, out into the hallway.

"Why are you so mean?" he said, rubbing his arm again. "That hurt."

I opened and closed my mouth seven thousand times. Finally I said, "Why did you follow me down here?"

"It's my job. Can you get that light out of my eyes?"

His whiny voice took away 87 percent of my fear. The tears welling up in his eyes took away the rest. I placed the flashlight on a stack of boxes near me so it shined at the ceiling.

"Your job is to follow me to the basement?"

"Not just the basement. Wherever you go."

"Why?"

"I told you, it's my job."

"I'm losing patience with this game. Explain yourself. Now."

"Your mom hired me to watch out for you."

"My mom? Why?"

"Because she was worried about you because of the trolls online."

"What trolls?"

"The ones she was arguing with on Twitter —"

"My mom's on Twitter?"

"Apparently."

"Let me get this straight. My mom got into an online fight with Twitter trolls?" This made less sense than her being on Twitter to begin with. "That's ridiculous." I reached into the box where I'd found the wobbly-handled skillet and pulled out what I believed to be a wobbly-handled crepe pan. I planted my feet and choked up on it. "Keep talking. But understand that this crepe pan has no more patience."

He took a strangled breath and let it out. "I'm a private investigator hired by your mother. After your agent was killed and you got all those crazy comments, your mom started replying to them —"

I let the crepe pan fall to my side and he flinched.

"She was trying to change their minds or something. But it just escalated. And there were threats —"

"To my mom?"

"No. To you. So she hired me to keep an eye on you here in Portland. Just in case."

"Just in case," I repeated, staring at him.

He swiped at his eyes.

"You're a private eye?"

He nodded and sniveled.

"Where's Clementine?"

"I don't know."

"I saw you grab her arm in the lobby. Where'd you guys go?"

"Down here."

"Why?"

"She made me."

"She what?"

"She made me. You know, figured out I was a PI and started grilling me right there in public about my job. I told her I couldn't talk about that. She said yes I could and then forced me to follow her. She said something about *the cloak of secrecy* and the next thing I knew, we were down here." He looked at me with wide eyes. "She scared me."

"Yeah, she kinda scares me too. But where is she?"

"Probably still down here somewhere. She lit up a joint and I high-tailed it outta here. Then I saw you in the hall and you started asking me questions. I didn't want to, but I had to come back down here after you to make sure you were okay." He wiped his nose on the sleeve of his white shirt and looked like he was eight years old.

I felt sorry for him. But just for a moment. He could be an accomplished liar for all I knew. I dug out my phone and checked for a signal. None.

"What's your name?"

"Billy."

Oh my God. He *was* eight years old. I thought for a minute.

"Well . . . Billy . . . here's what's going to happen. You're going to walk slowly in front of me while I use your flashlight to light the way. When we get to the top of those stairs, you're going to open the door very carefully. You're not going to talk to anyone. You're not going to run. You're not going to do anything but walk into the restaurant where we're going to sit and call my mother. Do you understand?"

He nodded forlornly.

"Okay, let's go. And no monkey business."

"Yes, ma'am," Billy said.

He did exactly as I instructed. In the restaurant, I ordered another Dead Guy Ale, and Billy did too after showing both me and the waitress his ID.

I dialed my mom's number. She answered on the second ring. "Bug? Is everything okay?"

"You tell me, Mom. Did you hire a child named Billy to follow me?"

"He's a private investigator with good references."

"Really? Good references?" I shrugged apologetically at Billy, who shrugged back.

She paused. "Well, he's my friend Linda's boy. He's just starting out and he was pretty cheap . . ." She trailed off.

My feelings were a bit hurt that she'd hired a cut-rate PI to keep me safe. I shook it off. "Mom, why were you fighting with trolls?"

"After that ugliness with your agent —"

"You mean the ugliness of her murder?"

"Yes, and how everyone was thinking you did it —"

"Not everyone."

"No, dear, not everyone. But lots of people. Well, they were just saying such rude things about you online and I was afraid it would make people not buy your books, so I tried to reason with them and get them to change their minds."

"Only you would try to change the minds of online trolls."

"They threatened you, Bug! You should read some of the horrid things they said. And then, out of spite, they started posting bad reviews —"

"Why do you think I don't read my reviews, Mom?"

She didn't answer.

"Mom, did you tell Lance about any of this? If there were threats, you should have reported it to the police."

"I didn't want to worry him. Besides, I'm sure they didn't mean those things they wrote."

"Then why am I looking across the table at a private investigator?"

"Maybe I believed them a little."

Billy leaned across the table and spoke

loudly. "I'm sorry, Mrs. Russo. I told you I've never tailed anyone before when you hired me. Will I still get paid?"

"Don't you pay him one dime, Mom."

"Oh, Bug, that's not fair. What would I tell his mother? I'd never be able to show my face at book club if I stiffed him."

I sighed. "Mom, we'll talk about this later. But quit worrying about me. Everything's fine."

"Okay, Bug. Love you."

"Love you too, Mom."

The waitress brought our beers and I glared at Billy until she left. Then I glared at him some more while I took a long sip of my much-needed beer.

Finally I said, "Since my mom is going to pay your fee, and probably give you a nice tip, you're going to do something to earn it."

"What?"

"Help me find Clementine." I wasn't entirely sure he had told me the truth about what happened between them, but I was convinced he didn't have it in him to kidnap anyone. "Tell me more about your argument."

Billy sipped his beer, making a face that made me think it was his first taste of alcohol. "I told you. She figured out I was a

PI. But she thought I was following you, not trying to protect you."

"Why would she think I needed following?"

"Because of your dad."

I sipped my beer and almost choked. "What about my dad?"

"She wanted to know what prison he was in."

I swallowed hard. "Prison?"

"Yeah. For robbing a bank and killing the bank manager."

Good grief. The lies and fairy tales that were out there! I fought to control my temper, taking another sip of beer to buy some time. "You are really bad at your job." I said calmly. "There are articles and photos online of my dad's funeral thirteen years ago."

Billy's face reddened. "That's what I told Clementine! But she said they were obviously doctored."

I didn't explain any further about my dad but wondered where Clementine had gotten such bad information. I mulled it over while nursing my beer. Billy sipped his, too, making a sour face.

And then it came to me. Lily.

I drained my beer, then said, "You go find Clementine and bring her to me." I stomped off to talk to Lily.

Billy called after me, "Can I finish my beer?"

"I doubt it!"

EIGHT

I went back to the workroom, where it was quiet now that everyone had gone home, and called Lily. Her voicemail came up. "Hi! It's Lily! I will definitely call you back! Leave me a message! Have a GREAT DAY!" I was not having a GREAT DAY and I didn't want to leave a message.

I called Clementine's number but she didn't answer either. I wasn't too concerned about her. First, because I didn't think Billy was lying about her smoking a joint in the basement, and second, because I was fairly certain she could defend herself against the likes of Billy.

It was late. I gave up and went to my room. This whole situation was getting so weird. I picked up the phone to call my brother again, fully intending to tell him my theory about Viv's intentions with the conference funds. But I didn't. What if there really was a kidnapping and they found out

I involved the police, even if it was just my brother in Colorado? A long shot, but ever since Melinda's murder I was always on the verge of paranoia — taping over the camera on my laptop, changing my passwords obsessively, and scrutinizing every driver who passed me. And now I had to start worrying about my online trolls. If I called Lance, I'd have to tell him about Billy and the whole thing with Mom, and I really didn't want to do that.

Instead, I called Ozzi. All I wanted was to hear his voice in my ear. I listened, contented, while he told me all the mundane details of his day. No Viv, no conference, no kidnappers, no hard questions, just normal conversation. We'd been dating long enough for convivial chatting, but not so long that we knew the entirety of each other's stories. And certainly not long enough to finish each other's sentences. He told me a funny story about Peter O'Drool. Seems the pug cornered a rabbit in the juniper bush under my kitchen window, but instead of running away like usual, the bunny made a stand against tyranny and it scared the bejeebers out of Peter. He ran, the rabbit chased him, and Peter ended up cowering on the third floor of Ozzi's building in our sprawling apartment complex, afraid to come down.

"So I returned him to Don and Barb and they insisted on repaying me by making me dinner."

"What did you have?"

"Meatloaf and mashed potatoes. Just like my grandma used to make."

"I love having the Singers right upstairs. I pretend they're my grandparents."

"Barb made cherry pie, too, and told me how fond they are of you. Said to tell you they hope you're having a marvelous time. So are you having a marvy time?"

I deflected, telling him, "You wouldn't believe me if I told you. I'm tired. Tell me what's on TV."

He flipped through channels until I stopped him at an episode of *The Simpsons*. He narrated the last half, complete with commercials.

I finally fell asleep after the longest Wednesday of my life. At least the longest one since I'd been a murder suspect. That was never far from my mind, but I'd been holding it at bay until Lily mentioned it. I could continue to ignore any questions or discussion on the topic, but it would be marvelous if she'd drop it — and any talk of my dad — completely.

I startled awake the next morning to loud,

113

happy voices in the hallway discussing where to have breakfast. Food seemed a distant memory to me. My stomach rumbled but I couldn't face another package of Oreos or granola bars. Twenty minutes later, I sat in the hotel restaurant trying to decide between the *Baccon and Egg Speshal* and the *French Tost* on the *Thursday Breckfast Menu,* not sure whether I should thank or curse those hallway voices for waking me.

I wondered if it was too early to call Lily. Not because it might be impolite, but because I wasn't sure I could handle her so early without sustenance. I voted for sustenance.

While pouring my coffee, the waitress talked me into the bacon and eggs, commiserating with my horror at the awful spelling and reminding me of the power of protein to fuel my day.

"But the spelling! The terrible, terrible spelling!" I wanted to shout. I understood they'd had to simplify and print up a new menu due to the sudden loss of their regular chef, but how many writers at the conference would find their heads exploding as they read this? Every single one who found themselves reading it, that's how many. I thrust the vile paper back into the waitress's hands, glad to be free of such a demonic hellhound of a page.

I watched her refill mugs as she meandered around tables toward the kitchen. As she got there, the swinging doors came at her full-force and she had to jump away to avoid being hit.

Roz the catering manager stormed from the kitchen into the dining room, face so full of fury I don't even think she saw the waitress standing, shocked, off to the side, coffeepot held aloft. Roz turned and held the swinging doors open while she argued with someone in the kitchen.

After a few moments Roz swiveled to the dining room, shouting, waving her arms in the air as if to clear it of stupidity. "— No proof they got food poisoning here. If I'd known they were going somewhere else, then I would have used my own —" Suddenly she noticed the waitress standing like a statue and all the breakfast diners watching the show. Her eyes raked the crowd, ending with me. She promptly reorganized her suit jacket and stormed out of the restaurant. I watched as she fled, but couldn't tell if she left the hotel or not.

The pin-dropping silence ended as people went back to their breakfasts, clinking forks against plates and resuming their chatter. Someone else's drama is never as riveting as

115

a hot breakfast right in front of you. Unless you're a mystery writer.

I replayed Roz's scene while I waited for my food. Was any of it a clue to my real-life mystery? Was it simply a frustrated workplace outburst? Or did Roz know something about the food poisoning?

When the waitress brought my breakfast, I didn't even wait for her to put it down before I peppered her with questions about the ruckus. "What was that all about? Why was Roz so mad? Who was she yelling at?"

The waitress looked around, then lowered her voice. "She just found out the chef was fired yesterday." She put my plate in front of me.

Was it possible Roz had been truly unaware of this? I'd assumed she simply didn't want me to know. "She's the catering manager. How come she just found out?"

"The general manager fired him, and he says he called her. But everyone knows — even the GM — that Roz always ignores his calls." The waitress moved the ketchup and hot sauce closer to my plate.

I remembered the call Roz had ignored yesterday while Jack and I were with her. "Isn't the GM her boss? He's okay with her ignoring him?"

"He thinks it's funny." The waitress refilled

my cup. "Or at least that's the impression I get. He's probably happy not to have to talk to her. Besides, he doesn't need Roz's permission to do anything." She said Roz's name with a sneer.

"You don't like her?"

The waitress lowered her voice even further. "She's awful."

"Why do you say that?"

She shrugged as another waitress came out juggling plates for a nearby table. It was clear to me she didn't want the other woman to know we were chatting about something other than *breckfast speshals.* "Is there anything else I can get you? Juice? Toast?" she asked loudly.

"No, that's okay."

She started to walk away, but I stopped her. If she was willing to talk about Roz this way, maybe I could get information about Jack and the mystery girl. "Wait. Toast actually sounds good. Sourdough when you get a minute? No rush."

The restaurant got busier and busier, and the two waitresses raced around like roller derby jammers. I was finished with my bacon and eggs and down to the last cold swig of coffee but my toast hadn't yet appeared. I gave up on it and instead tried to get someone's attention to bring the check.

117

While I waited, Lily plopped herself down at my table.

"Good morning, Charlee! How are you? Did you sleep okay?"

"Why did you tell Clementine my dad was in prison?" I whispered.

"Because she wanted to know," Lily whispered back. "Why are we whispering?"

"He's not in prison."

"Are you sure? Because I think he is."

"No, he's not. My dad is dead."

"Oh, Charlee! I'm so sorry! How awful! Was he shivved? Mob hit? Did he turn snitch?"

"No!"

The people at the table next to us stopped talking and stared at us.

I leaned closer to Lily and lowered my voice. "My dad was never in prison."

Lily whispered back. "So he never robbed a bank, killed the bank manager, and got a life sentence in a federal penitentiary in New Jersey?"

"No!" I said loudly, drawing more stares from our neighbors.

"Hmm. I guess there must be another guy with his name!" Lily beamed at me.

"And you told all this to Clementine?" I asked.

Lily nodded. "Well, she saw it on my

computer. She wanted to write a true crime story about it."

"Why were you searching for my dad on the internet?"

She wrinkled her brow like the question confused her. "Because not all the information was in the newspapers."

She was right. The information reported was a bit obscured by the police. And I sure wasn't going to give any interviews — not now, not ever — to set the record straight. I pulled out my phone and searched my dad's name. Yep, there was a guy with the same name whose story was exactly as Lily described.

"How was breakfast?" Lily pointed at my empty plate. "I've never eaten here before!"

So much energy. So early in the morning. "Hard to screw up scrambled eggs and bacon."

"I guess!"

"Hey, Lily, speaking of screwing up food . . . when did everyone get food poisoning?"

"Hmm . . . pretty sure it was Tuesday."

"Daytime? Were they here? Like at a meeting?"

"I don't know. I thought I heard it was in the evening." She smiled and waved at nearby diners.

I turned to look. "Conference buddies?"

"Nope. But they look like real nice folks."

She truly was a people-person. I brought her back to the topic at hand. "Why do you think it was in the evening?"

"I don't necessarily *think* it was in the evening. I might have been told that, but I don't really remember. Why?"

"I don't know. Just wondered."

"There are lots of meetings in the evening. Most volunteers have day jobs."

"Do you?"

"Yep. I get to play all day! I'm a buyer for a toy store!"

"Of course you are." I tilted my head. "So why are you here today? And yesterday? Don't you have to go to work?"

"I had vacation saved up since I never take it. But I figured I could help out more here. I love to help!"

"I know you do!" Her sweet enthusiasm was disturbingly contagious this morning. Must be the protein. "Well, if I'd ever get my bill, we could get back to it." I waved again toward the servers.

"Oh! I almost forgot why I came over here! I didn't really want to disturb your breakfast, but we got a phone call."

"We?"

"Well, the conference. There was a note

taped on the workroom door this morning."

"A note? Who would have left a note?"

"I don't know. Maybe the front desk?"

"Was this note on hotel stationary?"

Lily fished it out of her pocket and inspected it. "It was! No wonder you write mysteries! You're so good at finding clues!" She handed it to me.

It read simply *travel agent,* with a local phone number underneath.

I handed it back. "And?"

"And I called them!"

"And?"

"And they're the conference travel agents!"

"And?"

"And there's a big spring storm due to hit the East Coast tonight with, like, three feet of snow expected, and what did we want to authorize them to do?"

"About what?"

"The travel arrangements."

"For who?"

"All the agents and editors who are supposed to fly in."

"Are you trying to tell me that all of the agents and editors are stuck in a snow storm?"

Lily giggled. "No, silly goose. One is from San Diego! No snow there!"

"So how many from the East Coast?"

"Only, like, four or five."

"Out of how many?" I'd seen the faculty list but couldn't remember how many of the names belonged to agents and editors.

"Like, six."

My words stuck in my throat. "Do you mean all but one of the editors and agents will be stuck in the snowstorm and won't be able to get here tomorrow, and everyone who signed up for a critique or a pitch appointment will be disappointed?"

Lily blinked three times. "Not everyone. Some people signed up with the one from San Diego."

"So. Just ninety percent of the people."

"But ten percent will still be happy!"

Ah, Lily. So optimistic. So wrong. "What about the authors on the faculty?" I asked. "Are any of them stuck?"

"Two! Isn't that great?"

"Great? Why?"

"Because it's only two! And you're so smart, you can teach their workshops!"

"What are their workshops?"

Lily consulted the conference schedule. "One is 'Science Fiction Tropes' and the other is 'Compose Like a Renaissance Poet.' "

"Oh, good. At least those are my areas of

expertise."

"Really?"

"No!" I took a breath. "Can you please call the travel agent and tell them to get our faculty here? Make whatever arrangements have to be made. Tell them to shovel the runway if they have to. And if the editors and agents can be persuaded to leave New York before the storm hits, check with the front desk and make sure they have rooms."

"And if they don't have any rooms available, they can stay with me!" Lily took the travel agent's phone number from me and stood, no doubt already planning the slumber party she was going to have with the East Coast faculty.

"And for heaven's sake, find a Renaissance poet!"

As she turned to leave the restaurant, Lily almost ran down Orville, who had come up behind her. She gave him a hug and sat back down. "You don't look good, Orville. Do you need some breakfast?"

"The wife made me oatmeal. Like always." Orville pulled out the chair across from me. Before sitting he asked, "May I?"

"Sure, but I'm leaving as soon as they bring the check." I waved at my server and at least got a head bob when I mimed signing my bill.

Orville sat down, moved the ketchup and hot sauce away from him, and leaned toward me, hands gripping the edge of the table.

"Are you okay, Orville?" I asked.

"Actually, I'm not having any luck with the registration website."

"Did you call them?"

"Just now."

"And?"

"And I didn't understand a word they said." He pulled a folded piece of paper from his shirt pocket. It was scribbled with notes. "Some nonsense about browsers and if I've plugged in and if my Earl was optimized."

"Earl?"

He checked his notes and pointed. *URL.* He offered me the paper but when I shook my head, he crumpled it into a ball and flung it to the table. "And then they asked if I had any cookies. Like I'd offer them snacks after all that."

I stared at him for a bit. "Orville, honey." I patted his hand and spoke softly. "You don't know anything about computers, do you? You're not really what anyone would call a techie, are you?"

He sighed and straightened up in his seat. "I thought I did. I did spreadsheets all the time back before I retired. And I can do the

Facebook."

"You're on Facebook?"

"More than a dozen friends." His chest puffed up.

Lily pushed buttons on her phone. "I'm friending you right now!"

"I guess we can't do much about the online registration this close to the start of the conference," I said. "The people who already registered will show up and the people who had issues will probably email through the Stumptown Writers website —"

"Or they'll contact the registration place themselves." Orville smiled. "Then I'll be off the hook."

"Or they'll show up furious and ready to kill us." I turned to Lily. "Is there some sort of website or message group or some way that all the Stumptown writers share information?"

"There's a Facebook page and an email group."

"Can you post a note in both places? Say something like we're having registration problems, but regardless, come on down to the conference and we'll get it straightened out."

"Sure!"

"And maybe contact the website administrator for Stumptown Writers and get them

125

to post something right on the front page of the website?"

"Absolutely!"

"Good. That way, anyone who is having trouble with late registration won't have to miss the conference because of it." I tipped my head back and briefly closed my eyes. Nice to have a victory — albeit a tiny one — and cross that problem off my list.

Before I could bask in the glow of dubious accomplishment, Clementine strolled into the restaurant looking in the opposite direction from where we sat, trailed by Billy. She was decked out in her hipster costume, today consisting of black leggings, lacy elastic top, chunky jewelry, crocheted beret, and Hello Kitty rain boots. She carried a very full canvas shopping bag from Fred Meyer and walked straight toward us without making eye contact. She only acknowledged our presence with a barely perceptible nod when Lily jumped up to hug her.

Without thinking, I stepped up to hug her, too. She made a sour face and stepped back.

"Where have you been?" I asked her. "I was worried."

"Why?"

"I heard you . . . took that secret door down into the basement." I was suddenly treading dangerously embarrassing waters.

Busybody narc or concerned elder stateswoman?

"So?" She narrowed her slightly red eyes and adjusted her rhinestone-studded eyeglasses with no lenses. "Not that it's any of your business, but I fired up a blunt there last night because I think my ferrets are allergic. Trying to keep my apartment a doobie-free zone. And then when I walked in this morning, this hired dick is waiting for me at the door and says I have to talk to you."

I turned to Billy. "You just waited for her to come back? I could have done that."

"Your mom told me not to leave you."

I shook my head and turned to Clementine again. "My father is not in prison for killing some guy. You got faulty information." I cut my eyes at Lily. She must not have caught my sarcasm because she simply smiled at me.

"Bummer." Clementine rearranged her glasses on the bridge of her nose.

"Wait. How did you know this guy was a PI in the first place?"

"He looks exactly like that guy on *Mindhunter.*"

I had to think a minute before placing the show she referenced. "That guy was an FBI profiler."

She flicked her hand dismissively. "Whatever." She turned and held the shopping bag out toward Lily and Orville, who gathered around her to get a better look.

"Dude." I pulled Billy a few steps from the table. "You need a better look. Especially since you're working for me now."

"Doing what?"

"Finding a kidnapper," I whispered.

"No way. That sounds dangerous." He pulled his phone from his pants pocket and pushed some buttons. "Mrs. Russo? I'm off the case. This was way out of my purview. I see that now . . . Yes, she's fine . . . No, I won't be back until Christmas . . . Yes, I absolutely will . . . That's very generous of you. Thank you, Mrs. Russo. Goodbye."

"You absolutely will what?" I asked.

"Go see her next time I visit my parents in Santa Fe."

"So that's it? You're done? Just like that?" I sputtered in his ear. "You're not going to keep an eye on me or help me find a kidnapper?"

Billy shook his head and rubbed his ear. "You should really call the police. That sounds pretty serious." He turned and walked away.

Call the police. Gee, why hadn't I thought of that?

Clementine stepped out of his way, then sat in the closest chair, arranging the overstuffed bag at her feet. Lily and Orville sat on either side of her. "So," she said, picking up the hot sauce. She uncapped it and poured a few drops on her index finger. I thought she was going to taste it. Instead, she wiped it on a napkin. We watched as she did the same thing with the ketchup. When she noticed us staring, she said, "What? I wanted to compare the colors."

"Okay. . . ." I said, desperate now for my breakfast bill.

Clementine stared at the finger she'd poured the condiments on, clean now. Without looking up, she said, "The books for the on-site bookstore haven't all come in yet. People are mad."

"What people?" I plopped wearily into my seat.

"People. You know. The authors, the bookseller. People."

My mind raced. "Is there anything we can do?"

"Nope."

I was oddly relieved, mentally crossing off a problem I didn't even know I had. If only they were all like that. "Okay, then." I stood to leave. Maybe if they thought I was going to dine-and-dash they'd finally allow me to pay.

Clementine pulled something from her Fred Meyer bag and I sat back down.

"What now?" I asked.

"I just found these in the Clackamas Room." She held up a T-shirt in one hand and a patch with the Stumptown Writers' Conference logo and tagline — *Don't be stumped by writing* — in the other.

I recognized them from my exploration of the workroom last night. "Oh. Were they supposed to go in the swag bags?"

"Yes," Clementine said.

"I'm sorry. I thought maybe they had to be bought separately. Luckily I didn't get too far with filling the bags last night. We can all get that done today, though." Finally a problem I could solve.

"They need to be ironed first."

"What needs to be ironed?"

"They're iron-on patches," Lily explained.

"So?"

"Ironers got food poisoning," Clementine said. "So these still need to be ironed onto the T-shirts."

"No they don't. Just plop 'em in each goodie bag. People can iron their own when they get home."

"That's not how we do it," Clementine

said. "That's not how we've *ever* done it."

"They won't feel our love if they have to iron them on themselves!" Lily's hands fluttered in the air like they wanted to leave her wrists.

"Get someone else, then. We have enough to worry about."

"There's nobody else." Clementine picked up the bag, scooped out all the shirts and patches, and held them out to me. "These are yours." Addressing Lily and Orville, she said, "Yours are still in the workroom."

Lily nodded in the excited way she did. Like she was a Golden Retriever offered a tennis ball.

I shook my head. "I'm not good at ironing. I always make everything more wrinkled than when I started. I don't even own an iron. When my clothes get wrinkled I throw them out."

Lily laughed because she didn't realize I wasn't joking.

Orville buzzed his lips. "Send them to the dry cleaners. That's what my wife does."

"Will your wife pay for them?" I asked.

"No. We're ironing," Clementine said. "That's that. We're all helping out."

"Can I have the bag?"

"No."

I took the load of shirts and patches from

her. Great. Someone was finally taking charge of something and this is what they chose. Extra work for everyone.

As we scooted away from the table and prepared to start our day of toil in the Clackamas Room, the middle-school-looking cook hurried over with a large tray.

"Wait, wait. You're the conference people, right?"

"Yes. Like pod people but with better grammar." I dropped the T-shirts on the chair next to me.

"You came into the kitchen yesterday, right? I've been working on the food for the conference, using Chef's notes. He didn't have recipes, but I think I figured it out." The boy beamed and I wanted to pinch his widdle cheeks. "I'm Jerry, by the way.

"You're the sous chef?" By elevating his possible job in the kitchen, I hoped to avoid being rude.

"What's a sous chef?" Lily asked.

"Second-in-command in the kitchen," Jerry said. "And, no. I'm part-time breakfast prep." He must have seen my face change because he quickly added, "But I've stepped up when nobody else wanted to."

He had me there. Clementine arched her eyebrows the teensiest bit at me. I was properly chagrined.

"What's all that?" Orville eyed the tray brimming with plates and bowls.

Jerry's grin split his face. "Your conference menu." He set the tray on the table next to us and motioned us to sit back down. With a flourish he set each plate and bowl of food down while naming it. "Grilled Fennel and Lemon Tacos. Simmered Soy Lasagna. Baked Fennel and Orange Pie. Blanched Egg and Coconut Home Fries. Steamed Fennel, Cloves, and Mushrooms. Avocado Crumble."

"Extra shipment of fennel this week?" I asked as he handed each of us silverware wrapped in a cloth napkin.

"This is gonna be great!" Lily said.

"Not what the wife cooks," Orville said.

When everything was ready, Jerry swept his hand over the feast, took one step backward, and clasped his hands behind his lower back, awaiting our verdict.

We placed small dibs and dabs of everything on our plates and began sampling.

After a couple of bites Orville pushed his plate away. "The wife would kill me if she knew I was eating between meals."

Clementine turned her fork over on her plate, then wiped the corners of her mouth with her napkin. "Gotta go." She strode from the restaurant without a backward glance.

"You really tried hard!" Lily said. "Did you have any, um, help with this?"

"Not a bit." Jerry beamed, still at attention, hands behind his back.

I took miniscule tastes from several plates, trying to formulate what I wanted to say. Couldn't very well blurt out "Yuck!" Thanks to my cohorts taking the easy way out, the final decision was left to me. I eyed the samples and did some calculations. We needed lunch on Friday, Saturday, and Sunday and dinner Friday and Saturday. Breakfast was already scheduled to be continental — yogurt, pastries, and fruit.

"Jerry, this is all really . . . great. You went to a lot of trouble, but since we're kind of in a time-and-effort crunch here, could we simplify this?"

"Of course. Which dish?"

"All of it?" I made an apologetic face. "And I hate to be *that* person, but I think I might be allergic to fennel."

Jerry's face fell.

"Continental breakfasts, right?" I asked.

He nodded.

"And for lunches, since it's so . . . um . . . rainy and dismal . . . what about a few huge pots of tomato soup with make-your-own-sandwich stations?" I knew it would screw up the timing of the day to have three hundred people making their own sandwiches, but it was better than fielding three hundred complaints about fennel tacos.

Orville and Lily nodded encouragingly, hoping Jerry would agree.

He spoke slowly. "People don't want to make their own food when they go out to eat. They want —"

"They want autonomy," I offered.

"Control!" Lily added.

"Something that tastes good."

Lily and I shot Orville a look.

"He means," I explained to Jerry, "something they feel comfortable with. After a hard day of learning, people want comfort food. Hey, I know! We can speed things up by having your staff — since you're the boss now — slap together, er, make peanut-butter-and-jelly sandwiches to go with the tomato soup. Everybody likes those."

"Some people are allergic to peanuts," Lily said. "And we'll need some gluten-free bread. And sugar-free jelly."

I glared at her. "For anyone with dietary considerations, we can have *them* make their own sandwiches." I turned to Jerry. "Would that work okay?"

"Sure, I guess. But I really thought those

tacos were an excellent choice. I'm almost positive it's why Chef had all that fennel. I don't know what I'll do with it now."

"I'm sure you'll think of something," Lily said.

I was equally sure he would. But it wouldn't taste good.

Jerry brightened. "Besides, there's still both banquets."

"Yeah, about that. I had a thought," I said. "What if we did the banquets family-style? You could make each table a tuna-noodle casserole and they could serve each other."

"That's a great idea!" Lily clapped the tips of her fingers together.

"The wife buys ready-made stuff at Costco when we have the family over. Lasagna, enchiladas, twice-baked potatoes, fried chicken."

"Orville, that's genius!" I turned to Jerry. "That would be so easy!"

Jerry frowned. "No, it wouldn't. How would I pay for that?"

"Good point." I thought for a moment. "Could you and I go see what's in your freezer? It must be full if the chef was getting ready for this conference."

Jerry shrugged. "I don't think he'd ordered everything yet. He was probably going to do it the day he got fired."

"Then how were you going to make all this?" I swept my hand across the table.

"Oh, I made some substitutions. You know, just to get a feel for it."

Ah, that explained why the Blanched Egg and Coconut Home Fries tasted like carrots.

"Can I please take a peek in the freezer?"

"I guess."

We helped him clear the table.

When we finished, I loaded my pile of T-shirts and patches into Lily and Orville's arms. "Please put these in the workroom for me. Then find Clementine and any other volunteers or friends of the conference you see."

"Friends of the conference?" Lily asked.

"People who may not be technically volunteers but they come to all the Stumptown Writers' events. People who know stuff. People who know people. People with nothing to do."

Lily nodded knowingly.

Orville adjusted the Velcro on his shoe.

"We need to finish stuffing those bags," I said. "But first, organize the faculty packets with their workshop schedules so they know where they're supposed to be — assuming they get here before the storm hits. But first, call that travel agent. And make some signs so everyone knows which room each workshop is in. But first, see if you can find any documents about the workshops. Some of the rooms might need projectors . . ." Oy vey. We had too much to do today. I shooed them away.

Jerry and I went to the kitchen, where he showed me the walk-in freezer. I wondered again at the abrupt timing of the firing of the chef. Hadn't Jack said this was the hotel's biggest conference? Why would they fire their chef right before the big event? I couldn't imagine in what way, but could his firing have had anything to do with the kidnapping? The timing was so coincidental.

I shook the thought from my head and pulled a small notepad from my bag. "Just start calling off what's in there and I'll write it down."

When Jerry was finished, we toured the rest of the kitchen to see what he already had on hand. I added it all to my list. He explained what he knew about how the kitchen worked, what he could order and get right away, and how and where all the prep and cooking was handled.

We made some notes, ending with a plan we could both live with.

Once the food was organized, I wondered again about the chef's firing and why Roz had apparently been caught completely by surprise by the news. It made no sense.

"So, Jerry, any more info about why the chef was fired?"

He shook his head. "Not a word."

I returned to the Clackamas Room. Lily was dealing with the faculty travel issues, Orville and Clementine were designing and printing signs on the computer. Actually, Clementine was designing and printing signs. Orville was adjusting his Velcro and occasionally pointing out a spelling error.

The mountain of swag for the attendees' bags remained piled on the table just as I'd left it the night before, so I again circled the table, dropping items in the bags and arranging bags in the corner.

It was hypnotic, brainless work and my mind drifted. The ACHIEVE acronym popped into my brain. Of course, I got stuck on the A. Like yesterday, again today all I could think of was *agility*. Forget the other letters.

I pulled out my phone to check my notes. A was for *ability*. Duh. I glanced at the entire acronym, then clicked away. But my thoughts were on Hanna, not my keynote speech. Maybe I could apply ACHIEVE to the kidnapping, perhaps finally making sense of it.

Ability — who had the ability to kidnap Hanna?

Courage — I hoped Hanna was being brave and not freaking out, wherever she was.

Hocus-Pocus — if Hanna was bound, I hope she could figure out how to remove the duct tape or whatever was securing her.

Imagination — I need to think outside the box if I want to figure anything out.

Editor — I need help.

Voice — If Hanna screamed, would anyone hear her?

Earnings — Was there a ransom note? Would the police have to get involved if there was a ransom? Surely Viv would have told me if she'd received a demand from the kidnappers since the original call. I made a mental note to ask her. If she'd got one, I could talk to Lance again. If it really was a kidnapping, not involving the police was a mistake. Why couldn't Viv see that?

I went up and down and over and through the scant information I had. Why had I offered Viv my help? I barely had enough information to form questions, much less any answers. She'd said Hanna was kidnapped. She'd said her relationship with her daughter was complicated. But she'd never told me why anyone would want to kidnap

Hanna. Viv owed the IRS money. She said the police couldn't be involved. She didn't get food poisoning when all her key conference volunteers did.

Jack told me he didn't know Hanna, but Viv had said they were friends and I overheard Jack and that girl mention Hanna's name. Was it a different Hanna? If so, that was a mighty weird coincidence on this particular weekend.

All these disjointed facts — if they even were facts — swirled around my head while I shuffled around the table stuffing swag into bags.

At some point Orville began helping me, but I didn't notice until I ran into him when we both dropped our filled bags into the corner. I looked around the workroom and saw that Clementine had set up an ironing board and was attaching conference logo patches to T-shirts. Lily was working on her laptop and quietly singing off-key with the iPod playing on the table next to her.

Before I placed another load of empty bags on the table, I took a moment to stretch. I raised my arms straight above my head and did a swan dive to touch my toes. I held the pose until the tightness in my back and legs disappeared. When I straightened, I checked the time. "Ohmygosh. It's almost two."

"I'm starving," Orville said, abandoning the bag in his arm.

Lily's eyes got wide and she pointed at her iPod while singing along to the lyrics, which coincidentally involved cheeseburgers and paradise. She stopped the music but her eyes remained surprised.

Jimmy Buffett's song wormed its way through my brain and I wiggled my hips. "I could eat."

"You know how Viv does all that volunteer work?" Clementine said without looking up from her ironing board. "You might not know it, but she's as generous with her money as she is with her time. If she were here, she'd probably require us to stop for lunch." She turned her head and looked at me.

I couldn't tell if a smile danced around her eyes. Probably not. Was she trying to guilt me into buying them lunch?

I didn't take the bait. "Hey, yeah. Want me to go get Jerry's samples? I think there were plenty left." I pretended to leave the workroom.

"No, that's okay," Lily piped up. "We'll order something."

"Don't tell the wife." Orville plopped into a nearby chair and pulled the Velcro from

142

his shoe. Riiiiiip.

"I know just the place." Clementine pulled out her phone. As she scrolled for a number, she said, "Watanabe's."

"Ooh, I love that place!" Lily clapped her fingertips together.

"So. Not cheeseburgers." I reset my taste buds. "Fine."

Twenty minutes later, a grim-faced Jack ushered a tough-looking twenty-something guy into the workroom carrying a large open box filled with brown bags, tops folded over and stapled. Biceps bulged. He announced, "Delivery. Watanabe Yatai."

Jack crossed his arms and waited near the door.

Lily and I hurried over to help collect the food. We placed the box on a table while the man handed the bill to Clementine. She placed the credit card slip on the nearest table and I saw she signed her name "Clement!ne Sm!th."

How adorkably hipster. It hadn't been Lily's overly enthusiastic notation after all.

The delivery guy lifted each bag from the box, announcing the items as he did so. "*Okonomiyaki,* sometimes called As-You-Like-It-Pancake. But it's more like pizza to me. This one's shrimp, this one's pork. *Takoyaki,* like doughnut holes, but with octo-

143

pus, ginger, and scallions. *Yakisoba,* which is noodles, pork, and vegetables. Fish cakes. And last but not least, two large ramens."

He ran a hand through the hair that had flopped down on his forehead. I suddenly recognized him. He was the guy I'd watched from my balcony having a fight with his girlfriend.

He collected the credit card slip, removed a handful of paper-wrapped chopsticks still in the delivery box, and then left with the empty box.

Jack turned to follow him out, but he stopped when Lily whispered, "Sweet potato pancakes, he's cute."

Clementine nodded. "Michael Watanabe is as important to his parents' restaurant as the food is."

Jack shook his head. "Watch out for him. Even though he claims he doesn't use anymore, we call him Michael-What-A-Druggie. He's bad news."

I opened up the bag with the shrimp *okonomiyaki* and inhaled deeply. "Someone who makes food this delicious simply can't be bad news."

"He's a small-time hoodlum drug dealer when he's not delivering food. He gets kids hooked. One of them was my best friend from high school. Made her do awful things." Jack's voice cracked.

"He must be small-time if he's still driving around delivery orders." Clementine handed out the sets of chopsticks.

"Just watch out for him. Oh, and I'm supposed to tell you that you're not allowed to have outside food sent here. We have a restaurant, you know."

"Yes, we know," I said. "Want some?" I held out the container of octopus doughnut holes.

Jack reached in and pulled one out. "Yes, please. Just one, though." He took a bite and turned for the door before spinning back for another. "Okay. Maybe two."

After we ate our fill and ponied up cash to reimburse Clementine, I excused myself, telling everyone I'd be back in a little bit.

"Good idea! Why use a public restroom when you can use the one up in your suite?" Lily clapped her fingers together again.

"Sheesh, Lily. Can't a girl tinkle in secret?" I had my hand on the doorknob when I heard Clementine clear her throat in the way people clear their throats when they really just want to get your attention without saying anything. I glanced back at her.

She jerked her head toward the pile of T-shirts and iron-on patches. "You could take these with you now, so you don't forget."

I almost said, "But I want to forget." Instead I said, "I'll get them later."

Clementine's eyes were hot enough to brand me.

As I crossed the lobby I saw Jack and a young woman, who still wore a maid's uniform of dark blue scrubs with her exotic headwrap, deep in what seemed to be a serious conversation. They were in a quiet corner of the restaurant. I wondered if it was the same girl I overheard talking with him yesterday. It certainly was the same girl I saw arguing with Michael Watanabe from my balcony. I veered away from my path toward the elevator and made a beeline for a stack of free newspapers on the counter outside the restaurant. I picked one up and pretended to be fascinated by an article on page three. They were too far away for me to hear their conversation clearly. Maybe she was the friend from high school Jack had mentioned.

Hugging the edge of a long, built-in planter overflowing with ivy, I inched closer and closer with my back toward them until I could make out a few words here and there. Their conversation seemed unimportant and a tad ridiculous until I heard

Hanna's name again. That couldn't be a co-incidence. Not twice, anyway. I still didn't know why Jack had lied about knowing Hanna, but it was time to find out.

Keeping my back to them, I folded the newspaper and tucked it under my arm so I could pull my phone from my bag easier. I walked back into the lobby, but turned around as soon as I was out of sight. I returned to the restaurant, put the newspaper to the top of the stack, and headed straight for them with my phone at my ear.

"Oh, there you are!" I said to Jack as I faked hanging up. "Viv asked me to ask you to call Hanna. She's having car trouble and needs help."

Without thinking, Jack pulled his phone from his pocket saying, "I wish she'd get a better car. That one is always breaking down."

"Aha!" I pointed my finger at him. "That was a trick! You said you didn't know Hanna." I stared down at them.

Jack and the girl exchanged a quick look, but neither said anything. Silence wasn't really an option for me. Not part of my plan, such as it was.

Jack held his phone in midair. "So she's not having car trouble?"

"No."

He pocketed his phone and glared at me. After a bit his face softened. "Fine. Yes, I know her. Hanna and I have been friends since eighth grade. Viv got me this job."

"Why did you tell me you didn't know her?"

"I don't know you, and I didn't know why you wanted to know." Jack cocked his head. "Still don't."

This put me in a bit of a bind. I wanted to know everything he could tell me about Hanna, but I couldn't let on she was missing. If Hanna really had been kidnapped, Jack would worry and might do something rash. If Hanna wasn't kidnapped, and this was some weird scam by Viv, Jack shouldn't know that either. And if Jack was somehow involved, I didn't want him to think I suspected anything. I had to come up with an acceptable fib.

"I was just making small talk. I heard you say her name, so I was curious. I'm a writer, remember? I'm curious about everything." I glanced at the girl's headwrap. "Actually, now that I think about it, it was you who said Hanna's name, not Jack. Do you know her too?"

The girl cut her eyes at Jack and didn't answer, instead attaching a name tag to her navy blue scrubs. Nervous? Buying time to consider her answer? She adjusted her name tag one last time, then lowered her hands and looked at Jack.

I leaned a bit closer to read her name. "Sarah, yesterday didn't I hear you say that Hanna isn't getting her way about something this time?"

She looked at me but didn't respond. I suddenly felt conspicuous standing there at their table.

"It's pronounced saRAH," Jack said.

"What?"

"You put the emPHAsis on the wrong sylLABle," Jack explained.

Portland really is weird, I thought. But I said, "Am I being punked?"

Instead of answering, Jack said, "Why do you want to know about Hanna?"

I contemplated my response. "Viv hasn't heard from her in a few days and she's worried. When was the last time you heard from Hanna?"

Another look passed between Jack and saRAH, and they had an entire conversation with their eyebrows.

Finally Jack said, "The last time I talked to her — must have been Monday or Tuesday — we got into a huge argument."

"About what?"

In a quiet voice, saRAH finally spoke.

149

"About me."

"Like I said, Hanna and I have been friends since eighth grade." At my raised eyebrows, Jack added, "Nothing like that. Just friends. But she's very protective of me and didn't want me to date saRAH. She thinks she'll break my heart." Jack took saRAH's hand. "We're in love, so we're keeping our relationship a secret from her. Just for a little while —"

If Jack and saRAH were in love, how did Michael Watanabe fit in? Were secrets being kept from Hanna *and* from Watanabe? Interesting.

"But Hanna must have heard rumors or something," saRAH said. "We needed to work up the courage to tell her."

"Why are you both so afraid to tell her you're dating? Maybe if she met Sarah, I mean saRAH —"

saRAH gave a tiny snort. "Hanna and I are best friends."

"Then wouldn't she be happy for you?"

"Hanna has a temper," Jack said.

"And she always gets her way," saRAH added.

Just like Viv. Mother and daughter must butt heads a lot. Maybe that was the difficult part of their relationship Viv mentioned.

"Hanna sabotaged the last three girls Jack dated," saRAH finished.

"So," I said to her, "you and Hanna are more like frenemies now?"

She shrugged.

I thought for a moment, then asked Jack, "Was it Hanna you were talking about when you said Michael Watanabe got your friend hooked on drugs?"

Jack nodded. saRAH dropped his hand and studied her shoes. Jack reached for her hand. He squeezed it gently and then rubbed his thumb on the back of it.

After a moment, she raised her eyes to mine. "I introduced Hanna to Michael. But I didn't know he was a drug dealer."

Jack stared at his thumb rubbing the back of her hand. "Hanna checked herself into rehab twice."

"Where?" I asked.

"I don't know. Nice place, somewhere on the coast."

"Could she have gone back?"

"I think she was clean," Jack said.

"She was," saRAH said. "The place was called ReTurn A New Leaf. There's no way she went back."

"No way." Jack shook his head.

"Then why haven't you heard from her?"

"I told you, I talked to her Monday or

Tuesday."

"And you?" I asked saRAH.

"Me what?"

"When did you last talk to Hanna?"

saRAH shrugged. "I don't know. Before that." She looked up at me. "How often do you talk to your friends?"

Hmm. Trick question. I thought about AmyJo back in Denver. Even though we were in a critique group together, we also had a long-lasting friendship. We went to movies. Out for coffee. On stakeouts. Well, just the once, but still. I racked my brain. When *was* the last time I'd talked to AmyJo outside of our critique group? I couldn't quite put my finger on anything specific. But that's to be expected, right? I was thirty, after all, with a real job — assuming you could call writing a real job — and, of course, I spent much of my time with Ozzi. But this wasn't about me.

I remained unconvinced that they were telling me everything. I had so many questions. Had Hanna racked up some debt because of her drug use? Owed the wrong guys? Would saRAH do something to Hanna to keep her from meddling in her relationship with Jack? Was Jack lying about something else? Why did he lie to me about knowing Hanna, really? The two of them didn't seem worried that they hadn't spoken to her recently. And what had saRAH been arguing with Michael Watanabe about?

Jack straightened saRAH's name tag and I remembered that they weren't that much younger than me, after all. They had real jobs and a significant other too.

They weren't acting like anything was amiss with Hanna, but I'd just met them. How would I know if they were telling me the truth? That's why I never played poker with strangers. Not since that scary night on the book tour with Viv, anyway. You didn't know their "tells." The way they scratch their cheek when holding only a pair of deuces. Or the way a waitress averts her eyes when she swears the salmon was flown in fresh this morning. Or the way your mom smiles when she tells you everything will be okay, then chases an Ambien with a glass of pinot noir.

I heard voices from the kitchen right behind me. Turning to see if I needed to move out of the way, I was surprised to see Viv walking backward into the dining room as she finished a conversation with someone in the kitchen. She pivoted and saw me.

"Charlee, hi . . . I was hammering out the menu details with what's-his-name. Justin?"

"Jerry," I said automatically. "Viv? What

153

are you doing here? I was just talking to Jack and saRAH —" I wanted to warn her that I hadn't said anything specific to them about Hanna and motioned behind me.

But they'd disappeared.

NINE

I was trying to keep my surprise in check at seeing Viv in the hotel. "What are you doing here?" I repeated in a whisper, following her across the restaurant.

"Why are you whispering?"

"Because you're here working on the conference instead of trying to find your kidnapped daughter."

Viv stopped walking and stared at me. Her eyes were red and ringed with dark circles. "I'm still freaked out about Hanna and I haven't heard anything more — from anyone, about anything — so I thought checking on conference details would keep my mind occupied."

"Have you gone to the police yet?"

"No. And I'm not going to. I told you that already." She grabbed my hand. "Have you? I told you not to —"

"No. Of course not. You told me not to. Besides, what would I tell them?" The

Portland police would probably be even less helpful than Lance.

She covered my hand with both of hers and held me tight for a moment before starting across the restaurant again. I followed on her heels, all the way to the Clackamas Room.

She threw open the door and called a cheery, "Hello, everyone!"

Lily, Orville, Clementine, and two middle-aged women I hadn't seen before greeted her, everyone chattering at once.

One of the women said, "How are you? I've heard food poisoning can make you want to shoot yourself."

"Oh, don't worry about me." Viv pulled out a chair next to where Orville had Lily's laptop open. It didn't escape my notice that Viv had neither confirmed nor denied that she'd had food poisoning.

"Hey, Viv," Lily said. "When is Garth getting here?"

All the women spoke at once, acting like preteens backstage with a boy band. Viv rolled her eyes and held up one hand, traffic-cop style. "Late tonight, I think. But that won't matter if we're not ready for the conference by then. Clem — can I call you Clem?" Viv reached into her purse.

"No."

Viv pulled out some papers stapled at the corner. "Um . . . Clementine, I heard there's some problem with the bookstore. These are the books we absolutely must have by tomorrow afternoon." She handed the pages to her. "Can you make sure they have these? And tell them if they don't, they better get them in stock if they want to run the conference bookstore next year."

"Pretty sure I won't tell them that. But I will check with them." Clementine folded the papers in half lengthwise and tucked them into her left Hello Kitty rainboot.

"Thank you." Viv grasped both of Clementine's hands in hers, just like she'd done with me earlier.

Clementine pulled away, acting like Viv had foisted a dirty diaper on her. She left the workroom with a shudder.

Viv didn't notice because she'd already turned to Lily and the two new volunteers. "Are all the signs made?"

"No," Lily said. "We only got halfway through. Then the printer jammed or ran out of ink or something."

Viv turned to Orville. "Can you go see what you can do about the printer?"

"Sure," he said.

"Or maybe Lily can do that." I waved at Lily. I had serious doubts that Orville could

157

extricate a sheet of paper from the jaws of the printer, given that it wasn't made of Velcro. But he probably could create a spreadsheet in no time at all showing the myriad ways paper could jam.

"Absolutely I can!"

"Okay." Viv glanced at me, but I shook my head ever so slightly. "Well, can the rest of you start putting up the signs we do have? And are all the workshops for each room, for each day, listed on the sign?"

Lily nodded while she shuffled through some papers. "Here's the Columbia, Willamette, and Multnomah Rooms." She handed the signs to Orville.

"And what about the name cards for all the speakers?" Viv asked.

"Done." One of the women held them up.

"Great," Viv said. "After you hang the workshop signs, can you three get the name cards into each workshop packet for the moderators?"

The two women looked at each other. "Workshop packets?" one asked.

"Moderators?" the other asked.

"The people who introduce the faculty at their workshops," Viv said.

Lily said to Viv, "Charlee didn't tell us to do that yet."

Viv looked at me. "Why not?"

"Well, two reasons I guess. One, nobody told me to do it. And two, I didn't know it had to be done. Oh, and three, I didn't know it had to be done!" My voice screeched a little bit when I repeated myself.

"Calm down. Geez." Viv turned to Orville and the two women. "Do you know what I'm talking about with the workshop packets? The big envelopes that hold the speaker introductions and the announcements and stuff?"

The women nodded. Orville did not. Perhaps he was wondering if his sneaker suddenly felt inexplicably too loose or too tight.

Viv continued. "Okay, get started on that as soon as Lily gets the printer fixed." As the group gathered up their things to tackle their respective jobs, she added, "Oh, and Lily? If you can't get the printer fixed right away, you'll have to use the one in the business center. It's on the third floor —"

"I already asked, but they said I can't."

"But I'm telling you that you can. And you must. We're running out of time." Viv shooed them all away before pulling the laptop in front of her. "If you hurry, maybe you'll be done before Garth gets here."

The two women giggled as they followed Lily and Orville out the door. Viv and I were

159

alone in the workroom.

"Who in the world is Garth?"

She typed while she spoke. "A flake I invite to speak every year so I can keep tabs on him."

"Why do you need to keep tabs on him?"

"Because he's a small-time criminal."

I frowned. "Is he talking about crime writing?"

"No. He's my ex-husband. I like to make sure he's keeping out of jail."

In all the time I'd known her, Viv had never mentioned her ex to me before. "Is he Hanna's father?"

She put her finger to her lips but didn't look up from the computer screen. "Shh. Don't tell him. He doesn't know. And neither does she."

A million thoughts raced through my brain until I landed on one. "Maybe he does. Could he be involved in the kidnapping?"

Viv stopped typing and looked directly at me. "Of course not. I told you, he's small-time. Just some disorderly conduct. Snuck into a Trail Blazers game, then made a nuisance out of himself trying to get them to drop the charges. Cops called it harassment." She stared over my left shoulder, lost in memories. "And then there was that silly misunderstanding when he recorded some movie at a premier. And once he harvested some cedar without keeping a record. I think they impounded his truck for that."

This conversation confused me. "Cedar?"

She shrugged. "This is lumberjack country. People have a close, personal relationship to their trees."

It all was beginning to seem less and less like a kidnapping. "Sounds like he's a grade-A hustler," I said. "How can you be sure he's not involved in Hanna's . . . disappearance?"

"Because I know him. He's petty."

"Maybe so petty he'd try to get back at you for keeping Hanna a secret from him? Surely he's not so stupid that he couldn't figure it out. Or maybe Hanna did and tracked him down."

The two middle-aged volunteers returned to the workroom. Viv gave them a smile and a half-wave, then whispered. "Even if he did figure it out AND wants to get back at me AND was smart enough to plan a kidnapping, I still need to raise the ransom money."

Viv's voice had gotten louder, and the women glanced our way. One of them pointed to the leftover takeout food. "Is that for anyone?"

"What?" Viv asked.

"Looks like it's from Watanabe's."

"Fantastic! Yes. I love their food." Viv jumped up and grabbed a container and a set of chopsticks. She returned to the computer, set the food between us, and logged in to the registration page.

"You got a ransom note?" I whispered.

"Another phone call," she whispered back.

"How much?"

"$339,000."

I repeated the amount back, unsure I heard correctly.

Viv took a bite of cold *yakisoba* and nodded.

"That's a weird amount. What's the significance? What does it mean?" My voice had risen, so I pointed at the computer screen to justify my part of the conversation in case the women were watching.

"Shh. No idea."

My mind whirred. The ransom demand turned this into a kidnapping the police could investigate. I watched with unfocused eyes as Viv typed on the laptop. I tried to formulate an argument compelling enough for her to finally involve the authorities, despite the kidnappers' death threat against Hanna. Her furious typing captured my attention, though. I watched, alarmed, as the realization of what she was doing finally sunk in.

"Viv, you can't."

"Charlee, don't you understand?" Viv spoke fast and pitched her voice down a notch. "This registration glitch was fate. I can use it to pay the ransom for Hanna."

"No, you can't," I whispered. We kept our voices low and our eyes on the computer screen while we talked.

"I can. I have access to the online bank where the registration money goes."

"I don't mean that you don't know how to. I mean you shouldn't." My pulse quickened.

"Charlee —"

"Viv. You can't. If you take all that money, how will you pay for the hotel and the food and all those honorariums? I'll donate mine, of course, but —"

"It's the only way."

"It can't be the only way."

Viv dropped her chopsticks and shoved the carry-out container away. "Do you want to give me $339,000?" She turned toward me, eyes flashing.

"Viv, some of that money isn't even real. If people are overcharged, they're going to call their credit card company and dispute the charges. Those numbers will be a computer glitch. Not actual funds. And I think that's embezzling."

"It's my only option." She turned back to the screen.

"No, it's not. You could go to the police."

"I already told you I'm not doing that."

We were at an impasse.

I tried once more to thrust and parry with my sword of logic. "There's probably not even enough money in the registration account anyway. You'd be committing however many crimes this is and still not be able to pay the ransom."

She didn't look at me. "Charlee, I'll figure it out. Everyone will get what's owed them. Just don't tell anyone."

Don't tell anyone? Who would I tell? Who would believe me?

This was the moment Viv made the switch from concerned mother to embezzler. And she was going to do it on Lily's computer. She was going to take that money. And it was clear she couldn't pay it back.

I glanced at the two women foraging for Japanese food leftovers. They sensed a rift between us and were surreptitiously straining to hear our conversation.

Viv studied the computer, then again reached for her chopsticks and the takeout container.

I placed my hand on her forearm, lowered my voice, and spoke in code. "I really don't think you should take that . . . *yakisoba.*"

Viv looked at me, then at the takeout. I tipped my head toward the computer, then toward the two volunteers. She nodded.

"I'm just borrowing, er, tasting it."

One of the women glanced our way.

"But what if something goes wrong?" I asked. "Can you . . . give it back?"

Viv nodded furiously. "Of course I can . . . give . . . it back. Don't worry. Everything will be . . . delicious."

"This is delicious," the volunteer called. The other one had her mouth full and simply gave a thumbs-up.

"I don't know, Viv. People have gotten locked up in jai — the hospital for . . . eating bad things."

I'd lowered my voice, but apparently not enough. One of the volunteers had a bite of food halfway to her mouth and set it down without eating. She pushed the takeout container away, emitting a small choking noise.

Viv smiled at her. "Don't mind Charlee. Nobody is going to . . . the hospital. I promise." She turned back to me. "Quit worrying, Charlee."

The ominous tone of her voice silenced

me and I thought about the V in ACHIEVE. Voice makes writing memorable. There's no mistaking Raymond Chandler's voice for Stephen King's, or Shakespeare's for Mark Twain's. Atticus Finch does not sound like Hercule Poirot.

But at this moment, Viv sounded exactly like Hannibal Lecter. Cold. Calculating. Caustic.

I watched the disconcerted volunteer eat the Japanese food, although with a little less gusto. Viv clicked away on the keyboard. Both made my stomach churn. Viv's phone rang and she dove for it. She didn't say hello. Didn't speak at all. Her eyes widened and she tucked herself into a protective huddle.

I mouthed, "The kidnappers?"

She retreated from the room and motioned me to follow. By the time I reached the hallway and shut the door behind me, Viv had already hung up.

"If the ransom isn't paid by noon on Saturday, then starting at one o'clock, one conference attendee per hour will be killed until it is paid."

I glanced at the closed workroom door. "Did you transfer the funds already?"

"They said the ransom had to be paid in full."

"Viv, you have to cancel this conference."

"It's already" — she looked at her phone — "3:40. The conference starts tomorrow. People are already trickling in. It's too late to cancel. I'd have to return everyone's fees, maybe even their travel costs, and I'd still be on the hook to pay for the hotel and speakers and food. You know I can't afford that. We've had this argument and I don't want to keep having it!" She brushed me aside to return to the Clackamas Room.

I stood in the doorway and watched her log out of Lily's computer and collect her things. As she shoved past me she whispered, "Besides, I'm sure they're bluffing about killing people. How would the kidnappers know who was a conference attendee and who wasn't?" She rushed away down the hall.

I stared at her back, stunned. Then I glanced at the table containing the pile of Stumptown Writers' Conference name tags awaiting lanyards.

How would they know? Because every attendee would be wearing one of those.

Like sitting ducks.

I recovered from my shock when I realized that Viv had never answered my question about whether she'd transferred the funds. I raced down the hall after her but didn't see her anywhere in the lobby. I rushed out the revolving door, hoping to make her see reason before she drove off. Hurrying through the portico, I skidded to a stop behind a pillar when I saw Viv having words with Roz. They were too far away for me to make out their conversation, but it was clear by their body language and faces that they were arguing. Something behind them caught their attention and they both bolted. Viv to her car, where she roared away, and Roz to behind a pillar that matched mine on the other side of the large circular drive.

I peeked around my pillar to see what had scared them. Jack? He was struggling to place a large, lumpy duffle bag into the back of the hotel van. My imagination fired up. Was there a body in the duffle? Was he strong enough to carry a body like that?

After Jack closed up the van, he went back to the side of the building, where he'd come from. Roz popped out from behind her pillar, looked furtively around, and then hurried toward the van and drove away.

I returned to the lobby, surprised to see Jack already back at his desk. I walked nonchalantly toward him. He flashed me his thousand-watt concierge smile, which I returned. Or tried to. I could only work up to a dim forty.

"That was some big duffle bag. What was in it?"

His wattage flickered like his electric bill hadn't been paid. "Nothing. Hotel business."

A guest walked up to Jack before I could find out if he was strong enough to lift a dead body in one hand. I wasn't sure how to go about that short of loading myself into a bag and asking him to deliver me to my room.

I moved away from the concierge business being conducted. Pushing aside two throw pillows, I plopped myself down in one of the plush loveseats in the lobby. I wanted to make a list of everything, to help clarify my thinking and perhaps see some solutions, but I didn't have a notepad with me. Instead, I stared into the nothingness across the lobby. Before I could have a good think, though, I heard a voice say, "Do you mind if we use this?"

A border collie with a woman attached stared intently at me. "Do you?" the woman repeated, pointing at a hassock near me.

"No, I don't mind."

The dog danced beside her as the woman pushed it across the lobby toward two other hassocks. She maneuvered these three, then a fourth, situating each exactly ten heel-to-toe lengths apart. She called the border collie over, pointed at each of the hassocks, and upon some magic command, the dog took off like he was shot out of a cannon, sailing over each hurdle with precision. When he finished, he circled to the woman's side and sat gazing up expectantly. She gave a tiny nod and he raced to leap over them again.

I watched them do this eight times in a row. I grew tired of it, but the dog and his handler looked like they could do it until Christmas.

The handler noticed that others were waiting for a turn on the obstacle course. She stepped aside and pointed at her border collie, who sat. Then she walked behind the dog's back, pulled something from her pocket, and tucked it under a chair. She did it again, this time tucking it inside a couch cushion. She hid treats in four more places, then went back to her dog, who hadn't moved a muscle. She said "Search!" and the border collie took off, finding and gobbling the treats one after the other.

A man escorted by a weimaraner asked if I was using the pillows I'd pushed aside.

"Take whatever you want." I stood and

waved my arm magnanimously.
I had a plan.

TEN

I strode across the restaurant, flinging my messenger bag bandolier-style across my chest. The room was mostly empty this late in the afternoon and nobody saw me push open the swinging doors that led to the kitchen. I didn't recognize any of the kitchen staff, and I hoped they wouldn't toss me out like wilted lettuce.

"Is Roz here?" I asked, knowing full well she wasn't.

A server leaned on a stainless steel prep table swiping on her phone. She didn't look up. "Nope."

"Do you happen to know if she left the menus for us in her office?" I also hoped this was where Roz's office was, but you know what happens when you assume.

"Nope." Again, no eye contact. I could be a crazed murderer carrying an axe, a pipe bomb, and a half-starved Siberian tiger and the server wouldn't have been able to identify me.

"Do you mind if I go back and look?"

"Whatev."

I accepted that in the same manner I would an engraved invitation. Hoping I wouldn't meet any inquisitive kitchen staff, I held my breath past the walk-in freezer, a storage area, and a door identified with only a generic *Executive Chef* nameplate. I exhaled slowly when I reached a door marked *Catering Manager.* Slipping into Roz's office, I pulled the door closed behind me. No lock on the knob. I'd have to work fast. I surveyed the small area. Desk covered with file folders and scattered papers. Credenza stuffed with binders and cookbooks, scraps of paper, and Post-It notes sticking at crazy angles from most of them. Since I had no idea what I was looking for, unlike the border collie, I didn't know where to start. I only knew that the duffle bag, Jack's demeanor, and the argument between Roz and Viv made me suspicious.

The desk was closest to me, so I began there. I lost no time shuffling papers, flipping files, rooting through drawers, and moving practically everything I could reach, sure the door would fly open and Roz would catch me. After what seemed like forever, I clasped three items to my bosom.

The first was an unopened letter addressed to Roz from ReTurn a New Leaf, Hanna's rehab place. Why would Roz have anything to do with Viv's daughter's drug rehab? I desperately wanted to open it, but tampering with the mail was a federal offense. Clasping it to my bosom undoubtedly made me some sort of desperado, but if I got caught, maybe I could argue entrapment. It was right there in plain sight and leapt into my arms. Kind of.

The second item was a manila folder stuffed with photos of storefronts and attractive young women in their mid-twenties, like Hanna. Some sort of high-class prostitution ring? Escort service? None of the women were posed suggestively, and all wore proper and modest clothes. It didn't matter to me what kinky thing Roz was into, unless it might involve this situation with Hanna.

And the final paper I clutched was the original catering contract Roz and Viv had signed for the conference. At the top was scribbled *Never again.* A threat from Roz? From Viv? It didn't look like Viv's handwriting, but I couldn't be certain.

I found a stack of oversized mailing envelopes and shoved my evidence, or theft, or contraband, or whatever they'd call it when they arrested me, inside one. I shoved the envelope into my bag. I peeked from Roz's office into the kitchen. The only soul there was still the server playing on her phone. I walked past and neither of us acknowledged the other.

My plan was to march over to Jack's concierge station and demand information, but my hands started to shake. I veered to the bar and asked for a glass of water. I forced myself to sip the entire thing mindfully, willing myself to calm down.

Sure, I'd stolen stuff from Roz's office, but it had to be done, right? Roz and Jack were both acting so suspiciously, lying about this and that, and Viv was being completely wacko. I was the only one who could get to the bottom of this fiasco.

Right?

Was I?

I drained my glass, feeling less and less sure of anything.

"Anything else for you?" the bartender asked.

I studied the rows and rows of bottles behind him. "Give me a shot of that." I pointed to his left, at a squat bottle made of clear glass with a silver stopper that resembled a pineapple. Or maybe a pinecone. The bartender lifted it down by its neck and I saw two silver hands clutching the sides of the bottle. Or maybe they were two silver leaves.

"You're a tequila gal?"

"I am today."

After my shot — okay, fine, two shots — I summoned courage to my sticking place — or sticky place, since my shaky hands had spilled a bit of tequila — and marched across the lobby to where Jack worked at his desk.

He saw me coming and retreated to the reception desk in a poorly masked attempt to act busy far away from me. I met him there, leaned toward the desk clerk, and said in the sweetest voice I could muster, "I'm so sorry to drag Giacomo away, but I have a problem only he can help me with." I held Jack's upper arm and saw the clerk's mouth twitch. She got a knowing look on her face and nodded the teensiest bit. "No! Not that," I said, dropping his arm. "I have some questions only he can answer."

The clerk's nod became more emphatic. "I hear you, sister," she muttered before walking away.

I turned to Jack, both of us fire-engine red and clutching ourselves as if we had been caught naked in math class.

"Thanks. Thanks a lot," he said.

"It's not my fault your handsome is right out there for everyone to see."

Jack used his arm to wipe his brow. "What was it you wanted?" I could tell from his voice he'd rather I didn't actually tell him.

"I have more questions about Hanna. I need to —"

Cutting me off with a finger in the air, he pulled me away from the reception desk. He dialed his phone and whispered into it, "Meet me downstairs." He marched to the hallway leading to the meeting rooms and I followed.

Was he taking me to Hanna? Was she hiding in the hotel? Or was he taking me to the kidnappers? I stumbled in front of the Deschutes Room but he only gave me a cursory glance over his shoulder.

When we got to the Clackamas Room, before the hallway made its ninety-degree turn, I stopped. The chances were good not many people were in the other, more distant parts of the hallway. "Where are we going?"

Jack had already turned the corner with his long stride, but stepped backward toward me. "Downstairs."

"Why?"

"You said you had more questions about Hanna."

"Why can't I ask them here? And who did you call?"

"saRAH. Better for her. Lots of people happy to rat us out."

"For what? Dating? Besides, I told the front desk clerk I had a problem. I'm sure she assumed it was work-related."

Jack turned the corner. "Are you coming or not?"

Was I? No, I wasn't. I considered diving into the workroom, and all the tasks waiting to be done. That's what I should be doing. Not this, whatever "this" was. I took a hesitant step toward the Mount St. Helen's Room. But what if Hanna was down in the basement? What if she needed help? What if Clementine hadn't gone down there to question Billy the PI or smoke weed after all? What if that was just a story? What if I could mop up this mystery in the next hour, then get back to putting this stupid conference on?

Courage. Sticking place. Suck it up, Charlee.

I turned the corner and saw Jack gripping the handle of the hidden door.

I looked behind me. I looked at Jack.

Then I followed him through the door.

ELEVEN

Jack reached behind me to shut the door. As before, the dim yellow bulb cast the short hallway in a weird, unnatural sort of twilight. Jack moved faster than I did and the darkness swallowed him. I hurried to catch up. When I did, I saw him waiting at the stairs, which descended into even more darkness.

"Watch where you step. Sometimes there's rats. Or worse."

Worse than rats? I shuddered to think what I would have done if I'd seen any rats when I was down here alone.

Of my two choices, to go back or to keep following Jack, I knew one thing. Neither was a good decision.

I chose to follow him down the stairs. But as I did, one eye watching for rats, I pulled up Lily's number on my phone. I'd only talked to her twice on the phone since I'd been at the hotel, but I knew that if there was trouble, I'd only have to hit one button and in half a second I'd hear her standard cheery greeting: "It's Lily! Thanks for calling! What can I do for you?" Unless I got her voicemail, that is. Still a cheery greeting, but absolutely useless for my purposes.

Of course, I was assuming I'd have cell service. I checked my phone. Two bars. I drew a breath.

We reached the bottom of the stairs with nary a rat, mouse, or worse sighting. The yellow caged light bulbs were set farther apart, making the light even more dim. I hurried to keep up with Jack, who expertly picked his way through the maze. Only the darkness seemed familiar from before. We twisted and turned so many times I knew I probably couldn't make it back to the Clackamas Room even if I wanted to. And I was beginning to want to.

Jack stopped suddenly and I crashed into his back. I took two steps backward when he reached for a door. It opened to the outside of the hotel, and I peeked over his shoulder as he blocked the threshold, looking right then left. It seemed to me like an underground parking area, maybe for deliveries. But there were no vehicles or people there, and he closed the door and continued through the maze. It was bright above my head now, the dim yellow bulbs replaced with higher wattage white ones. I tried to memorize our location in case I needed to make a run for the outer door. I snapped a few quick photos, but they showed only the washed-out back of Jack's head ahead of me and darkness behind. As I checked the photos, something caught my eye.

Zero bars.

Jack was out of view and I hurried after him, longing for daylight.

After a few steps, the bright light disappeared and the hallway was plunged back into the eerie twilight. I pulled up my flashlight app and used it to better light my way.

As I followed Jack, I realized the bowels of the hotel, from the looks of it, were mostly used for storage. Jack zigged, zagged, and then finally stepped into a room filled with furniture that matched some of the pieces in my room on the eighth floor. Three loveseats covered in the same fabric, but the cushions were torn. Several rolling desk chairs missing some of their wheels. Armoires with broken hinges. And one desk broken completely in the middle, as if someone had taken a sledgehammer to it.

"What?" a voice behind me said.

Simultaneously I heard a bang on a wall.

The hallway and storage room blazed with fluorescent light.

I jumped directly out of my skin and did an awkward pirouette toward Jack.

I saw saRAH and Jack staring at me. "Why didn't you do that on the way down here?" My terror made me sound petulant, which maybe I was.

"Do what? Turn on the lights?" Jack said.

I nodded and tried to regain some dignity.

"Why would I do that? I knew where I was going. The emergency lights save energy."

There was no sign of Hanna or kidnappers or anyone else down here. I plopped myself on the nearest torn loveseat and took a deep, cleansing breath. I powered down my flashlight and noticed I was at 38 percent power. "Why did we come all the way down here?" I still sounded petulant, but I was fine with that. Better than having them know how close I was to peeing my pants.

"It's obvious. I have the run of the place, but maids don't. Ever seen a uniformed maid in a hotel lobby? It's easier for saRAH to sneak down here."

"She was in uniform in the restaurant," I pointed out.

"I like to push the envelope. Live dangerously," saRAH smirked.

Suddenly I jumped up from the loveseat. "Do you guys come down here to —"

"Gross!"

"No!"

To cover my embarrassing imagination, I said, "Sorry. I thought it would be a good place to, you know, live dangerously . . . sneak a smoke."

"Oh," Jack said. "Well, yeah, we do that."

"What's this all about?" saRAH asked, lighting a cigarette.

Since it didn't look like I was going to rescue Hanna or get whacked, I said, "I need to access Hanna's social media."

saRAH expelled a smoky breath that would have been right at home in a film noir from the 1940s. "Hanna doesn't respond to calls or texts unless she instigates the conversation."

How convenient, I thought.

"She might respond to a direct message from me," Jack said. "Why?"

"I told you before. Viv wants to get in touch with her."

"Maybe she's avoiding for a reason." More smoky words from saRAH.

I fought the urge to wave my hand in front of my face because I suspected that was exactly what she wanted me to do. "Maybe. But wouldn't you like to know?"

Instead of answering, she blew smoke slowly and deliberately into the air and then panicked when she realized she was directly under the smoke alarm. She and Jack frantically fanned the smoke away. When it had dissipated, saRAH stubbed out her cigarette and dropped to the arm of one of the love-seats.

"What's her username on Facebook?" I pulled out my phone. Still no bars. I'd have to check her profile later.

saRAH snorted. "Facebook? She's not ninety." She raised one perfectly threaded, disbelieving eyebrow.

"Fine. What's her social media platform of choice?"

"If you have to ask, you probably aren't on it." saRAH fiddled with her pack of cigarettes, closing and opening her hand until the package was crushed. I didn't even think she noticed.

"Instagram, then."

"Nope."

"Twitter? Tumblr? Snapchat? Weibo? Reddit?" I raised one finger and smiled, convinced I had it. "LinkedIn."

saRAH started to answer but Jack interrupted. "Actually, it's Symwyf."

"Sim Whiff?"

"Speak Yo Mind With Yo Friends."

"Never heard of it."

saRAH tucked her crushed cigarette pack into the couch cushion. "Not surprised."

"It's new," Jack said.

I won't lie. It hurt that he gave me a verbal pat on my forty-years-in-the-future blue-tinted grandma hair.

He pulled his phone from his pocket. "I'll DM her right now and tell you the minute she responds." When he finished he looked at me. "Want me to also send a tweet to our friends and ask if anyone has seen her?"

I wondered if he had really direct messaged her. He had bars but I didn't? "No. I don't want to alarm anyone," I said, even though these two were not the least bit worried about Hanna. But if there really was a kidnapper paying attention, I wouldn't want him — or her — to get a whiff of anything. Especially not a Symwyf.

"I don't know why you're so worried about her," saRAH said. "Hanna goes AWOL all the time —"

"Mostly to get away from her mother," Jack added.

"Where does she usually go?"

"Once she followed a boyfriend to Hawaii on the surfer circuit," saRAH said. "And another time she went to hike the Appalachian Trail on a dare."

"Who dared her?"

"Me." saRAH rubbed her throat with one hand.

"Why would she run off without telling her mother?" I wanted to understand Hanna and Viv's relationship.

"Their relationship is . . . complicated," Jack said.

"That's what I hear. How is it complicated?"

saRAH ticked off the reasons on her fingers. "Viv doesn't like Hanna's boyfriend, doesn't like that Hanna dropped out of college, doesn't like that Hanna doesn't do what Viv wants her to do, doesn't like that she has a part-time job that doesn't come close to paying her bills —"

"How does she support herself?"

Jack and saRAH exchanged an uneasy glance.

"I don't know, but it's probably got something to do with her boyfriend." Jack spat out the word like it was a bite of Jerry's Avocado Crumble.

"What's Hanna's boyfriend's name?" I asked.

They answered in unison. "Michael Watanabe."

"The drug dealer?"

Again they nodded in unison.

saRAH and Jack exchanged a kiss in the dark hallway outside the storage room after the fluorescents had been turned off. She went one way and I followed Jack the other. The trip back to the lobby seemed to take a fraction of the time it had taken to get down there. Fear and an unknown destination play tricks on your senses, I guess.

Jack went back to work. I plopped into an overstuffed chair in the lobby with a good view of the revolving door and dialed the Watanabe Yatai takeout number. While I waited for Hanna's boyfriend to deliver my order — and maybe some answers — I watched dogs and their handlers run through a small agility course they'd set up with props from the lobby. The hassocks were still there from before, joined by sets of throw pillows leaning together in inverted Vs.

I watched the dogs leap over the different types of hurdles. I laughed out loud when the smaller dogs jumped onto the hassocks and struck a pose worthy of a Milan runway. I craned my neck when I realized part of the course had been out of my view. Chairs from the restaurant were set up with jackets draped over them to create a tunnel for the dogs to crawl through. I watched a brindle greyhound start through the tunnel but worried when it didn't come out the other end in the amount of time I thought it should. Apparently the handler was worried too and dropped to his knees at the end of the tunnel. He called out, "C'mon, Shasta. This way!"

Shasta seemed to get spooked by the tunnel and in her haste to get out, knocked over two of the chairs and got tangled up in the jackets that fell.

With a start I realized that Jack and saRAH really could have whacked me down in the basement. I would have been hidden like Shasta but nobody would have known to look for me. I'd been scared of them, then I wasn't, and now I was again. Were they toying with me? They didn't seem to think it was weird that I kept asking about Hanna. Or did they? Were they just hiding it? Were they hiding her? Were they trying to lull me into some false sense of security so they could whack me later?

So confused. So paranoid.

My paranoia only intensified when Michael Watanabe arrived with the food I'd ordered. Even though I was fairly certain he didn't remember me from earlier, I stammered nervously, "You got me hooked!"

As soon as I said it, I wanted those words stuffed back into my mouth. Probably not appropriate to say to a convicted drug dealer. Even though I was talking about the *yakisoba* and those delicious octopus doughnut holes.

He ignored me, instead holding out two plastic bags with Watanabe's logo stamped on them. "This one's the —"

"When was the last time you saw Hanna? Or heard from her?" I blurted, without taking the bags.

He froze.

"Do you guys live together?"

No answer.

"Does she work for you?"

He hadn't moved. Still held out the bags.

"Is she on drugs?" I asked, quieter.

His eyes flickered. Fear? Regret? I couldn't tell.

He stepped toward a nearby table and deposited the bags. I realized my paranoia had made me come on too strong. He was ready to hightail it out of here and I'd never see him again.

But he didn't. He moved right in front of me and squared his shoulders. "Are you a narc? Because I've done my time. Out of the biz."

I calmed myself by filling my lungs with air and then slowly releasing it. He'd given me a second chance. "I'm not a narc. Hanna's mom and I are looking for her."

"She's disappeared before." Michael Watanabe walked away, then said over his shoulder, "Always comes back."

I stared as he pushed through the revolving door, and long after he'd gone. He, too, was completely unconcerned by Hanna's disappearance. Alleged disappearance. I couldn't help but think that all of this had nothing to do with Hanna and everything to do with Viv. But what? It would sure explain why Viv was more than happy to embezzle from the conference but not to get the authorities involved with her daughter's kidnapping. Alleged kidnapping. Did Viv have something to do with the glitch that charged people almost four thousand bucks for this conference? And why would the kidnapper know or care about the Stumptown Writers' Conference? It seemed targeted to make trouble for Viv. Or at least gave her some, what . . . plausible deniability? My brain kept circling back to the fact that none of Hanna's friends were worried about her.

I jumped when someone touched my shoulder.

"Pardon me. I'm sorry to intrude, but. . . ." Bernice from the front desk glanced pointedly at the takeout bags from Watanabe's. "You're not supposed to bring outside food in since we have a restaurant." Her Southern belle charm dimmed her smile appropriately at being forced to reprimand me.

I'd completely forgotten about the food and realized Michael left without being paid. I flashed her a grin and handed her the bags. "I actually got this for you guys, to thank you for working so hard to . . ." I heard the handlers calling commands and encouragement to their dogs. "To thank you for working so hard to correct the double-booking situation." I had absolutely no idea if they were doing anything to correct the double-booking situation, but if they were, great, and if they weren't, maybe now they would. Win-win.

Bernice took the bags. "Well, bless your heart. Thanks!" She walked away with a smile that came close to splitting her face, calling to her cohorts behind the desk, "Hey, ya'll. That lady just bought us dinner."

I waved at them and hurried away in the opposite direction to avoid any further discussion of my generosity. Alleged generosity.

Not sure where exactly I was headed, I stopped when I saw the revolving lobby door to my right. I wasn't satisfied with my conversation, if you could call it that, with Michael Watanabe. Why wasn't he more concerned about Hanna? Why had he been arguing with saRAH outside? Was he still using or dealing drugs? What didn't he want me to know?

Maybe our conversation had spooked him and he might show his hand in some way. I wished now that I'd thought to follow him right away. But if I went to Watanabe's now and he was there, it would show he hadn't gotten spooked at all and was just back at work. And if he was back at work, I could justify being there to pay him for the food he delivered.

I turned back toward Bernice at the desk. "Hey, Bernice, where is Watanabe's exactly?"

"It's on the corner of . . . I want to say it's at Multnomah and Grand, but it might be at Seventh." Jack had returned to his desk from the luggage room, so she called out to him across the lobby, "Jack? Is Watanabe's on Grand or Seventh? This lady is asking for directions."

Jack looked at me and cocked his head. "Grand."

Bernice nodded. "Multnomah and Grand. Not too far from here. If you're walking over, you can borrow an umbrella." She gestured toward a stylish bucket filled with half a dozen different colored umbrellas.

"Yes, that would be —"

"But didn't you just get a delivery from Watanabe's?" She glanced toward the door where the food had been spirited away by the staff.

I flashed her what I hoped was a winning and charming and not at all suspicious smile. "Like a dummy, I forgot to pay him."

"He didn't hand you a bill? Watanabe's is so old school. They should ask for credit card info when people order." Bernice leaned forward on the front desk. "Especially since everyone knows how . . . flaky their delivery boy can be."

I leaned on the counter too. "Flaky how?"

"Oh, you know." She waved a hand around her head. "Forgetful. Marches to his own drummer."

"How do you know him?"

"Michael? Everyone knows Michael." The phone rang, so she excused herself to answer it.

Puzzled, I walked toward the umbrella

bucket and drew out a pretty one. Why would everyone know Michael Watanabe? I considered possibilities, all simply conjecture, as I crossed the lobby to the revolving door. I passed one of the front desk clerks on his phone and he almost swerved into me. "Excuse me, ma'am," he said as he sidestepped.

Ma'am. Ouch.

Outside, I opened up my pretty green and blue umbrella, dismayed that it was festooned with the Seattle Seahawks logo. I hoped this wouldn't revoke my Denver Broncos fan card.

I turned left down Multnomah just as the rain picked up. How do people live here, I wondered, missing the dry Colorado weather. I splashed the direction I thought I was supposed to go, not seeing anything but my feet except for the times I raised my umbrella at intersections to read the street signs. It was twilight and the streetlights were on, casting weird reflections in the puddles and bouncing off all the lights, from the street, from cars, from shops. People were bustling all around me, very few carrying umbrellas. Just me and the old people. That guy's earlier "ma'am" stung me again.

I plodded along through the rain, raising my umbrella every so often to search for

Grand or a sign for Watanabe's. I was still amazed by how different Portland rain is from Denver rain. Most of our rain comes on summer afternoons, quick and harsh thunderstorms sailing toward us from the mountains in the west. Those storms are often violent and destructive, bringing hail, lightning, torrents of rain and wind. If they aren't violent, though, they are always noisy. Hard rain falling fast, blitzing in and then out of the state just as quickly, over the mountains from the west out to the plains on the east, bada bing, bada boom. Kansas's problem now.

But here, in Portland, the rain was softer. More insidious. Like it wanted to get to know you, stick around for a while. A long-term loving relationship versus a raucous one-night stand. I smiled at my analogy and listened to the few sounds around me, mostly just cars whooshing and splashing past. No voices. Everyone seemed to be on a mission to get somewhere. All I heard around me were my footsteps and the occasional trickle of rain down the nylon fabric.

I listened, a bit hypnotized, until I became aware of another set of footsteps, matching mine in perfect rhythm. I glanced quickly over my shoulder but only saw a red umbrella bobbing behind me. My paranoia was on high alert. I slowed down. They slowed down. I sped up. They sped up. I raised my umbrella to see I was mid-block, between intersections. I ran across the street, dashing dangerously between cars, splashing loudly in puddles. When I got to the sidewalk I raised my umbrella to look at the other side of the street.

No red umbrella. Had my imagination taken me into dangerous traffic or was someone actually following me? Did they open a door to their destination or were they watching me from some hidden vantage point?

Either way, I was anxious to get to Watanabe's. I hurried to the next intersection and saw it was Seventh. If Bernice couldn't remember if the restaurant was at Seventh or Grand, I must be close. When I got to Sixth, I saw a tall sign that said *Japanese Food.* I decided that even if it wasn't Watanabe's, that's where I was going. I could get a cab from there.

I crossed the street again and ran the last block, flinging the restaurant door open, relieved to see *Welcome to Watanabe's* on it. As I burst in, startled diners stared at me. I tried shaking my umbrella outside the door, but only succeeded in flinging water all over the vestibule.

The elderly hostess hurried toward me, gently taking the umbrella from me and dropping it into their stand. "Table for one?" she asked.

"Um . . . actually, I'm looking for Michael."

She gave me a serious once-over, then went to the saloon doors into the kitchen and called to him. He came out wiping his hands on an apron he wore. When he saw me, he turned on his heel and returned to the kitchen.

The hostess watched this, then stomped over to me, grabbed my elbow, and hustled me to the furthest seat at the sushi bar. She was tiny but strong and pushed me into a stool. "What you want with my grandson?"

"I . . . I . . . wanted to pay him for some food he delivered earlier."

"He bring you food? You no pay for?"

"I didn't mean to. I just forgot. We both forgot."

She stared at me for a long time before finally nodding. "Yes. He do that." She bustled off to the kitchen.

My eyes traveled around the interior of the restaurant. Even though the aromas were deliciously Asian, the decor was decidedly not. Throughout the entire restaurant were photographs and newspaper clippings of a wrestler, almost always holding a trophy. I slid off my stool to take a closer look. They were all of, or about, Michael.

Michael Watanabe, Japanese food delivery boy and drug dealer, had been a high school and college wrestling champion several years in a row. No wonder Bernice said everyone knew him.

As I was bent over reading one of the articles, I heard him say, "Here's your bill. You can pay my grandma at the register." He turned and walked away.

I wanted to talk to him some more, to continue our conversation from before, but I couldn't come up with any questions I hadn't already asked. And it was obvious his feelings for me hadn't grown any more hospitable.

Since he was wearing an apron and had been involved in the kitchen when I arrived, it didn't seem that he'd stopped anywhere on his way back from delivering food to the hotel. Clearly he hadn't been spooked by our encounter. Or if he had been, he didn't detour anywhere that would have shown me his hand. I paid, tacked on a sizable tip, and waited at the sushi bar for a cab back to the hotel.

Michael Watanabe was still no less of a

puzzle to me. But now I could add "Was I being followed?" to my list of concerns.

Jack knew I was going to Watanabe's, because Bernice had told him when she verified the location. Had he followed me? And if so, why?

When I got back to the hotel, I immediately looked for Jack. I wanted to see if his shoes and hair were wet like mine. He wasn't at his desk.

As I slid my Seahawks umbrella into the bucket, I asked, "Bernice, do you know where Jack is?"

"He went home for the day. Is there anything I can help you with? I'd be happy as a clam to do so."

"No. Nothing. Thanks though. I'll talk to him tomorrow."

I was striking out all over the place. And I was hungry. Since I'd given the desk staff the dinner I'd ordered from Watanabe's earlier, and I hadn't thought to order anything while at the restaurant, I grabbed one of the bowls of trail mix sitting out in the lobby and scooped a hefty dose into my mouth. As I turned, chomping, I almost tripped over Scout, her huge German shepherd frame enthusiastically leaping over some of the inverted pillow obstacles. I caused her to knock them over, and as I attempted to right them, she modified her performance with some random enthusiastic leaping, now combined with a new trick — competitive face-licking.

Every time I bent over to balance the pillows, she'd knock them over trying to kiss me and steal some trail mix from my bowl. The more I laughed, the more exuberant she became. Finally, Scott walked over. With Brad Pitt beside him.

"Scout. Sit."

She stopped mid-lick and mid-bounce, sitting as still as Lot's wife at Scott's side.

Her handler turned to me. "I'm sorry about that. She gets a little excited. But I think she likes you."

I rubbed Scout on the side of her face. "I like her too."

One inch of her tail flicked back and forth.

"I should be that lucky," Brad said.

"My secret's out. I love getting my face slobbered on." I rubbed Scout some more, bending closer. "Sorry, baby. You're not slobbering and I didn't mean to imply such a thing."

Flick, flick, flick.

I offered Brad and Scott some trail mix. When they both declined with grimaces, I said, "More for me" and nibbled another handful.

We watched a couple of dogs run through the makeshift agility course. Then Scott said, "Okay, Scout. Want one last turn?"

Without waiting for a command, she raced around the course. Scott didn't even tell her what to do, but she completed it exactly as the two previous dogs had. But faster, much faster, despite almost catching her girth inside the tunnel of chairs. She wiggled free and galloped toward us, skidding to a stop at Scott's feet.

"She's amazing," Brad said to Scott.

I bent to nuzzle her. "Yes, you are. Who's amazing? Who's an amazing girl? Is it you? Yes, it is. It's you!" Scout and I had a moment until I realized how silly I must sound. I straightened and felt my face flush.

"You love her." Brad chuckled.

Scott nodded. "Scout has that effect on people."

"Can she teach me?" Brad waggled his eyebrows.

"Scout or Charlee?" Scott teased.

"There's an idea." Brad turned toward me. "Wanna slobber on my face?"

"Tempting, but no."

"Aw, c'mon. Have a drink with me. I'm not ready to go up and deal with my roommate yet. Being awfully cranky." He batted his eyes melodramatically. "You're not cranky at all."

"We'll leave you two to it. Come on, Scout. Bedtime."

I said, "Bedtime for me too," but wished I hadn't when Brad waggled his eyebrows again. "Geez, you're relentless. Go find someone else to flirt with. Maybe you'll wear *them* down." I fluttered my fingers goodbye to him and met up with Scott and Scout waiting at the elevator.

"No nightcap?" Scott asked.

"Nah. I've got a boyfriend I'm on my way to call right now."

"Does he know you have a boyfriend?" Scott ticked his head toward Brad, who was walking into the bar area.

"Yeah. Brad's a big flirt," I said. "Probably wouldn't know what to do if his lines worked on anyone."

"You're right. Come to think of it, seems whenever I see him, he's hanging out with guys. Just a big talker."

We both glanced over at Brad, now sitting at the bar talking animatedly with the bartender.

The elevator came and as the doors were closing, Brad gave us a happy little wave. Scott waved back, but both Scout and I reached for the button for the eighth floor.

Me with an index finger, her with a snout.

"You're on eight? We are too, aren't we, Scout?"

Scout replied with a thump of her tail.

"You taught her to push the button?"

"No, she already knew that. I just showed her which one was eight."

I let Scout push the button.

We got off on eight and walked together. I realized Scott might be escorting me to my door and I waved him off. "I'm okay. You don't need to walk me home."

"No, I'm down this way. 811."

I blushed. Of course. I stopped at 809. "Good night, you two." I fished my key card from my back pocket and unlocked my door.

"G'night, Charlee. Say good night, Scout."

Scout gave one solid bark. Then another. Then a third.

"What a good girl you are," I said. "*Bark* back atcha."

A woman with an angry face poked it out of a door down the hall. When she saw the full impact of Scout staring at her she pulled back inside and closed the door without a word. I felt a vindictive delight that Scout's bark annoyed her as much as her always-needing-filled ice bucket annoyed me.

"Good girl," I said again and gave her a

good-night thump on her side.

I peeled off my clothes and changed into my comfy brushed-cotton pajama bottoms and an oversized T-shirt of Ozzi's I'd stolen from him. I took a good long sniff of the shirt before pulling it over my head. It still had a trace of his scent, a cross between freshly mowed grass and pancakes. I always thought this odd, because even though he ate pancakes — boy, did he eat pancakes — he never mowed grass. But there it was.

A weird noise caught my attention. I stood still and cocked my ear to determine if it originated in my suite or not. It was a rhythmic thumping and squeaking, and I shuddered to think I was hearing the Ice Lady shaboinking someone. But no, it didn't quite sound like that.

I stepped toward the bedroom wall and listened again. It was coming from Scott and Scout's room next door. Faintly, I heard Scott laugh and then say, "Okay, that's enough. I know the rules have been a bit lax lately, but I don't think it befits a show dog of your caliber to jump from bed to bed. Now get down and eat your dinner."

I heard two squeaks and one last thump and I pictured Scout's sweet face staring adoringly at Scott, who, I was sure, forgave her misbehavior immediately.

Thinking of Scout eating dinner made my stomach growl and again I kicked myself for not getting some of that Watanabe food when I'd had the chance. Multiple chances, in fact. The minibar was an option, but not a good one. The armoire door hung open, so I closed it when I passed by to dig out the room service menu from the padded three-ring binder of hotel information. After thoroughly perusing it, I settled on clam chowder and a grilled cheese sandwich. I had a million problems, but lactose intolerance wasn't one of them.

I was startled to see that my share of the T-shirts and iron-on patches were folded in a neat stack on the loveseat. Clementine must have seen that I'd forgotten them and asked Jack or housekeeping to deliver them to me. My scalp prickled to think that someone had been in my suite for some reason other than to clean it. I grabbed the three-ring binder again and sidled over to the floor-length curtains at the sliding door. I held the binder as far away from me as possible and used it to flip the curtains away from the wall. Of course nobody was behind them, but it made me feel the teensiest bit better to check. I did the same thing with the shower curtain in the bathroom and the open door into the bedroom.

Certain I was alone, I searched the suite for an electrical outlet so I could charge my phone while I talked to Ozzi. As I passed the armoire, the door had opened again and I knocked my head against it as I felt around the nearby wall. The armoire was where the TV and mini-fridge lived, ferpetesake. No electricity supply? Did they run solely on fervent wishes?

I hadn't been able to find an open outlet the day before either, but I'd thought it was just fatigue. Again, I plugged my phone into the only outlet I could find and sat on the closed lid of the toilet to dial Ozzi. I'd decided while following Jack through the dark bowels of the basement that I'd tell Ozzi everything that was going on, despite what Viv wanted. I needed a second opinion, a voice of reason, a sounding board. However, I resolved not to mention that perhaps I'd been followed to Watanabe's. If I was going to use Ozzi as a sounding board, I needed him to be unemotional. I was emotional enough for the both of us.

I didn't want to dive right into my problems, so we chit-chatted a bit and he told me about the project he'd completed today. I only understood about two-thirds of what he said about his computer job. It always sounded to me like my boyfriend was a hacker, but he'd assured me he was not (despite that time he'd hacked my laptop) and that everything he did was completely legitimate, virtuous, and wholesome.

Well, maybe not everything was wholesome. As I drifted away from Ozzi's words and let his voice wash over me, I suddenly wished I was in his bed. And that we were doing something other than talking.

A loud knock jolted me back to the Pacific Portland Hotel.

"Room service."

"Hang on, Oz. My dinner's here." I put the phone down next to the sink and opened the door.

The waiter waltzed in with a large tray and, without asking where I wanted it, placed it on the short coffee table in front of the loveseat. He handed me the ticket. I quickly calculated the tip, signed it and handed it back, and then escorted him toward the door. As I neared it, I banged my upper arm against the armoire door — hanging open yet again — and then closed it so he wouldn't bump into it.

"Thank you, ma'am."

Really? Another "ma'am"? I had to quit wearing sensible shoes. "Thank *you*. It

207

smells delicious." I wondered who'd made it.

I closed the door behind the waiter and saw the armoire door had eased open for the ten-thousandth time. I picked up the white napkin folded neatly on the tray and tried to loop it around the knobs in an effort to keep them both closed. The knobs were small, the napkin was thick, and I couldn't make it happen. Plus, Ozzi and my dinner awaited. I draped the napkin over the open armoire door. If it was going to hang open, at least I could tie a surrender flag to it.

Grabbing the bowl of chowder with one hand and the plate with the diagonally cut sandwich in the other, I returned to the bathroom to finish my conversation with Ozzi.

"Okay, I'm back." I took a big bite of the sandwich. A sharp crunch, then a delightful combination of hot, gooey cheddar and pepper jack oozed into my mouth. I swallowed, then took a spoonful of chowder. I must have made yummy noises because Ozzi asked, "Are you eating or do you just miss me a lot?"

"I do miss you, but lordy, this chowder is delish!"

"I bet Portland has good chowder. Are

you seeing any of the city?"

"Not much. I took a walk a little while ago but mostly I haven't left the hotel since I got here." After eliciting a solemn — heart-crossing, mother's life and such — promise not to breathe a word of what I was about to tell him, I filled Ozzi in on what was going on with Hanna's kidnapping, the suspicious behavior of everyone, and the new threat hanging over the heads of conference attendees if the kidnappers' demands weren't met by noon Saturday. "And now, all I want to do is figure out a way to cancel this conference without everything backfiring on me — and on everyone else — in a grand and spectacular manner."

"What are your options?"

"I could call in a bomb threat," I suggested.

"I think they call that domestic terrorism."

"Wreck the power supply at the hotel? I know where the basement is. That's probably where everything is."

"Illegal."

"I could give everyone food poisoning at lunch tomorrow."

"Illegal and derivative." Ozzi made that unconscious noise he makes when he's thinking. "Maybe you could make a surprise announcement at lunch tomorrow that the conference is cancelled and everyone needs to clear out immediately."

"Then I'd be on the hook for all of Viv's costs. I'm sure I'd be the first one named in her lawsuit." I finished the last couple of bites of my dinner. "I don't see how I can cancel the conference."

We talked a bit more about how I might be able to convince Viv to cancel or involve the police, but it seemed fairly hopeless. I told Ozzi I needed to call my brother too, and we said our goodbyes. Again, I wished I could do it in person.

When Lance answered my call, I filled him in and told him about the ransom, the ticking clock, and Viv's weirdness about the money. "Will the police get involved if there's embezzlement?" I asked.

"Any evidence?"

"I don't have any."

"Then still no."

"Will the police get involved if . . . someone . . . calls in an anonymous bomb threat, or shuts down the hotel power, or if everyone at the conference gets food poisoning?"

Lance was quiet for a moment. "Yes, but not in the way you want. Don't do any of that, okay?"

"Fine."

"Fine."

"Lance, seriously. Does this sound like a kidnapping?"

"Seriously? No. Why would this girl be kidnapped? Sounds like she disappears regularly. And that ransom amount? Sounds bogus to me. I wouldn't be surprised if it's the amount of a tax lien against Viv."

Lance had verbalized everything I'd been thinking.

After we hung up, I left my phone charging in the bathroom but moved out to the living room. The pile of T-shirts and iron-on logos sat there in a heap, accusing me of neglect. Reluctantly, I knew I wasn't going to solve any mysteries that night and might as well do the ironing Clementine demanded of me.

"There have to be more outlets in this stupid room," I muttered, dropping to my knees. I crawled the perimeter of the living area, indeed seeing the hint of an unreachable outlet behind the armoire. I followed another cord snaking out and traced it to the lamp on the desk. The lamp near the loveseat had a light fixture attached to a wall switch. I crawled into the bedroom. If there wasn't one in there I'd have to iron in the bathroom. I crawled the perimeter there too, and on the last available wall, the one on the far side of the bed, I finally found an open outlet I could reach. Kind of.

I dragged the ironing board from the closet into the center of the bedroom and after several tries, got it set up. It seemed wobbly but it would have to do. I carried it to the side of the bed where the outlet was and tried to slide it into the gap between the bed and the wall. I finally succeeded in wrangling it into place by standing with it on the bed, then lowering it down as if I was a construction crane and it was a load-bearing I-beam in a skyscraper.

To plug in the iron, I had to twist myself into a master yoga position that involved a complicated process of breathing some space into my hips and softening my inner groin. But I finally did it.

As my reward, I dialed up the True Crime channel on the TV in the bedroom and settled in for some *Forensic Files* while I knelt on the bed to iron on those stupid patches. The instructions on the patches advised me to use something called a press cloth. I almost certainly didn't have one, and opted instead for a washcloth from the bathroom.

When the iron was hot, really hot, probably too hot, I placed it on the dry washcloth, which was placed on the iron-on patch, which was placed on the T-shirt, perhaps even in the correct position. It made an alarming sizzly noise but I held it on for thirty seconds, per the instructions. When I pulled off the washcloth, it smoked. The patch had a perfect nubby imprint of the washcloth. It was crooked on the T-shirt and one corner was bent up. Most of it adhered to the shirt, but it wasn't pretty.

"I told her I'm not good at this," I muttered.

I ironed long into the night, kept company by all manner of true crime stories but barely making a dent in my piles of T-shirts, mainly because I had to give myself a mental pep talk before tackling each one. I finally turned off the iron around midnight, my legs tingling with pins and needles, and collapsed into bed. My last T-shirt looked no better than my first.

I thought I'd be able to sleep, since every part of me was exhausted up to and including my spleen, but I was wrong. The body was willing but the brain wouldn't relax.

There's something about the middle of the night that makes everything — and I mean, everything — seem worse than it could ever possibly be.

Glaciers melting. Fires raging. Snipers. Politics.

That freckle? At two in the morning, obviously skin cancer that had metastasized.

That noise? A marauding army coming to drag me off to Camp 1391.

That bill from Mastercard? Debt so deep a backhoe couldn't dig me out.

Misplaced car keys? Clearly dementia.

That gray hair sticking straight out of my chin like a tiny flag? Impending geezerhood, incontinence, and sensible shoes for the rest of my life.

And now, in addition to all that, I had a kidnapping that might or might not be a kidnapping to solve, with someone who really didn't want my help in solving it.

I grabbed my phone from the nightstand and groaned when I saw the time. I held it, gently rolling it from my right hand to my left and back again.

I should call the police and demand they investigate. But what if it wasn't really a kidnapping? What if there wasn't really any ransom? I'd look dumb, they'd look dumb, Viv would look dumb. Or worse, we'd look like criminals. I set the phone back on the nightstand.

But what if it was a kidnapping? I picked up the phone again. Was this just overblown, melodramatic middle-of-the-night angst? Would insisting on an investigation get Hanna killed? The cops would require some kind of evidence, which I didn't have and Viv would deny. I set the phone down.

That freckle was not skin cancer, there was no army near Portland, and I had plenty of time left to take a heroic stand against sensible shoes.

Things would look better in the daylight.

Because they couldn't look worse.

TWELVE

I woke Friday morning with a serious crick in my neck from jolting awake in the wee hours when the ironing board collapsed. The clamor had launched me from my bed like a scud missile. The buckled ironing board could lie there forever for all I cared, slowly becoming buried under eons of dust and neglect. Or the maid could deal with it. Either way, it was dead to me.

Another drizzly, overcast day matched my mood, but I harbored high hopes that pancakes would lighten it and somehow strengthen my resolve not to return to bed. Hiding under the covers remained just on my horizon, but I willed myself to greet the day.

While waiting for the elevator, I hummed the silly advertising jingle for Glu-Pocalypse, the epoxy everyone in the world had in their junk drawer and which had served to implicate me in the murder of my agent. I tried to get the tune out of my mind, but it was insidious, as all good advertising jingles are, and I simply couldn't help myself. I jutted my hips side to side to punctuate the final "Glu-Poc-A-Lypse!"

The elevator dinged on the final syllable. As I stepped inside, so did a man carrying a briefcase. It startled me and freaked me out a bit. He'd come out of nowhere! Had he seen me dancing to music in my head?

"Going down?" My finger hovered above the panel of buttons.

He glanced over. "Same."

With everything going on, I wasn't sure if I was being paranoid or prudent, but I plastered myself against the far side of the elevator.

At least he ignored me instead of turning into one of those creepers standing too close, or worse, telling me I'd be prettier if I smiled. Or worse yet, calling me "ma'am" again.

I felt myself getting angry even though he'd done none of those things. I was so relieved when the elevator opened at the lobby. I guess I should have thanked him for chasing the Glu-Pocalypse song from my head.

When I stepped out, my nose tingled with the scent of wet dog. It wasn't overpowering but floated at the periphery of my senses. More alarming was the large crowd of writers milling about. How did I know they were writers? Because every single person in the lobby not attached to a dog was attached to a notebook, binder, or computer of some kind.

Clementine passed by in today's hipster costume of miniskirt over strategically torn red tights, Uggs, and oversized man's tuxedo shirt cinched with a wide, stretchy, faux animal-print belt. I gave her a wave and a wide smile. She gave me a wave and a grimace. My campaign of earning a smile from her was failing miserably. She rounded up a wayward group of writers and hauled them away, presumably to put them to work.

I found a table at the back of the restaurant, where I desperately wanted to sit with my back toward the lobby, hiding until after my pancakes and coffee kicked in. Unfortunately, my father had impressed upon me at a very tender age the police officer's habit of sitting with their back to a wall so they could survey a room in its entirety. I did the same. Couldn't change even if I wanted to.

The man with the briefcase was being led to a table for four. After he sat, he opened up a newspaper and walled himself off. I thought about Billy the PI doing this same

218

thing and wondered if my mom had sent another mercenary to watch over me. After everything that had happened in the past twenty-four hours, I wouldn't be so cavalier about dismissing his help.

While the server poured my coffee, I ordered pancakes with bacon and two scrambled eggs. The grammatically horrifying menus had disappeared and I crossed my fingers that the hotel had either hired a new chef or Jerry had stepped up his game.

A woman kissed the man with the briefcase and sat down next to him. He set his newspaper aside and gave her his full attention. Clearly not surveilling me.

I was on my own once again, so I considered the events of the last two days.

It was absolutely clear to me now that Hanna's "kidnapping" was nothing of the sort. Everything pointed to Viv's activities rather than Hanna's. I was sure Hanna was perfectly safe kayaking through the Columbia River gorge, or at some music festival in Bolivia, or happily trapped on Tom Sawyer's Island at Disneyland. But I couldn't figure out why Viv thought it was a good idea to manipulate me in whatever nefarious financial plot she was devising. Our friendship was strong, but probably not embezzlement-abetting strong.

Was I her alibi? Scapegoat? Diversion?

And what did she need so much money for, if it wasn't for some bogus ransom? Could her debt to the IRS really be six figures?

Maybe Hanna had gone back to rehab.

My breakfast came and I immediately crunched an entire strip of bacon, practically weeping with joy at its perfection. Maybe today wouldn't be terrible. After wiping delightfully greasy fingers on my napkin, I used the internet browser on my phone to search for the ReTurn a New Leaf website. No costs were listed for their rehab treatment plans. I guessed it was like wondering about that beautiful cashmere sweater in the boutique. If you had to ask, you couldn't afford it.

Many clicks and bites of breakfast later, I gleaned that rehab costs in places like ReTurn a New Leaf — in-patient spa settings on an Oregon beach — could be anywhere from $20,000 to $80,000 per month. Hanna had been in-patient at least twice, and three-month treatments weren't unheard of. I did the math with the help of my calculator app, then felt foolish, since I could certainly have multiplied eighty thousand times three in my head. At the high end, $240,000 for each of her two prior visits would be $480k, a tidy sum. If Hanna was there again, and not in Bolivia or Disneyland, Viv could be looking at $720,000 in total, in addition to her tax problem.

If I could whistle, this would have been the time to let out a low one. Viv could be a million bucks in debt. It made my money problems seem pretty insignificant.

I stabbed the last bite of scrambled egg and almost choked when someone appeared beside me without my noticing. So much for seeing a room in its entirety.

Lily squealed in my ear, "There you are!"

"Um, yeah." I coughed to clear the wayward egg from my throat. "Here I am."

Lily stepped to the side and gesticulated wildly at someone across the restaurant. "Here she is!"

I watched a middle-aged man walk toward me. He'd surely stepped right off the pages of *Guru International Magazine.* Flowing, floor-length, flowered kaftan in a brown-on-beige batik. Matching harem pants, pegged at the ankle. Huarache sandals. Unkempt stubble. Wavy, shoulder-length salt-and-pepper hair parted in the middle. The stone tablets were the only thing missing.

As he walked toward us, Lily could barely contain her excitement and bounced on the balls of her feet while gripping the back of a chair, probably to keep from floating away on the wings of her palpable joy.

When the man reached us, he placed his hands in prayer position and gave a slight bow, directed at Lily, and then gave a second one in my direction. "It's an honor to meet you, Charlemagne Russo. I recognized you from your book covers."

That seemed like a lie, since Lily had directed him over here. I filed it away as a character trait I could use in my writing and took the high road. "Call me Charlee. And you are?"

"Garth. Just Garth."

Ah. Viv's ex. The author all the volunteers went moony over. "Nice to meet you, too."

He sat down without being invited and motioned for Lily to do the same. The waitress refilled my coffee while Lily politely turned over a cup and moved it to the edge of the table to make filling it easier. The waitress tipped the pot toward Garth's cup, but he placed his hand over it. Lily placed her hand over her cup, too, and returned it to its original position.

"Is this coffee fair-trade from sustainable plantations?" Garth asked.

The waitress rolled her eyes. "Yeah, sure."

"And is it brewed with . . . tap water?"

"No, sir. It's brewed with artisanal free-range water collected in a hand-crafted well built with individually hewn stones and hand-dipped, using only the finest eco-friendly biodegradable bamboo cups by children rescued from African orphanages." She glared at him, forcing him to move his hand from the top of his mug with only the power of her world-weary mind.

I made a mental note to overtip her.

Lily didn't wait to be glared at. She picked up her cup and held it out, accepting coffee with a downward cast of her eyes.

"So," I said after the waitress left. "You're one of the local speakers at the conference?"

"Local?" Garth projected his voice, leaned in aggressively, and went full arrogance. "I, dear Charlemagne, am a citizen of the world. I spend some time here in Portland to recharge my batteries and coffers, but the rest of the time I'm in some far-flung country." He sipped his coffee, then set his cup down with a disdainful sneer. "Plus, there are people in Oregon I miss when I'm not here."

"Ah, Viv."

"I come here *despite* Viv's presence."

A look of embarrassment passed over Lily's face, but whether it was for Viv or Garth, or maybe me, I wasn't sure.

"I'm sorry. I assumed that because you

223

spoke at Viv's conference —"

"Viveka and I have a . . . complicated relationship."

This was getting interesting. "But a good one?"

"A complicated one."

"She told me she pays for you to come speak at this conference every year? Even though you've been divorced for so long?"

"Like I said, complicated." He took another sip and made another face, but it seemed like it was more directed at me than the coffee made from icky ol' tap water.

"Where have you been traveling?" Lily asked him.

"Let's see." Garth stroked his beard exactly like I knew he would. "Kathmandu, Kyoto, Caracas." He held up one finger. "And Cartagena." He rolled his *R* from here to Colombia and stretched out the second half of the word exactly like I knew he would.

"On a comedy tour of the world?" I asked.

"Um . . ."

"Everyone knows that words with *K* sounds are the funniest."

"Phuket."

"Excuse me?"

"Phuket."

"You don't need to be so —"

224

"On the Bay of Bengal. Bewitching place."

"Ah."

He toyed with his cup, clearly miffed that we had no follow-up questions, or much interest in his travels.

But I didn't want him to clam up despite how annoying this conversation was. Maybe he was an important key to unlocking the things I didn't understand about Viv. Plus, I really wanted to know whether he was aware that Hanna was his daughter. I knew I couldn't ask, though, so I tried a different approach, something all writers love to talk about. "So, Garth, what do you write?"

Lily giggled, and Garth smiled at her like they shared a secret.

"You mean books?"

I nodded, sipping my perfectly acceptable coffee.

"I haven't written any books. It's all in here." He tapped the side of his head with his index finger.

"Not even travel guides?" I rolled my *R* in solidarity.

"Travel guides are for flabby American tourists who simply want to say they've traveled but aren't willing to step away from their comfortable bourgeoise lives."

"Oh." Jerk. "So you don't write, but you speak every year at a writers' conference?"

He shrugged while smiling at Lily benevolently. "What can I say? I resonate with the masses."

I tried to wrap my brain around that.

Clementine appeared at Garth's side and collected him for a sound check for the opening night banquet. I turned and watched them walk out of the restaurant and through the growing number of writers milling about in the lobby. Garth worked the crowd like he was Jesus — greeting everyone, patting heads, bestowing benedictions, embracing, awarding air kisses. Everyone, men and women alike, visibly swooned.

I turned back to Lily, who had a look of pure rapture on her face. I snapped my fingers in her face until her trance was broken. "What's his speech tonight . . . the Sermon on the Mount?"

"It's called 'The World Is Your Frog, Lick It.' " Lily's glassy eyes sought out Garth. She was a junky in need of a fix.

"Why does he speak at a writers' conference if he's not even a writer?"

"I don't know." She shook her head as if to prevent his aura from taking complete control of her. "But he's so deep I wouldn't be able to understand half of what he wrote anyway."

Something was deep, anyway. Like what

226

I'd stepped in the other day.

Lily stood to leave. "I need to . . . I just want . . ."

"Yes, go." I shooed her away and she scurried off. *Follow him. Hang on his every word. Let him baptize you with his Zen-like arrogance.*

I waved for the check, still wondering about Garth. He was Hanna's father but didn't know it. Or did he? He was traveling all the time. Did the weird ransom amount have something to do with a foreign currency exchange rate?

I began googling the countries and exchange rates he'd mentioned.

Kathmandu, Nepal. One dollar equaled 107.89 Nepalese rupees, so $339,000 would be 36,575,998.2 rupees.

Kyoto, Japan. One dollar equaled 114.13 yen, so $339,000 would be 38,690,578.5 yen.

Caracas, Venezuela. One dollar equaled 9,946.86 Venezuelan bolivars, so $339,000 would be 3,371,986,557 bolivars.

Cartagena, Colombia. One dollar equaled 3,003.76 Colombian pesos, so $339,000 would be 1,018,274,640 pesos.

Absolutely no useful information except that now I knew how to work my currency converter app. What I'd hoped to find was that $339,000 was exactly one million of one of the other currencies.

I had one left, but my currency calculator needed to know the country and I was woefully ignorant about where exactly "fuk-et" was or how to spell it. I typed "Bay of Bengal" into the magic machine I held in my hand and enlarged the map until it told me that Phuket was part of Thailand. It also told me it was pronounced "poo-ket" and not "fuk-et," like Garth had said.

Had he actually traveled there? It didn't seem so, given that he didn't know how to pronounce it. Had he been to any of the places he'd mentioned? If not, where had he been? And why would he lie?

THIRTEEN

I called Viv. "We have to talk about Garth."

"Well, come to the workroom. I'm trying to track down a gluten-free bakery."

"You're at the hotel? Again?" But she'd hung up.

I scribbled my room number on the bill as Brad Pitt walked up.

"Can I join you?" he asked.

"I'm just finished. And now I have work to do. No rest for the weary."

"I thought it was no rest for the wicked."

"Same thing." I hurried away but heard him call out for a rain check. "Maybe!" I flapped one hand over my shoulder.

I dodged writers and agility dogs through the lobby, passing the bow-tied hotel manager, who was chastising a woman with a standard poodle on a leash. He didn't know whether to speak to the dog or the woman, so he switched every other word. "I know it was our mix-up, but we simply can't conduct our business with this cacophony of barking. I must put my foot down."

I didn't hear any barking, but the noise from the writers could be described as a cacophony. I guessed it was easier to keep dogs quiet than writers.

In the hallway near the Columbia Room, I passed the conference registration desk, where volunteers scurried like mad even while attendees waited in line to check in.

"Just give us a little bit longer, folks," one harried woman called out. "We need to finish getting these bags stuffed." She waved her hand at half a dozen volunteers violently throwing pens, notepads, brochures, and bookmarks into the swag bags.

I hurried down the hallway to the Clackamas Room, where more volunteers buzzed around, caroming off tables and each other like a bunch of drunken toddlers. I pulled a folding chair close to Viv and plopped into it. She was scrolling on a laptop through a listing of Portland-area bakeries.

"You're here?" I whispered. "Working on the conference? Not trying to find your daughter? Not cancelling the conference so none of these nice people get murdered? What is wrong with you?"

Viv didn't look up, didn't seem surprised at my outburst. "My therapist says it's my default coping mechanism. I'm sick with worry but not coping well." She stopped and met my eyes with hers. "I think I'm disassociating a bit."

"Ya think?"

"I need to do stuff I have control over, Charlee."

"Like cancelling the conference?"

She returned to the laptop. "I told you I can't do that. Please don't bring it up again."

"Okay, then let's talk about Garth." I tried to control the anger in my voice. "He told me he's been all over the world, but didn't know how to pronounce Phuket."

"So?"

"So he obviously has never been there."

"So?"

"So why would he lie?"

"I told you. Small-time hoodlum."

"That's not what hoodlums do. They steal bikes or hit people over the head for their wallet or leave the liquor store without paying for their six-pack of Pabst. Now you tell me the truth. If Garth wasn't in Thailand or Japan or Venezuela, where was he?"

We had a stare-down, eyes narrowed.

Finally Viv said, "How would I know? You should ask him."

An involuntary gurgle of frustration escaped from deep in my throat. Next thing I knew, all my questions poured out like a gush of water from a rusty pipe that snapped. "How come you didn't get food poisoning, Viv? Why aren't you more worried? Why are you HERE? What are you doing to find Hanna? What's with you and Garth? What were you and Roz arguing about? Tell me about Hanna's rehab. Do you need money for another stint at ReTurn a New Leaf?"

Viv glanced around the room to make sure no one was listening. "How do you know about that?"

"Is she using again?"

She glared at me. "Fine. I'll tell you." She swallowed hard, wet her lips, and spoke quietly. "I went out to the rehab place after I dropped you off from the airport, but Hanna isn't there, or so they said. They've lied to me before, though, at Hanna's request."

"Do you think she's using?" I asked again.

Viv slumped in her seat, eyes welling with tears. "I don't know. She didn't seem to be the last time I saw her."

"Would she have gone to a different place for rehab?"

"No way. She liked them there. They really helped her."

I cocked my head. "If she didn't seem to be using, why did you think she'd gone back out there?"

Viv didn't answer, just rubbed her hands like they ached.

I placed a hand on her forearm and asked, quieter, "What does Roz have to do with Hanna's rehab?"

"What?" Anger flashed across Viv's face and she straightened up. "I don't know. Nothing." She paused, probably trying to make some connection between Roz and the rehab place. Finally she shook her head and pleaded with me. "Please lay off the questions about rehab. People might get the wrong impression."

This had gone far enough. Maybe if I pushed her, I'd have enough evidence to go to the police. "The wrong impression of what? Hanna? Roz? Rehab?" I raised my voice, then glanced around to see which volunteers were listening. No one paid us any attention, lost in their own tasks.

Again, tears sprang to Viv's eyes. "Please, Charlee. I know I asked you to help find Hanna, but now I don't think it's a good idea. Besides, I told you. I have a plan. Could you just help with the conference? Please?" She used a knuckle to staunch a tear that threatened to spill.

233

I didn't know what to do. Clearly, Viv was in over her head with something and didn't want me to know what. But it was equally clear she needed help. I gave her a feeble nod.

She turned back to the computer, then jotted something onto a small notepad. She tore it off, grabbed her purse, and yelled, probably for show, "Found a gluten-free bakery! I'll be back later." Nobody responded, everyone busy with their own crises.

I considered chasing after her, to once again try to talk her into reporting everything to the police, and/or cancelling the conference, and/or asking my unanswered questions again, but I knew it was all pointless. Viv had an agenda and she would not be swayed.

My feeble nod was not a binding agreement. If Viv could have a plan, so could I.

Now I really wanted to know if there was a relationship between Roz and Hanna's rehab place. I used the computer to look up the phone number for ReTurn a New Leaf, jotting it on the pad Viv had left behind. I called and asked for Hanna Lundquist.

The voice on the other end said, "I'm sorry. I don't recognize this number. Who are you?"

I hung up, since they clearly used Caller ID to screen incoming calls.

On a hunch, I went to Roz's office. The light was off and I assumed that meant she hadn't come to work yet. At least I hoped that's what it meant. Using her office phone, I called the number for ReTurn a New Leaf. The person who answered didn't even wait for me to ask to speak to anyone. Simply said, "I'll put you right through, Roz." I listened to the voicemail for the Operations Manager at ReTurn a New Leaf, but I didn't leave a message.

How could this have nothing to do with Hanna?

FOURTEEN

Three hours after I'd stopped sleuthing, we'd finally finished stuffing freebie bags, gotten all the signs listing the weekend's workshops hung outside all the rooms, compiled information for all the faculty and moderators, and gotten the early arrivals checked in for the conference. We did not, however, finish ironing logos onto the T-shirts, but we had enough, and a few to spare, for everyone who wanted one today. When I handed the ones I'd completed to Clementine, she pursed her lips while shooting me a disappointed stink-eye, which only intensified when I suggested we could have the rest done by Sunday lunch, just before everyone left.

But now I needed more coffee, since I wasn't quite nervous or jittery enough. I grabbed a yellow legal pad and headed out to the bottomless hotpot in the lobby. I debated between the paper cup and the ceramic mug. It seemed that the paper cup was bigger, so I chose it, silently promising the environmental gods that I'd reduce and reuse something else to make up for it. I could at least rebel, rebuke, and repent if it would help. I'd certainly refill.

Garth sat in the center of an overstuffed loveseat in the far corner of the lobby, away from the dogs and their trainers. Three women and two men sat at his feet, looking every bit like apostles learning life lessons as they gulped in the words from the Parable of the Hippies.

I let him finish making his point before I interrupted. "Garth, could I speak with you for a minute?"

He gestured with an open palm at the floor next to his chair.

"In private?" No way was I kneeling at his arrogant, patronizing, and presumably unwashed feet.

If narrowed eyes shot bullets, I would have immediately needed to plug ten gaping holes in my chest. But he rubbed the back of the woman closest to him and said, "We'll continue this later."

His disciples stood and brushed themselves off, each one shooting me a silent curse.

I moved closer to the loveseat. Garth

didn't move, fully expecting me to sit at his feet. He was as wacky as his apostles. I smiled and pointed at one end of the seat. With a resigned grunt, he slid over. At the last second before my butt landed, he yanked the flowing edge of his kaftan around him. Clearly he didn't want me to sit on it and trap him into a conversation he might otherwise flee from.

"We'll save you a place, Garth," one of his acolytes called to him.

He turned to her and raised his hand in benediction. "I will look forward to it like a monk awaits nirvana."

Gag.

"What can I do for you, Miss Charlemagne?"

"Charlee."

"Ah, yes. The diminutive."

Uncalled for, but I chose to ignore his comment.

"I'm interested in hearing about your travels. Tell me again where you've been these last few months?"

"Malaysia, Japan, South America. I met the most fascinating character there named El Guapo. He and I —"

"Where were you in Malaysia?"

"Phuket." He pronounced it incorrectly again.

"What is their currency there?"

"Currency?"

"Yes. What's their money called?"

"Are you writing an international banking mystery?" He gave me a condescending smile while he picked some fluff from his kaftan.

"No." I condescended right back, but he was too engrossed in his fluff to notice. "I was thinking they use shillings in Phuket." I pronounced it as he had.

Garth nodded, still plucking at fluff.

"Or do they use bahts?"

"Perhaps for baseball."

"Perhaps, but also for money?"

"They'd need very large wallets." He smiled at his witticism.

He wasn't going to make this easy. I flashed him a smile so sweet and fake it could have been made out of aspartame. "I have to check, otherwise this is going to bug me." I pulled up the currency converter for Thailand on my phone and pointed to where it showed bahts as the currency. "And you should probably know that Phuket is in Thailand, not Malaysia, and it's pronounced poo-ket."

He stood, placed his hands in prayer position, and gave me a slight bow. "If you say so."

As he turned to walk away, I jumped up and held his arm. "You've never been to Phuket, have you? Or to Thailand or Malaysia or Venezuela or Colombia."

His eyes pierced mine until it felt like he was probing my brain. Finally he said, "But I have been to British Columbia."

I pulled him back to the loveseat. "Where were you? Why lie?"

He gave a wide sweep of his arm toward the gaggle of writers knotted across the lobby staring at us. "These people expect me to come here every year and regale them with epic tales of adventure and intrigue. I couldn't . . . wouldn't . . . disappoint them."

"Why would they be disappointed?"

"I don't understand your question."

I tried to be as precise as possible. "Why . . . would the people at the Stumptown Writers' Conference . . . be disappointed . . . if you didn't travel?"

He furrowed his brow. "Because I'm Garth."

"But . . . why?"

"I just am."

"No, not why are you Garth. Why would they care?"

"That I'm Garth? I don't know, child, they just do."

His circular argument made me dizzy. I

240

sat gaping for long enough that he must have believed the conversation was finished. He waved his acolytes back over and they plopped down at his feet, not before giving me another stink-eye for the interruption. I excused myself as they peppered him with questions about his upcoming banquet speech.

Phuket. I was halfway across the lobby before I realized he never gave me any answers.

Where was he, if not traveling? And why lie to me about it?

I found a quiet corner where I could see the dogs running through their paces but couldn't hear the commands from their trainers. I sipped my now-tepid coffee and tried to make sense of my conversation with Garth. Unfortunately, it made no sense. Would his banquet speech tonight be any more coherent?

I supposed it couldn't be any worse than mine would be on Saturday night. Oh my gosh, that was tomorrow. I hadn't really put any brain cells toward ACHIEVE since I'd arrived, what with all the chaos. Plus, I was quite disappointed that the keywords to match the acronym hadn't stuck in my brain or helped me clarify any ideas. I'd really thought that the guy at the airport was on to something. He had made it sound so perfect. So simple. Just think of stuff for each letter, he'd said. You'll remember your entire speech, he'd said. It'll be easy, he'd said.

But again, my speech was the least of my worries. What was I missing about Hanna and Viv? About Jack and saRAH? About Roz and the rehab place? About Garth?

Anything? Everything?

Writing it down would help. I've always thought more lucidly on paper. I turned to a fresh page on my yellow pad and doodled ACHIEVE down the side. I tried to clear my mind of everything, like I do when beginning to brainstorm the plot of a new novel.

I let my tongue droop from my mouth and shook my head like a basset hound until the creaks and pops in my neck quieted.

I opened my eyes only wide enough to get things in the right place. After the capital letters, I added:

A ll
C ops
H ate
I t when
E very
V ictim

E nds

I stared at the way my pen had manifested my subconscious. And stared. And kept staring until I accepted what my brain was telling me to do.

Right or wrong, I had to talk to the police.

But not in the lobby where I might alarm attendees, volunteers, or hotel staff. I topped off my coffee and headed upstairs to my room to make the call.

Halfway to the elevator, I heard Lily's voice calling me. I turned and she caught up to me. Her enthusiastic arms were piled high with enthusiastic papers. "Hi, Charlee!"

I eyed the papers suspiciously. "Hi . . ."

"Remember that storm I told you about? That one headed for our East Coast faculty?" Her bright eyes danced. Because that's a thing enthusiastic people can do to themselves.

A smile slowly spread across my lips. The storm must have veered away. Finally. A problem Mother Nature solved for us. "It didn't hit?"

Lily's grin never faded. "No! It hit! Dumped like two-and-a-half feet of snow!"

My smile faltered but I remained hopeful. "But it didn't close airports or divert the agents and editors?"

"Oh, no! They're completely stuck! Probably won't get out of New York until late tonight or early Saturday morning!"

I gave her the classic palms upturned *are-you-crazy* gesture. "Then what are you so chipper about?"

Lily tilted her head. "Because we have you!"

"I'm not an editor or an agent. I can't do what they do. Besides, I have something important to do."

"It'll have to wait!" Lily spoke in a sing-song voice while handing me the stack of papers from her arms. "You have to do their critiques starting in" — she looked at her watch — "twenty-seven minutes."

"Critiques?"

She nodded with gusto. "The attendees each submitted the first page of a manuscript and they want your input about it."

"My input?"

"Well, no." Lily looked pained. "They wanted the input from industry professionals." Then she brightened. "But they got you!"

I didn't want to do the critiques, but it nonetheless hurt my feelings that Lily didn't consider me an industry professional.

"Lily, I'm not the right person for this job. I'm too blunt. My mind is too scattered this

weekend . . . I'm going to traumatize somebody."

"Don't be silly! You're fantastic! Everyone
will be thrilled you stepped in!"

"I really don't think —" I tried to hand
the manuscript pages back, but she was
smarter than that.

"You're in the Multnomah Room from
one until three, then from three fifteen until
five fifteen in Deschutes." I started to ask
who else was available, but she stopped me
with a perky, "And then you're done!"

I realized arguing was pointless. "Fine." I
only had twenty-four minutes to call the
police and prepare to dash the hopes and
dreams of a room full of writers filled to the
brim with shaky optimism. Scratch that.
Two rooms. "I'll take these upstairs to read.
Where it's quieter."

"Oh, what a great idea! You ARE fantastic!
I'm so glad you agreed!"

Agreed. Riiiight. Saying no to Lily seemed
as likely as saying yes to Brad Pitt.

I got to my room and plopped the pages on
the desk before returning to hang the *Do
Not Disturb* sign out. Housekeeping hadn't
cleaned yet and I didn't want the maid
interrupting my call to the Portland Police.
The stack of manuscripts made me feel

245

guilty. I'd just have each writer read their own first page and improvise a critique during the session. I looked heavenward and whispered, "Please don't let me make a bunch of writers want to quit writing. Or cry."

I moved into the bedroom so I could concentrate on the job at hand without being judged by the stack of manuscripts. Sitting cross-legged in the middle of the bed, I found the number for the Portland Police Department. Before I could dial, I heard the door to my suite open.

I froze in place, a literal sitting duck. I very slowly straightened my legs. Silently scooted off the end of the bed. Tiptoed to the bedroom door. I stood behind it and peeked through the gap of the hinged side. All I could see was the alcove outside the bathroom, where the tall rolling luggage rack was parked. I heard indistinct noises. Was someone going through my things? Searching? For what? It must have something to do with the kidnapping, but what?

Suddenly a blast of dark blue passed by. I gasped and hit my head on the wall.

Somebody else gasped and glass shattered.

"Oh no!" The girl's voice sounded familiar.

I slowly maneuvered my eye to see the

alcove. saRAH knelt, plucking the large shards of a drinking glass off the tile and into her open palm. Next to her was a stack of towels with a set of tiny bottles of lotion, shampoo, and conditioner lying on top.

"Why didn't you knock?" I peered at her from behind the door, through the gap.

She gasped again and dropped the shards, breaking two of the more sizeable ones. She looked into the bedroom, then into the bathroom, then back out toward the living area. She didn't know where I was.

I cautiously stepped from behind the door. She rose and moved into the bathroom, away from me. Without taking my eyes from hers, I slowly squatted and picked up the largest remaining shard of glass and held it like a weapon.

"Why didn't you knock?" I repeated.

She shrank farther into the recesses of the bathroom. "I did knock. Nobody answered."

I looked at the door to the suite, which she'd propped open using the security bolt. Keeping my eyes on her, I stepped over the broken glass in the alcove and sidled toward the living area. The curtains were pulled open all the way now, but everything else looked untouched. Had she been signaling someone, using my curtains?

247

"What were you doing out there?" I asked her.

"I opened the drapes."

"Why?"

"I'm sorry. Did you want them closed?"

"Why'd you open them? Who are you signaling?"

"Signaling? Nobody." She sniveled. "I'm sorry."

"For what?"

"Trying to clean your room?" Sniff, sniff.

"Why would you clean my room when I left out the *Do Not Disturb* sign?"

"People leave it out all the time. But then I get in trouble for not cleaning." She had moved even farther into the bathroom. "Please don't tell."

"Don't tell what?"

"I don't know. I'm not sure what's going on."

I exhaled deeply. "I'm not either." I crossed to the bathroom and dropped the piece of broken glass I held into the trash can.

saRAH jumped, eyes wide as Frisbees.

"Are you sure you're just here to clean?"

She nodded so hard I was afraid her head-wrap would fly across the room.

"Then let's get this cleaned up."

From her housekeeping cart she collected

248

a whisk broom and dustpan, which I held as she swept up all the glass. She insisted on shining a flashlight around the alcove to make sure no slivers remained. I reached for the towels and toiletries to place into the bathroom, but she stopped me.

"Those might have glass in them."

"In the shampoo?"

"Well, on them." She took everything from me and retrieved all new supplies from the cart. After she'd placed them in the bathroom, she asked, "I'm happy to make the bed while I'm here."

When I left that morning, I'd yanked the blankets up like I did at home. "No, that's fine. Everything's fine."

She made no attempt to leave.

"You can go."

She stared at me.

"Really. It's fine."

More staring.

"I won't tell anyone."

She let out a big breath. "Thank you!"

She closed the door behind her, making a show of replacing the *Do Not Disturb* sign on the outside handle.

It all seemed innocent enough, and her explanation was logical, but everything had been so confusing that I didn't exactly know whether to believe her. I guessed I had no choice for the moment.

I barely had time to call the Portland PD now. Those writers would just have to wait.

"Can I speak with a detective?"

"Regarding?"

"A kidnapping."

"Your name?"

I paused, debating if I should go real or fake. "Charlemagne Russo."

"One moment."

"This is Detective Kelly. You're reporting a kidnapping?"

I told him the story as best I could, leaving out everyone's names.

"You didn't hear these alleged phone calls?"

"No."

"This girl is twenty-five?"

"Yes."

"And has disappeared before?"

"Apparently."

"Do you have any evidence that a crime has been committed?"

I was slow to answer, realizing where this conversation was going. "No."

"I don't mean to be rude, Miss Russell —"

I didn't correct his misunderstanding of my name, since this phone call suddenly seemed like a very bad idea. All the possible

outcomes flooded my brain. I'd been thinking all along that the police would fix
everything. A little piece of me kept thinking that Lance was wrong, that as soon as
someone reported the situation, it would be
out of my hands and into the hands of
people who could fix it. Who could do
something. Solve it.

But Detective Kelly's questions followed
the exact path that Lance's had.

Viv and her history of tall tales and money
problems loomed large.

Nobody was worried about Hanna. She
disappeared all the time. She was a twenty-
five-year-old with a history of drug abuse.
That's what we should be worried about.

And Viv? Her unpaid taxes and/or debt
from Hanna's stints in rehab would be
mentally and financially crushing. The bank
account for the Stumptown Writers' Conference would be an attractive cash cow for
anyone in her desperate position.

Detective Kelly was still talking but I
wasn't listening. Embezzlement was a bigger crime than false reporting, but not as
big as kidnapping. My brain whirred and
tripped over itself chasing these facts, or
whatever they were. Then it stopped as suddenly as if I'd flipped a switch.

How dumb could I be? I wore my stupidity like a bright red clown nose, finally seeing myself as Lance and Detective Kelly did. Of course there was no kidnapping, no kidnapper, no ticking clock, nobody going to be killed if the ransom wasn't paid on time.

"— call me if you get any useful information," Detective Kelly finished, then disconnected.

I don't know how long I sat with my phone in my hand, mind flipping and flopping about this kidnapping-that-wasn't. As I sat, though, I felt anger churning the bile in my stomach. My jaw ached from clenching. My knuckles were white around the phone.

Viv had kept telling me to butt out, so it was high time I did. Let her deal with her family and financial drama. It had nothing to do with me. Nothing. I'd promised her I'd help put on this conference, so that's what I'd do. Not for her but for all those enthusiastic, hopeful writers out there, coming to fulfill a dream, or scratch an itch of curiosity, or step into their destiny. That's who deserved my energy.

How could I have been so wrong? Granted, I had plenty of experience being wrong, but that didn't make it any easier or less disconcerting every time it happened. Crucial times. Life-changing times. I'd been clueless about my dad. Clueless about my agent's murder. Clueless about my critique group friends. And now clueless about Viv.

Fiction was so much easier than real life.

A banging on my door jostled me from my anger and self-reproach. I heard Lily's panicked voice. "Charlee! Charlee! They're waiting for you in the critique session! You're late!"

I opened the door and she grabbed my arm. "C'mon!" She yanked me into her crisis and out of my own. I grabbed the stack of manuscripts and raced for the elevator. At least I could remedy this crisis.

When I got to the Multnomah Room, I left thoughts of Hanna and Viv behind while I tried to channel my inner Lily, willing myself to be chipper and positive.

"Hey, everybody!" I spoke extraordinarily loud and scared many of them with my enthusiasm. I modulated to my indoor voice. "Change of plans. I don't know if you heard, but a big snowstorm stranded some of our faculty." At their groans, I added, "I'm sure they'll be here real soon, but for now, I'm taking over this Read and Critique session. I have your pages here, so when I call your name, you'll read from your copy and I'll follow along and make notes on these copies. We only have a few minutes for each of you, so let's get going!"

I called the first name. "James?" No response. I looked around the room. Twenty-seven terrified faces stared at me, but only one had a full-tomato blush going.

I didn't want to let on I was as terrified as they were. I'd have to listen closely to their first page — not even two hundred words — judge what worked and what didn't, and then explain myself, all while being constructive, kind, and brief. How was that even possible?

I nodded toward the blushing middle-aged man and said his name again. His eyes widened like I'd asked him to disrobe. He stammered and sputtered and finally reached for his computer. While it was firing up, I said to the rest of the group, "How 'bout all of you get your pages on your computer or out of your bag or whatever. I don't want to run out of time and have to miss anyone."

Actually, that was exactly what I wanted, but the option seemed unavailable to me at the moment. I didn't want to be responsible for crushing dreams or dashing confidence, and I knew that's exactly what could go down with these on-the-spot critiques. Because it had happened to me.

During my junior year, I paid twenty

bucks for this type of critique of my writing at a conference my college had organized. Even at the time, I knew not to submit anything that wasn't polished, but my naive idea of polished writing was definitely not the same as that held by the brusque New York editor who filleted and gutted both me and my manuscript like it was a Coho salmon. He yanked out my bones and ran a thumb up through my confidence, splattering it onto the floor where it disappeared, oozing into the carpet. I'd watched it fade into nothingness.

In less than three minutes, I knew I'd never be a writer. I sat frozen in my seat, rigid and numb for the rest of the session, then fled to my hotel room where I hibernated, huddled under the covers eating room service nachos and watching bad cable movies on TV for the rest of the conference. I never told anyone.

It took me six months to pick up that manuscript again, and when I reread it, I realized something. It was good. Not great, not perfect, but it had good structure, a roller-coaster plot, intriguing characters, and mostly the right words in mostly the right place. That asshole didn't know anything.

Three weeks later, I submitted a revision

of it to a New Voices contest and won first place.

So as I looked out at the terrified writers before me, I smiled. "Before we get started, I want everyone to take a deep breath." I led them in a cathartic lung exercise. "Now I want you to repeat after me: I am a good writer."

"You are a good writer," they intoned.

"No! Say I . . ."

"I . . ."

"Am a good writer."

Twenty-seven voices repeated.

"My writing may not be perfect, but it can be."

"My writing may not be perfect, but it can be."

"Criticism does not define me. I can take what makes sense and leave the rest."

"Criticism does not define me. I can take what makes sense and leave the rest."

"What that ninny Charlemagne Russo says about my writing is simply her opinion at this particular time on this particular day. She has been known to be wrong. In fact, she's usually wrong. She puts potato chips on her peanut butter sandwiches, so her opinion is dubious at best."

Everyone laughed and visibly relaxed.

"Ready, James?"

After a nod and shuffling of papers, James read the beginning of his science fiction. I was thrilled he did so many things right — intriguing first line that pulled us into the story immediately, no backstory. But he could have grounded us in the setting better, and I pointed out a couple of places where he could do that.

"Thanks," he said. "Maybe I'll have to try chips on my sandwich now."

Next up was a hackneyed young adult story with "frenemies" as the two main characters, of course, fighting over a boy, of course. I had a twinge when I thought about Hanna, saRAH, and Jack, wondering about their story. But the poor girl reading this one reminded me so much of AmyJo from my critique group. I knew that both aspiring writers wanted to ease the way into adulthood for some young reader and teach a tender-but-worthy lesson, but still, fiction for young people shouldn't make that its main goal. I pointed out some language that could be less preachy, which the girl seemed to appreciate.

So far, so good. No tears.

Next up was an overwrought high fantasy, heavy on the world-building and Daddy issues. I didn't know how to express how very terrible it all was. I stared at my page long after she'd finished reading. The hackneyed phrase "the tension was so thick you could cut it with a knife" seemed very appropriate.

Instead of offering a critique to her, I crossed the room. "I love the line about her clothes, but I need to think about this one a little more. Could you please email me the first three chapters? Put 'Stumptown Writers' Critique' in the subject line. I'd like to read more before I formulate an opinion." I wrote my email address on the dry erase board mounted to the wall. "That goes for all of you, by the way. One page is really hard to judge by, so I'd be happy to read more from all of you if you'd like me to. I know you paid for a critique, and if you want one from one of the other faculty members — you know, the industry professionals — I'll see if I can make that happen."

"Even Garth?" someone asked.

Garth? An industry professional? "Sure. Why not."

The author of the fantasy story smiled at me, relieved, perhaps knowing her work wasn't ready for prime time yet. I wanted to tell her that that's part of being a writer, too, but I didn't want to embarrass her.

We plowed through the rest of the submissions. More fantasy, more sci-fi, more young adult and middle grade, romance, memoirs, and mysteries — cozies, historical, and a private investigator premise that pissed me off due to no fault of the writer — read by all sorts of writers. Some overly confident, some so nervous it made me ache on their behalf. I had to restrain myself from wrapping them in a smothering hug and offering cocoa and a binky.

Some excerpts sounded perfect to me, some far from it, but all showed flashes of brilliance, whether plot or character or language or voice.

Five minutes after the session was supposed to end, we finished the last first page.

"I'm impressed with the talent in this room. You are all writers and deserve a round of applause. For your writing and your bravery." They clapped for themselves and each other, beaming and tittering with relief. "I want you all to remember that sometimes — whether you've written one manuscript or one hundred — you have to get the basic story down so you have something to revise. If there's no glob of clay on the pottery wheel, there will never be a ceramic vase. If there's no wool on the loom, there will never be a rug. The trick for a writer, of course, is to surround yourself with readers and writers who can help shape your work until it is a beautiful representation of what you envisioned. If you do nothing else this weekend, network with one another and organize a critique group if you don't have one, either online or in person. Your writing pals will be some of the best instructors you'll ever have."

I was sorry to have to end the session, and I think they were too, even though it had been mentally exhausting for all of us, but I had another session starting in five minutes. Most of the writers followed me to the Deschutes Room.

I walked to the dry erase board and wrote my email. As before, I turned to the wide-eyed, obviously anxious writers already sitting there. I smiled in what I hoped was a calming rather than profoundly creepy way, waiting as the room filled with the attendees streaming in from my previous session. All the chairs were taken. People leaned carefully against the accordion walls or sat in the aisles and wrapped around the front wherever there was empty floor space. I hoisted myself to a sitting position on the table in the front of the room. "So, we're going to do something a little different in this session. Every one of you is going to email me the first three chapters of your manuscript and I will critique it. And if you want a critique from a particular industry professional who got stuck in the storm, email me with their name and I'll try to make that happen, too. But for this session, let's talk about anything on your mind. You can read from your submission if you want, we can chat about the publishing business, you can ask me your burning questions about this crazy writing thing that turns otherwise normal and pleasant people into obsessive word zombies, or whatever else you want to talk about."

Nobody got filleted on my watch.

Again, the session sped by. The attendees thanked me on their way out of the room, some stopping to ask follow-up questions, but eventually everyone trickled out to have a drink with their newfound friends before the opening night banquet.

"Enjoy BarCon!" I called after them. Seasoned conference-goers know that all of the networking and most of the learning comes while hanging out with your tribe at the bar during a conference. Didn't matter if you drank, just that you were there, soaking it all up.

I considered joining them, but exhaustion slapped me silly. I needed to debrief the day to Ozzi, obsess over the weather back east, send snow-melting thoughts to the stranded faculty members, and then perhaps raid my minibar. Maybe not in that order.

The lobby was packed with writers, dogs, and handlers. It felt like I could dip a bucket into the El Niño of words and noises shifting and surging around me and carry them all away with me.

I picked my way through the thinnest part of the mob and saw what had drawn everyone's attention. The agility course had grown more massive and elaborate. In addition to the hassock and pillow hurdles and the tunnel of chairs, there were now bedspreads draping the chairs instead of jackets, creating a more complete tunnel experience for the dogs. There was also an area with eight large, leafy ficus plants pulled from all over the hotel and set about two feet apart. Dogs weaved through them like on a slalom course. In another area there were ironing boards balanced on boxes and crates and used as fulcrums. I watched Scout run up one side of an ironing board, balance a bit in the center, and then use her weight to tip it the other direction so she could run down. She then shimmied through the tunnel, leaped over the hurdles, and ended the course by racing through the slaloms. She skidded to a stop near Scott and pranced around behind him, soaking up the applause.

"She's great!"

I turned to see Brad Pitt next to me. I nodded. "Sure is. I'm glad it's raining so they have to practice in here. Otherwise I never would have believed this."

"I know. I was talking to Jack, the concierge?" When I nodded, he continued. "He told me the hotel is happy to let the dogs practice in here as long as there's no barking and they don't go into the bar or restaurant. He told me almost everyone here is either a dog person or a writer person."

"That's probably true. The dog people won't care and we writers spend all our time in the bar anyway."

"I'm no writer, but I have grown fond of that bar."

"You're not here for the conference?"

"Nope."

"I just assumed, since you're local. Why stay at a hotel in your own town?"

"I'm from the Portland area, but not Portland per se."

"Per se . . . you sure you're not a writer?"

"Almost positive."

"Then you must be a dog guy."

"Nope. Cats, actually. And too many of

263

them. Came with my brother."

"The cats also cramp your style?" Perhaps it was judgy of me, but Brad Pitt seemed too old to have roommates, even if some of them were of the unappreciated feline variety.

He sighed. "Yep."

"Bummer." I was curious about his living arrangements and wanted to ask more, but applause and cheering drowned out any further conversation. We turned our attention back to the dogs.

We watched as a terrier, then Shasta the brindle greyhound, then Scout raced through the obstacle course. A basset hound overturned the tunnel obstacle by getting tangled first in his ears and then in the draped fabric, so all action ceased while someone fixed it. The ears remained unaffected.

"She won the quarterfinals in her class today," Brad said, flicking his chin toward Scout.

"Oh, I was so busy with my own stuff I didn't realize their competition started already. They must have found some arena to use."

"Must have. Scott thinks she might take home some real prize money this weekend. Says it's pretty tall dough, too."

"Good for them," I said. "I know Scott was nervous about the competition."

"Speaking of competition . . . can I buy you dinner?"

"You're relentless, aren't you?" Before I could make an excuse, a blonde pushed through the crowd toward us.

"There you are! I thought you were taking me to dinner." She spoke in a babydoll voice that made my skin crawl. I wanted to shake her and say, *You're a full-grown woman — don't speak like a four-year-ld,* but I didn't want to insult four-year-olds.

"I was just looking for you, darlin'." Brad Pitt took her arm and steered her away, but not before he turned back to wink at me.

I shook my head after them, then negotiated my way to the elevator, ready to be alone in the quiet of my room. I sidestepped a knot of people. As one thanked me for my critique session earlier, I turned toward her but kept walking until I ran solidly into someone who let out a loud "Oof."

"I'm so sorry! I should have been watching — oh, it's you."

Viv stood in front of me rubbing her shoulder. "Where are you going in such a hurry?" she asked.

The sight of her made my earlier anger roar back. My face must have hardened

265

because she stopped rubbing her shoulder and asked, "What?"

"What?" I parroted. "Are you really going to ask me that?"

She pulled me toward the wall, out of the traffic lane. "Charlee, I know you want answers from me, but I don't have any to give. And you've made it abundantly clear you don't like the way I'm handling this, but I'm doing what I think is right. I can't talk about it now. I have things to deal with." She stepped away from me, but I grabbed her arm.

"What kind of things? Lying things? Secret things?" Viv didn't respond, which infuriated me even more. I raised my voice. "Embezzlement things?"

She shook off my grip. "Please keep your voice down." She tried to steer me farther away from the happy lobby people milling about, but I planted my feet.

"I don't know what kind of game you're playing, Viv, but I'm done. Out. Kaput. I'll help with this conference until the end of the weekend, but that's it. We're done. You've put me in the middle of your drama for the very last —"

In the middle of my tirade, Viv quietly pulled out her phone.

"Seriously?" I practically screamed at her

rudeness, unconcerned about drawing attention.

She thrust her phone at me. "Listen to that voicemail."

I put the phone to my ear.

"Mom? I don't know what's happening. He wants me to remind you not to call the police. Do you have the money yet? I'm okay, just scared. I'm blindfolded and don't know where I —"

I heard a man's muffled voice say "That's enough" before the call disconnected.

I felt the color drain from my face. "But . . . the police. Maybe they can trace that call."

Viv shook her head emphatically. "No. I'm not going to call them. I told you they said from the very start they'll hurt her if I do. And you heard her. She said she's okay. I told them I needed to hear her voice before I did anything else. Now I need to get that money."

So she hadn't taken the conference money. Yet. "You need to call the police."

"No."

"Then I will." *But this time I can give them hard evidence.*

Viv stared at me, then plucked the phone from my hand. Finally! My relief turned to horror when I saw that she wasn't calling

267

the police. Instead, she tapped and deleted Hanna's voicemail message.

"No cops, Charlee. I'm going to pay the full ransom and get her back."

She turned away and stomped through the crowd. I stared until she left the building.

Jack appeared from nowhere and asked if I was okay. Blinking at him, I said, "Did Hanna ever respond to you or saRAH on that social media . . . what was it? . . . Sip-Smell?"

"Symwyf. Nope. Neither of us has heard from her."

"Can you check again?"

He pulled out his phone, pushed some buttons, then shook his head. "Nope. Still no messages."

"Can I see?" I held my hand out for his phone. I could tell he didn't want to give it to me, debating in his head if he'd rather have Hanna mad at him or me. I hardened my face, narrowed my eyes, and curled my lips into a snarl, trying to show him I was his biggest nightmare if he didn't hand over that phone.

Whether he was frightened for his life or because I looked dyspeptic didn't matter. He handed over the phone. He showed me his direct message to her, with no reply.

"Let me see her profile."

"Push where it says 'Symwyf me.' That's her profile page."

Nobody should ever be commanded to simwhiff anyone, but that wasn't my concern right now.

It took a moment to load, but when it did, I gasped. A photo of me sitting next to Garth in the hotel lobby filled Hanna's page. There was no caption, and no indication why a photo of Garth was taken or why it was posted there.

Jack leaned over to see what I was staring at so intently.

"Why is this photo of Garth on here?" I asked him.

He cocked his head and pulled the phone closer. "That's a picture of you."

I yanked the phone from him and held it in front of my face while I studied the photo. Garth's presence had captured my attention right away, but I saw that I was centered in the frame, facing straight ahead. Garth was off to the side, with his head slightly turned, perhaps chatting with someone off camera? I tried to think back to my conversation with him. What had been going on?

The acolytes sitting at his feet. I'd interrupted and gotten the stink-eye from them. Garth said something about a monk awaiting nirvana to one of them.

Jack looked at me funny. "Is everything okay?"

Why was someone taking my photo? Was it even a photo of me? Even though I was facing forward and centered in the frame, it was a more interesting photo of Garth. His hair flowed, his kaftan flowed. It could have been someone simply wanting to capture his weird ensemble to show their spouse when they got home, or as a cautionary tale to their kids to stay in school and off drugs. *You don't want to end up wearing a dress in the middle of a mid-price conference hotel in the heart of downtown Portland now, do you, little Johnny?*

Jack touched my elbow and repeated, "Is everything okay?"

Not sure, I nonetheless nodded numbly, handing his phone back.

He didn't look like he believed me but excused himself and left through the same door Viv had.

Who took that picture? Who posted it on Hanna's page? And why? Jack had seemed as surprised as I was to see it there. But maybe it was a ruse. Maybe Jack was involved in this in ways I couldn't even imagine. Was he trying to scare me off? What was in that duffel he'd put in the van?

Why had saRAH really come into my room? Was she planting some kind of evidence? Money? Drugs? And what was Roz the catering manager's interest in ReTurn A New Leaf, Hanna's rehab place?

I called Viv. She picked up immediately. "Are you sure Garth and Hanna don't know about each other?"

"Absolutely sure."

I explained about seeing the photo of Garth and me on Hanna's Symwyf page. "Why do you think that is?"

Viv stammered, trying to land on a coherent sentence. Finally she said, "Maybe it's some subtle threat from the kidnappers, making sure we know they're watching us." She caught her breath. "Charlee! They must know you're involved!"

My mouth went dry. "But maybe it has something to do with Garth."

"Nobody but me and you know he's Hanna's father. He doesn't have anything to do with this."

I didn't share her confidence. "Maybe he's their next target."

Viv and I held silence.

Then she said, "Charlee, I don't know what to tell you. Let me talk to Garth and I'll get back to you." She disconnected.

Answers were elusive. No. Nonexistent.

There was no way I could figure this out. In fiction, I worked backward, beginning with the ending, with all the answers. Nothing like this.

I pushed the elevator button and breathed a sigh when the doors slid shut and I was mercifully alone. I slumped against the wall, berating the reflection I saw slumping back at me. Can't find any answers, can't find Hanna, can't convince Viv to get help from the police, can't help pay the ransom.

My pulse quickened. I straightened. Goose bumps popped on my arms. I don't have very many *AHA!* moments, but this was certainly one of them. *Money.* If I couldn't find Hanna or figure out anything about this mystery, maybe I could at least raise the ransom money without Viv having to embezzle from the conference.

The elevator dinged and I ran to my room, exhaustion gone.

FIFTEEN

With every step, my energy surged.

My plan had become more focused by the time I jabbed the key card in my door. All those places Viv volunteered for — reading to the blind, teaching Sunday School, tutoring — they should be thrilled for a chance to help her.

And that nonprofit. I racked my brain to remember what Clementine had called it. SIN was the acronym. I searched until I found the notepad I'd written the information on. *Strength in Numbers.* It taught groups to fundraise and organize letter-writing campaigns.

That's where I'd start. All those groups that Strength in Numbers had helped should be happy to return the favor, and those people probably had more disposable income than the blind or Sunday School kids did. It would be a modern-day *It's a Wonderful Life* moment, like when all of

Bedford Falls turned out to help George Bailey.

I got a little teary-eyed with the memory, and with the possibility of re-creating such a feel-good moment in real life.

While waiting for my computer to fire up, I saw a stunning sunset spreading sherbet hues across the sky. A bit of sky peeked through the clouds here and there. The rain had stopped, but the furniture on my balcony glistened with droplets. I grabbed a towel and my laptop and headed out there, thrilled to leave the hotel even if it was just three steps onto my balcony. I wiped off the filigree of the wrought-iron bistro table and one chair, opened my computer, and found the website for Strength in Numbers.

As I began to read, mist fell on my head, and I glanced across the balcony to the dry spot in the corner. I grabbed my chair to move out of the rain, which was picking up in intensity now. I tried to lift my chair twice before I remembered that everything was bolted down. Luckily I didn't have a sudden urge to hurl a bistro table through my balcony door.

I reassembled myself back inside the suite, at the desk. I scrolled through the comments and testimonials on all the posts on the SIN website, listing names on my notepad of everyone who had complimented and thanked Viv for her help with their various causes. I put an asterisk by the names of people who'd commented how they couldn't have reached their goals without Viv's help.

One of the project summaries caught my eye when it mentioned the name Greg Pitt. A quick image flashed in my mind of the actor Brad Pitt's less-famous, less-handsome, less-everything brother standing next to him.

I read that a little over three years ago, Greg Pitt, an attorney, had instigated a small-town neighborhood annexation fight. He wanted his neighborhood annexed into the town and finagled a vote on it, costing the town $15,000 that it couldn't afford. Nobody else wanted the annexation because their taxes would have gone up and the quality of their services down. But Greg wanted to live within the town limits so he could run for mayor. A group of neighbors asked if SIN could help them organize their fight to stop Greg and his proposal. With Viv's help, the annexation was ultimately voted down by a huge majority. Greg was made a laughingstock, and during his campaign for annexation he had pulled some stunts and made some claims that got him

275

disbarred. The most egregious of his activities was a series of frivolous lawsuits against his neighbors, presumably to intimidate and shut them up.

According to a comment thread on the website, Greg had to move out of his neighborhood. The specifics were unclear, but I could certainly see how it would be beyond uncomfortable to run into the very people you'd sued, lied to, and tried to hoodwink whenever you met them at the mailboxes or out walking your dog.

Do unto others, like Mom used to say. Or *what goes around comes around to bite you in the ass,* like Grandma used to say.

The last comment in the thread read, "Always remember, for every group SIN and Viveka Lundquist help, there's someone on the other side whose life is ruined. Like mine." It was signed B. Pitt.

Brad Pitt?

My brain buzzed.

It wasn't far-fetched to think the Brad Pitt I'd met here knew Viv. He was hanging around enough. He said he wasn't here for the conference, and he certainly wasn't here with an agility dog. But he'd never actually explained to me why he would be staying at a hotel near his home.

I reread the project summary, thinking

276

about everything Brad Pitt had said over the last few days. I kept circling back to him telling me that his brother had moved in with him and was "cramping his style."

Did Brad's style have anything to do with holding young women for ransom?

The more I thought about it, the more I convinced myself that it was the only answer. The Brad Pitt staying here at the Pacific Portland Hotel — the charming man who kept flirting with me — was a kidnapper.

Otherwise, it was too coincidental. Again I read the pertinent parts of the Strength in Numbers website, taking screenshots of the pages, solidifying my theory with each click.

Brad Pitt was a kidnapper. He said right there in his online comment that Viv had ruined his life, which must be why he targeted Hanna.

I called Viv and cursed loudly when it went straight to voicemail. I left a message that sounded at least 27 percent more hysterical than I wanted. "Call me as soon as you get this."

After about ninety seconds of holding my face in my hands, pressing my fingers into my forehead, I called the Portland Police. A desk sergeant answered. I asked for Detective Kelly, the one I'd spoken to earlier.

"Gone for the day. Can I help?"

"I really need to speak to him."

"And still, he's not here."

"Can you page him?"

"What's this about?"

The commanding tone of voice worked on me and I blurted, "I think Brad Pitt is a kidnapper!"

"And Tom Cruise is an axe murderer. I think I saw that one."

"I'm serious."

"What's your name?"

"Charlemagne Russo."

"Charlemagne?"

"Charlee. Two E's. But —"

"Listen, Charlee with two E's." His voice was less commanding now, and more soothing. "I need you to go look at your TV or your computer or whatever it is you're watching. Press pause. Go ahead. I'll wait."

"I'm not watching TV and you're wasting time. Didn't you hear me say there's a kidnapping?"

"Humor me. When you press pause — have you pressed it? — you'll see everything stops. Brad Pitt and Tom Cruise and everyone else will stop moving and talking. That's how you know it's pretend."

The hypnotic, dulcet tones of his voice made me reach for the TV remote until I realized the TV wasn't even on. It became clear to me that this officer had recently been through some de-escalation training and was practicing his skills on me.

"No, no, no, no, no. I'm not crazy! This is not a movie." My chest heaved and I tried to control my huffing and puffing since I was sure it would not move things in the direction I intended. I held the phone out to my right side and turned my head to the left. I took a huge breath and slowly released it.

"Let me start over." I explained the situation to him as I'd explained to Detective Kelly earlier, but this time I used names. "And please don't tell me there's been no evidence of a crime."

"But there's not."

"But isn't it weird that someone with the same name as that guy in the comments is staying at the very hotel where Viv is having her conference?"

"I thought you said that comment was signed with just the initial B."

"Yeah, but —"

"Hang on."

I heard typing in the background. Finally. Someone was taking a police report. Unless he truly thought I was a nut and had decided to trace this call. Could they trace my cell phone? Here, to the hotel? I heard my heartbeat pulsing in my ears and glanced at the door, expecting a SWAT team to break it down. Exactly like a movie with Brad Pitt and Tom Cruise.

I almost hung up, but then the officer spoke again. "There are 10,376 people in the United States with the last name Pitt."

"But how many in Oregon? Or Portland? Or this hotel? With the first initial *B*?" My voice fetched up at the end and I knew I sounded crazed.

"Ma'am? Charlee with two E's? I think your imagination is running away with you. Tell you what. Why don't you take a nice hot bath and get a good night's sleep. And in the morning, if you still think Brad Pitt has kidnapped someone, you come on in to the station and we'll get someone to talk to you about it."

"Look, mister. I am not crazy." Although I was beginning to doubt it the teensiest bit. "My imagination has not taken over my brain. I know what I know and —"

"And I know that nothing you've said constitutes evidence of any kind of crime. Quit wasting our time. Brad Pitt. Sheesh." The desk sergeant's dulcet tone and de-escalation training had disappeared. He hung up.

I tossed my phone to the loveseat with a bit more fury than planned and stomped back and forth in front of it. A few minutes of cardio raised my heart rate but lowered my resolve.

Was the cop right? Was this all my imagination?

I jumped when I heard voices outside my door. I tiptoed over and put my eye to the peephole in time to see the backs of two men pass by.

When my heart stopped racing, I decided to go about things systematically and pulled out my yellow tablet. Plopping into the desk chair, I listed all the facts I absolutely knew.

Hanna missing.

Hanna's voicemail. Was it really her? I didn't even know what she sounded like.

Viv in debt. I tapped my pen, then added, *I think.*

Jack and saRAH lied about knowing Hanna at first.

saRAH in my room even though Do Not Disturb sign out.

Hanna disappears a lot.

Hanna dating Michael Watanabe.

Watanabe was — perhaps is — a drug dealer.

Roz somehow linked to Hanna's rehab facility.

Chef mysteriously fired.

Garth is Hanna's father. I tapped my pen. *But does he know?*

Photo of me and Garth on Hanna's Symwyf page. Why?

Garth wasn't traveling the world.

Brad Pitt staying in this hotel.

Greg Pitt lost everything due to Viv helping those fighting against him.

B. Pitt's comment that Viv ruined this life.

Then I got stuck. Seriously? That was all I knew?

I drew an angry line bisecting the page. As I read each fact, I wrote a new list underneath it.

Hanna — disappeared herself.

Viv — faked the kidnapping with or without Hanna's help. To raise money?

Jack — angry with Hanna meddling in his love life

saRAH — ditto.

Michael Watanabe — got Hanna hooked again? Faked her kidnapping? Drug deal gone bad?

Roz — involved in drug deal and rehab?

Chef — ??

Brad Pitt — same as B. Pitt? Grudge against Viv?

Greg Pitt — Grudge against Viv?

Garth — found out Viv lied to him all these

years about Hanna?

This new list didn't clarify anything for me. In fact, it made everything fuzzier. But one thing was still as crystal clear as the fish tank in my dentist's swanky office.

I called Viv again. Voicemail. I wanted to call Ozzi and Lance, but I knew they'd both try to talk me out of what I knew I had to do.

I stepped out of the elevator in the lobby and searched the area. The bar was crowded and the dogs and handlers were either performing their tricks or standing around in clumps chatting or sniffing butts. I made a circuit of the lobby, ending on the side near the conference rooms. I didn't see who I was looking for.

I peeked into the ballroom, which had been created by the opening of accordion doors in the Willamette, Columbia, Mount Hood, and Multnomah Rooms. The opening night banquet was well underway. Round tables seating eight were piled high with mostly empty do-it-yourself bowls that once held toppings of bacon, shredded cheddar cheese, chili, chives, and sour cream. The majority of plates were scraped clean of their loaded baked potatoes. Seemed everyone had been pleased with Jerry's culinary offering.

The writers stared raptly at Garth, who was giving his banquet speech in a dressier kaftan than he'd worn earlier. It was midnight blue, imprinted with grinning gold suns and half-moons wearing spectacles, but this kaftan was knee-length. The angled side seams pointed toward his bare feet like two arrows.

I walked the perimeter of the room but still didn't see any sign of Brad Pitt. He wasn't in the lobby or the bar area, nor was he in the banquet room.

Garth rearranged the pointy arrow sleeves of his kaftan before leaning into the microphone. "Let me leave you with an original sonnet and interpretive dance I've written to mark this occasion —"

I was curious but feared I'd carry eternal scars from witnessing such a performance. I hurried for the exit and ran smack into Clementine.

"Did you finish those shirts yet?" she whispered loudly.

"Not yet." I tried to step around her but she planted one lime green stiletto in purple-striped stockings in front of me.

"You promised. We need them."

"Fine," I said. "I'll go right back upstairs and finish."

"You better."

I hurried away and hoped she wasn't watching as I veered to the front desk.

The name tag of the man working was crooked and I tilted my head to read it. "Good evening, Paul." I smiled what I hoped was a friendly looking smile and not something that screamed *UP TO NO GOOD.* "I've forgotten the room number of my friend, Brad Pitt. Can you please refresh my memory?"

"I'm sorry, ma'am. I can't give out guests' room numbers. But let me connect you to his room with the house phone." Paul clattered on his keyboard for a moment, then looked up and said, "We don't have anyone here by that name. You said it was Brad . . . Pitt?"

"Yes." I showed him my teeth again. "Are you sure?"

He checked again, then looked up, apologetic. "I'm sorry. No Brad Pitt here. No Pitts of any kind, in fact."

This time I grinned wide and meant it. "Thanks so much!"

Brad had checked out of the hotel. Either he'd never been involved in the kidnapping or, if he had been, he'd already collected the ransom Viv cobbled together and disappeared with it. I didn't know how she'd raised the money, but however she did it,

285

that was a bridge I could help her cross later. I only knew that Hanna was safe and that I didn't have to go upstairs and call all those people George Bailey–style tonight. I could actually do that ironing I promised Clementine.

I stepped away from the front desk and tried Viv's number again. Still no answer. A knot of unease formed, but just as quickly dissipated. Viv was probably reuniting with Hanna and didn't want to be disturbed.

The crowd surged out of the ballroom and into the lobby, signaling the end of Garth's banquet speech. I hoped everyone would recover from his interpretive dance. Please, dear God, for the love of all that is holy, let him have been wearing undies. Protect those fine, unsuspecting writers.

Clementine saw me standing there and gave me the stink-eye again, so I raced for the elevator to beat the hordes of people wanting to go to their rooms.

I made it to the eighth floor on the first elevator and felt lighter than I'd felt since leaving Colorado. Light enough that even wrestling the ironing board from where it had collapsed between the bed and the wall couldn't even make me cranky.

Sixteen

A smart woman would have remembered the rude awakening of the night before last, when the ironing board took a nosedive in the wee hours. Unfortunately, a smart woman was not staying in my room. I rubbed my elbow where I'd banged it during yet another frantic flight from the Ironing Board Monster.

I checked my phone for any calls or texts that had come in last night while I was sleeping. None. I turned the ringer back on.

That knot of unease returned.

I'd been sure that with Brad Pitt checking out, Hanna's kidnapping, or whatever it was, was over. But still not getting any calls or texts from Viv made me waver. Perhaps Brad Pitt wasn't involved after all? Perhaps I'd jumped the gun?

The *Do Not Disturb* sign remained on the outside of my suite door, and I contemplated removing it since it hadn't previously prevented saRAH from coming in to clean. But when I left, my hands were full of T-shirts and in-room coffee, so I decided to leave the sign swinging on the door handle for all to see. Besides, I had plenty of towels and tiny soaps and shampoos, and I figured the maids had enough to do with all the canine guests.

Juggling the T-shirts piled in the crook of one arm, I was halfway to the elevator when I heard a noise in the hallway behind me. Worried I'd been shedding a trail of shirts, I turned to check. No path of shirts, but I saw a figure duck down behind a maid's cart near my room. The noise I heard hadn't seemed to be the rumble of the cart, but it must have been. I continued toward the elevator.

I pushed the button with my elbow, trying three times before lighting it up. In the process, I lost my tenuous hold on the wobbly pile of T-shirts and they fell into a dismal heap on the floor, blocking one of the doors to the elevator. I knelt and scooped to collect them, raising my head toward movement down the hall, ready to apologize for the mess. Instead, I saw a floral print headwrap duck into my room. saRAH!

Again going to clean my room despite the *Do Not Disturb* sign?

I kicked the T-shirts up against the wall and away from the elevator, then tiptoed back down the hall. My *Do Not Disturb* swung provocatively exactly where I'd left it, visible to everyone walking by. The cleaning cart was three rooms down and my door was shut tight.

I slid my key out of my back pocket and in one deft movement was in my room with the door closed behind me. I stood frozen in the alcove, assessing the situation. A bit too late I realized I could be in danger. That's what happens when my curiosity leaps ahead of common sense.

saRAH was in the bedroom, and apparently hadn't heard me because I heard her unzipping my suitcase. I looked around for a weapon, but the only thing I saw was the telephone on the desk. I tiptoed over and unplugged the handset from the cord. How I longed for my parents' ancient rotary phone. That thing had some heft to it. When you angrily hung up our kitchen phone, the recipient of your ire felt it in their kidneys. This flimsy piece of plastic in my hand might squish a spider, but only if you were lucky and it was mostly dead already.

It was too late to seek out a new weapon, though, because suddenly saRAH came out of the bedroom. I raised the phone like a shield. She took a step back and gasped. I suspected it was because she saw me, not the toy phone.

"Why are you in here?" I waved the phone at her.

"I'm cleaning."

"Then why is your cart not outside?"

"I'm trying to get my steps in."

I checked her wrist. "No Fitbit."

"I use an app on my phone."

"Okay, then why don't you have any cleaning supplies with you or an armful of wet towels or anything?"

"Because I brought in new shampoos and soaps for you."

"Were you putting them in my suitcase?"

Our staring contest lasted either thirty seconds or fourteen years. Couldn't be sure. But she blinked.

"Fine. I'm not here to clean your room."

I waited for further explanation. And waited. "So what exactly are you doing in here?"

saRAH glided to the loveseat and folded her graceful legs under her. "Hanna has disappeared."

"But I thought she —"

"And I'm sure it has something to do with the drugs that you and Michael Watanabe are dealing."

I knew what every single one of those words meant, but strung together like that, the meaning stumped me. "Me? Drugs? Dealing?"

She stared through me until I almost believed that I was in the wrong here.

"I'm not dealing drugs!"

"Then what was in that bag he delivered to you on Thursday?"

"Food. From his restaurant."

"Twice in one day?"

She was tracking my calories? Not cool. I didn't want to admit that I'd had an ulterior reason for wanting to talk to Watanabe. Instead, I patted my belly. "It's so good! I might already be addicted to — oh! You heard me say he got me hooked!"

saRAH nodded. "I was picking up the linens from the restaurant."

"Well, he did get me hooked. On *yakisoba.*"

"Then why didn't you eat it?"

"How do you know I didn't eat it?"

"There was no trash in your room afterward."

"The front desk told me I couldn't bring outside food into the hotel, so to bribe them, I gave it all to them."

"After you took the drugs out."

"No!"

She raised her smug eyebrows.

"That was a trick question," I said. I realized I still held the phone in the air, so I slowly, perhaps even threateningly, lowered it to my side. "Let me ask you a question, and it's not even a trick. Even if I did buy drugs along with my *yakisoba,* what in the world does that have to do with Hanna?" If saRAH was wrong about me dealing drugs, she was probably also wrong about Hanna still being gone.

saRAH thought for a moment, all the while keeping her gaze on my face. "Hanna's been clean for eight months. You and Watanabe show up here at the same time she goes missing. He claims he's delivering food for minimum wage and out of the business. You claim to be a friend of Hanna's mom."

"I am a friend of Hanna's mom. But why would that be suspicious in any way?" This conversation seemed to have as much, if not more, to do with Michael Watanabe as it did with Hanna. Was all of this a jealous ruse to keep me away from Watanabe? Did saRAH think we had something going on? Well, two could play this game. "I saw you with Michael Watanabe by the pool. Does Jack know you're stepping out on him?"

"I'm not!"

"Then what were you doing with him, all

hidden out there?"

She burned me with her laser-like stare before answering. "I was asking him about Hanna."

"What a coincidence. I asked him that, too. But I didn't have to skulk around to do it."

"Coincidences are never just co-incidences," she said.

"Yes they are," I said.

A million examples raced through my mind. Identical twins, separated at birth, who go on to lead essentially the same lives. Norman Mailer, who wrote a novel about a Russian spy only to find out later that a real-life one lived upstairs from him. Mark Twain's dates of birth and death, marked by the appearance of Haley's Comet seventy-four years apart. Three of us on a panel at a writers' conference having the same birthday. Running into my neighbor last year in Santa Fe while at my mom's house for Christmas.

Or coming to Portland the same day that my friend's daughter was kidnapped.

"Coincidences are always coincidences," I said firmly. "And why are you all of a sudden so concerned about Hanna?"

"We're friends," she finally said.

I was unconvinced.

293

She kept staring at me.

"Did you find drugs in my room?"

She quirked her mouth as if the word was painful to say. "No."

"So, by your logic, Watanabe and I are dealing drugs, but you didn't find them. If there are no drugs, I would have had to sell them in, what, thirty-six hours?"

"That's how it's done."

"So maybe you're looking for wads of cash?"

"Yes."

"Did you find any?"

"No. But you interrupted me."

"By all means, continue your search. I'll even help." I waved a magnanimous arm, offering her the living area. I moved to the coffee table, right in front of her, and unscrewed the mouth and ear pieces of the phone's handset. I held it out for her inspection. "No drugs. No cash." She didn't move. "Go ahead. I'm waiting." I stepped toward the bedroom. "Did you finish in my suitcase? Although you must not think too highly of my drug dealer skills if you assume I'd toss everything in there on top of my undies."

We had another staring contest. I lost.

"I didn't buy drugs from Watanabe," I said flatly. "And I can't prove a negative. Ask him." I screwed the phone back together. "I did."

I didn't look at her. "What did he say?"

"That you ordered Japanese food."

"See? Another coincidence. Now get out of here before I tell your boss."

I ushered saRAH out of my room and watched her leave the hallway, ignoring the cleaning cart. A uniformed maid stepped out of the room two doors down and gave me a cheery greeting as she grabbed two drinking glasses and a roll of toilet paper. I sighed and tossed the *Do Not Disturb* sign on the floor inside my suite before heading back to the elevator and my discarded T-shirts.

I saw Jack at the far end of the hall, wheeling a large suitcase for a man carrying a Boston terrier. Jack was performing his concierge routine, just like he'd done for me when I checked in. He set the guest's suitcase down, stepped forward to unlock the door, gave a gentlemanly sweep of his arm to usher the guest in first, and picked up the suitcase to follow. Odd, then, to see him pocket the room key instead of handing it over to the guest, as he'd made a show of doing with me.

It wasn't my room, or my key, but it made me uneasy all the same. First, saRAH's odd beliefs and overwhelming need to search my room, and now Jack acting odd while doing his job. I fought the impulse to crawl into bed and tremble under the covers.

As I passed the open door of the suite, Jack bent down to pet the Boston terrier and didn't see me. I was glad, because I probably would have blurted something about saRAH, and I hadn't quite processed everything yet.

saRAH said that Hanna was still missing. Surely she would have heard if her friend was found. Wouldn't she? And now Viv being AWOL — on the very day the kidnapper had threatened to start whacking attendees?

Perhaps Viv and Hanna were debriefing, or celebrating now that the crisis — whatever it was — was over. But surely she'd call to let me know? Wouldn't she? Viv knew I was worried.

I was glad the pile of T-shirts remained heaped on the floor near the elevator where I'd kicked them. I didn't need an extra dose of Clementine's wrath if I had to tell her the shirts had disappeared. I loaded them into my arms.

Nothing made much sense. Not only were my old questions not answered but it seemed I collected new ones like T-shirts.

By the armful.

I pushed the elevator button, not sure if I wanted Jack to finish his business with the guest and join me or not. I couldn't form an opinion as to whether Jack was behaving mysteriously or normally. Moot point. The elevator door opened. I rode down alone.

When it deposited me in the lobby, I turned toward the restaurant, but a single bark drew my attention. Scout and Scott held court with a handful of people. I recognized some of the writers from yesterday. He was explaining something to them while Scout performed her repertoire of tricks. After each one, he gave her some of the lobby trail mix I'd been snacking on the last few days.

Jack's look of disgust as I'd crunched it that day — and every day since — made more sense now. I placed a hand protectively on my belly. I didn't think anyone had ever died from eating doggie kibble. It was probably healthier for me than most snacks I ate.

I continued on to get some breakfast but had to step aside for a large crowd emerging from a different elevator. As they passed, I yelped and stumbled, gawking as I watched Brad Pitt trailing behind them. He veered toward Scott and Scout when they greeted him.

Dropping my armload of T-shirts on a nearby table, I hurried over.

"Charlee, good morning," Brad Pitt said.

"I thought you —"

"Shh. You're just in time to see Scout's new trick."

Scott pulled a six-foot-tall rolling luggage rack close to our small group. It matched the one in the alcove of my room upstairs: shiny gold rails curved over the top, a carpeted base, and many convenient hooks.

Scout quivered with anticipation.

Scott snapped his fingers and the dog hopped onto the cart. I maneuvered for a better view. Scott waved at Scout and she waved one paw back at him, eliciting laughs from the crowd. Then he said, "Sing, Scout."

And she did. A gloriously goofy cross between howling and bugling.

The watching crowd laughed and cheered, as did people all across the lobby.

But three hotel employees race-walked over, clearly not as charmed by Scout's performance as we were. One was the bow-tied manager.

"Quiet," one of them scolded.

"That's enough," said another.

The manager adjusted his bow tie, turned to Scott, and spoke sternly. "While the Pacific Portland Hotel loves all God's creatures, we cannot tolerate this type of disruption. All my employees have orders to report any noise infraction. We've been more than generous to our four-legged guests, but we must draw the line some-where." He reached a conciliatory hand to pat Scout on the head, but she ducked him.

Good for you, Scout. Just because he wears a spiffy bow tie doesn't make him any less of a meany.

"You're absolutely right," Scott said. "I'm so sorry." To the crowd he said, "We didn't mean to disturb anyone. Forgive us."

Someone nearby said loudly, "Sing, Scout!"

And she did. Still loud, still funny.

I looked around to see who'd pranked the manager and saw Brad Pitt laughing behind his hand.

Scott attached Scout's leash to her collar and commanded, "Quiet," but you could see his attempt at keeping a straight face wasn't completely working. "On that note" — he paused to let the pun sink in — "we'll be off to the morning competition. Wish Scout luck today!"

He led her through the lobby, where

everyone wanted to stop and pet her. Most everyone. A couple of handlers stood off to the side with their dogs, conspicuously withholding their love. Jealousy is an ugly creature, whether in man or beast.

The crowd dispersed, leaving me with Brad Pitt. He offered me the bowl of kibble. "Hungry?"

"I can't believe you let me eat that."

"You seemed to enjoy it. Who am I to judge?"

I took the bowl from him and walked across to a nearby table to set it down. It gave me the few moments I needed to decide to relaunch my plan. I had to ask him if he was the B. Pitt who wrote that comment on the Strength in Numbers website, and, if so, in what way did Viveka Lundquist ruin his life.

"They told me at the desk you checked out," I said.

He waggled his eyebrows at me. "You were looking for me?"

"Yes." Seeing his grin, I quickly added, "No. Not like that."

"Are you sure?"

"Yes!"

"Yes, what?"

"Yes, I'm sure."

"Sure of what?"

"I'm sure it's not like that." I felt my face burn.

"Charlee, I'm sorry. I was just teasing."

I took a breath. He looked fairly adorable standing there like a scolded puppy. My conviction last night that he was somehow tied to Hanna's disappearance seemed so ridiculous this morning. My original assessment that he was a completely harmless flirt made much more sense.

"I'd love to spend the day with you, lovely Charlemagne, but I have things to do." Brad Pitt performed an exaggerated Shakespearean bow. "Love, peace, and bacon grease."

I wrinkled my brow. "Oh, like your brother always says."

I stopped myself from asking what his name really was. I wanted desperately to know, but if he said Greg, I might lose my mind. I needed to form a plan before losing my mind. And if I needed a plan, I needed some time. I couldn't just blurt things. AmyJo would be so proud of me.

"Hey, you want to have breakfast?" I asked.

"I just told you I had things to do." Brad Pitt gave a melodramatic pout. "You never listen to me."

"How about lunch?"

"I won't be back for a while. I have some business to attend to. Might be done around two. Late lunch?"

"Sure. I'll . . . um . . . look for you."

With a wave, he trotted to the revolving door.

I stared after him for a long time. He was using a false name, I felt certain. But he'd shown me his driver's license! I kicked myself for not asking his brother's name. I could have done it in a conversational manner. Did it matter to him if I knew things? Especially if things were clues? Were they clues? Was the charming guy act simply an act? Sociopaths were charming. Narrators could be unreliable. But Brad Pitt wasn't acting unreliable.

Still. That comment on the website. Viv ruined B. Pitt's life? Lost in thought, I chewed my lip until it hurt. He'd said he had important business to attend to this morning . . . right when the ransom was due. Was Brad Pitt the kidnapper after all? The enforcer? Some kind of hit man? Why else would he be hanging around the hotel under an assumed name? And if Brad Pitt *was* an assumed name, perhaps it had nothing to do with the B. Pitt on the website and the whole Greg Pitt annexation situation. Just a coincidence, right?

My litany of what-ifs had spun me up into such a state, it wasn't surprising that I jumped like one of the agility dogs when someone tapped me on the shoulder.

Clementine.

"Do you have those T-shirts?"

I pointed at the pile on the table, then raced for the door to the pool area. The sky was still overcast and drizzly, so I stuck to the covered portico near the building. I called Viv again to find out if Hanna was back. Still no answer. I fumbled through my caller history until I found the number for the Portland Police. I was glad that the desk sergeant from last night didn't answer. I asked for Detective Kelly's direct number, entered it into my contacts, and immediately called him.

"Detective Kelly here."

"Remember when I called the other day about a kidnapping?"

"Sure. The crime with no proof."

"Yes. I guess. But I think I have some now."

"Remind me of your name again?"

"Charlemagne Russo."

"Okay, Ms. Russo. Dazzle me."

"Brad Pitt isn't using his real name at the hotel."

I heard his long exhale and realized I

sounded like a complete nutjob.

"Wait. Let me start over."

"Ms. Russo, I don't know much about the Hollywood scene, but I do know that celebrities never use their real names at hotels. It's how they keep on the down-low."

"Somebody going by the name Brad Pitt is at this hotel, but not using his real name."

I heard Detective Kelly sigh again.

I was just as frustrated. Which made me veer off topic and stamp my foot. "Why do parents name their kids after celebrities?" Way off topic, since Brad Pitt told me he was born before the actor was. Which probably wasn't true anyway.

"Maybe their mom was a fan?"

"This Brad Pitt isn't a celebrity."

"Now, you may not like his work, but that doesn't make him less of a celebrity. I really enjoyed those Jack Reacher movies."

"That was Tom Cruise. But you're missing the point."

"Which is?"

"Brad Pitt isn't using his real name at my hotel!"

After ten seconds of silence, Detective Kelly said, "Ms. Russo. Are you calling to report a crime?"

"Yes. I guess. Maybe."

"Do you have any sort of evidence of a crime?"

I started to speak but he interrupted.

"That doesn't involve Brad Pitt?"

I went through a mental checklist of all the strange behavior over the last few days. "No."

"Then you have a good day now." Click.

I stared at my "call ended" screen. Really? Nobody was the least bit curious that there might be a kidnapping happening right under their noses? Wasn't that their job? It certainly wasn't mine. In fact, none of this was, and yet. . . .

A rustling of bushes made me glance over in time to see saRAH and Michael Watanabe walking past the hot tub, away from me. What was going on with them? She had to be two-timing Jack. I considered a second possibility. What if saRAH was dealing drugs with Watanabe and participated in getting Hanna hooked again? If her suspicion that I was working with him was just a cover story, what was she really doing in my room?

I gasped.

I raced through the lobby and stabbed the elevator button continuously until the doors opened. Why, when you're in a hurry, do elevator doors take an eternity to close?

When they released me on the eighth floor, I flew down the hall to my room. House-keeping had cleaned it already, but I tore it apart.

If saRAH had planted evidence, I was going to find it.

Searching every inch of the room and my belongings turned up nothing unexpected. Except eighty-nine cents in the couch cushions, a pair of sunglasses in the room safe, and a pizza flyer wedged way behind the extra pillows on a shelf in the closet.

No drugs, no wads of cash, no fake ransom note in my handwriting. I had to believe there was no evidence planted in my room. Because the alternative was impossible.

Back downstairs, I made my way toward the Clackamas Room. At least I could check in to see if there were any last conference-related emergencies.

Volunteers manned the registration desk checking in last-minute Saturday morning attendees. Clementine stood ready to hand them their T-shirts. All seemed calm. Same in the workroom, assuming the locked door meant all was well. Hopefully the volunteers had finished their work and were off attending the workshops.

I stared at Clementine calmly distributing the T-shirts. If it was true she'd lit up a joint after she and Billy the PI were in the basement, was it possible she was involved in harder drugs? Was she working with Michael Watanabe to deal drugs? Did she get Hanna hooked again? Maybe Clementine had a vendetta of some kind against Viv. Wasn't it Clementine who'd told me Viv made a lot of people mad? The surly hipster persona would be excellent cover if someone wanted to be inscrutable.

I thought harder about Clementine's story about looking into my dad's history to write some true crime article. Did that even make sense? Was that how writers researched for true crime? I racked my brain to conjure up someone I knew who wrote in that genre but came up empty. I couldn't think who to ask.

In the old days, a couple of months ago, I would have asked my agent. But with Melinda dead and her husband taking over the literary agency, my options were nil there too. I'd gotten off on the wrong foot with her husband and didn't have any confidence in his literary acumen. There was no way he would have developed contacts like that already, and he probably wouldn't tell me if I asked.

Clementine saw me staring at her and cocked her head. If it was anyone else, I would have thought it was an unspoken way to ask if I needed something. Instead it looked more like a challenge. *Keep staring and I will cut you into tiny pieces to put in my Hello Kitty purse,* she was probably thinking.

I turned away, unnerved. Still hadn't even made her smile yet. I was fairly certain I could make her cut me, but what would it take to make her smile?

There was still some time before I had to teach my workshop on dialogue, but I couldn't get that feeling of a ticking clock out of my head. If there really had been a kidnapping, and if Viv didn't get the ransom paid in the next couple of hours and the kidnappers weren't bluffing about killing someone every hour starting at one o'clock, then one of these poor writers was going to get killed.

And all I could do was teach them how to write compelling dialogue.

I meandered in the vague direction of the room where my workshop was to be held. Halfway there I stopped short, the pit of my stomach dropping. I hadn't called any of those people from Viv's SIN website! Last night, when I'd assumed everything was over and done with, I'd abandoned my entire ransom fundraising plan. And now, the day the ransom was due, I wasn't even sure Viv had raised it, and was equally uncertain about Hanna's situation. Viv would have told me by now if they'd been reunited. And she would be here to micro-manage what was left of the conference.

The lobby held one more chance to deter-mine if Brad Pitt was somehow involved in all this. I had a rudimentary plan that began with calmly asking him to tell me more about his brother. Beyond that, it was a bit fuzzier. Even though I'd seen Brad leave earlier, I searched his usual places and didn't find him. He must not have been ly-ing about having business to attend to. As I stood in the bar area contemplating my next move, I saw Bernice, the front desk clerk on duty, pull down the cuffs of her blue blazer and leave her post. The minute she did, Jack jumped up from his desk and hurried toward the meeting rooms.

The way he kept glancing over his shoul-der made it seem like he'd been waiting for her to disappear.

He ducked down the hallway.

I followed him. When I got to the start of the hallway, I peeked around the corner. Dammit. He'd disappeared. I didn't think he would have had time to get all the way to the hidden door to the basement, but maybe he sprinted. Although with all these people milling about, wouldn't that seem weird? Especially when it seemed he wanted to keep his activities on the down-low?

He must have gone to the basement, though, because everything else in these hallways was related to the conference. I edged around the corner, trying to be invisible so nobody would stop me to chat or ask questions about writing or books or the publishing industry. I kept close to the wall farthest from the meeting rooms, watching my feet, letting my hair fall loose across the right side of my face to hide me. Past the Columbia Room. Past Mount Hood.

"Miss Russo? Charlee?"

I pretended I didn't hear the woman's voice behind me as I neared the door of the Deschutes Room.

"Miss Russo? Can I ask you a quick question?"

Someone tapped me on the shoulder at the same time that Jack scurried out of the Clackamas Room and disappeared around the far corner. Now he carried a plastic grocery bag.

I turned. "I'm so sorry, I can't talk right now. Come to my dialogue workshop and we can chat for a bit then."

The woman fumbled with unfolding her schedule, then grabbed me by the upper arm before I could follow Jack. "Is this it? Here? In the Tualatin Room? I wasn't going to go to that one. I was planning on attending Garth's poetry writing workshop." She looked accusingly at me. "Your workshop is at the same time as Garth's."

I shook free of her grasp. Jack was getting away and I was being made second fiddle to Garth. As I hurried around the corner past the workroom, I called back to her, "I'll be around. Find me later."

Of course, Jack was nowhere in sight by now. I pretended to tie my shoe until a group of three conference attendees passed, then grabbed the handle of the hidden door. Tentatively opening it, I saw the short hallway was empty and slipped in, closing the door quietly behind me. I waited until my eyes adjusted to the low light while listening for Jack descending the stairs. Why was there no switch for the fluorescent lights?

I heard nothing but the hum of the behind-the-scenes workings of the hotel. Descending the stairs, I wondered what Jack had taken from the Clackamas Room. Was he a thief? Did he steal one of the volunteer's purses or something? Was it a bag he'd stashed in there earlier? Were plastic bags even legal in ultra-environmentally conscious Portland? I didn't think so.

Everything about Jack's behavior was suspicious. Add this disappearance to what I'd seen with the duffle bag in the parking lot on Thursday and the way he'd pocketed that man's room key this morning, and my spidey senses were tingling.

My knee buckled on the stairs. I wobbled but grabbed the railing before I fell. Was Jack's plastic bag full of ransom money? That would explain his hurry and the worried look on his face as he left his desk. I knew I was almost to the bottom of the stairs because the hallway darkened. Ahead of me lurked Jack and perhaps the solution to this kidnapping. Perhaps even the kidnapper. I clutched the railing.

Behind me was safety.

Before me, a kidnapper.

Kidnapper. Safety. Kidnapper. Safety.

Whenever I watched one of those awful women-in-danger TV movies I invariably yelled at the screen, "Don't be dumb! Why would you go in there? Run! Call for help!" And now here I was, being dumb.

I pressed my hip against the railing for balance and fished out my phone. I opened up my contact list, but there was nobody I could call. They'd all tell me the same thing: "Get out of there."

Detective Kelly wouldn't do anything, especially if he knew it was me. But what if I called 911? I could make an anonymous call and tell them something so they'd come down this stairway. I pushed the three numbers and my phone lit up. A bright red FAILED TO CONNECT filled my screen.

I checked for service and had none today either. Clearly it was a sign for me to get out of there, and I almost made the move back upstairs. Until I heard voices ahead of me. Was it Jack? Who was he talking to?

Suddenly I felt a blush creep up from my toes. Jack was down here to meet saRAH. He'd grabbed some munchies from the workroom and hurried away for a quick tryst. He had to sneak because it wasn't his break time. I pivoted and had my foot on the step when I heard another voice. A man's voice. Deep. Definitely not saRAH's. I pivoted again. They kept talking, so I tiptoed down the steps, thinking I'd stop when I got close enough to hear their conversation. Their murmur was low. I couldn't make out any words.

The stairs ended and I continued down the dim hallway toward the indistinguishable voices. I followed the maze with an ear

313

toward the murmur. Even though I couldn't hear what he was saying, I felt certain that one of the voices belonged to Jack. I continued toward it, formulating a lie if he caught me.

As I passed the storage rooms deep in the bowels of the hotel, the sounds from the voices echoed and bounced above my head. I passed the small room I'd ducked into on my first visit. I glanced inside at the boxes. The skillet I'd thrown at Billy was still on the ground. I picked it up.

I came to a room with the door closed, while all the other doors were wide open. I stopped and had a quick conversation with my gut. It told me Hanna could be hidden in this room. My head told me to run far and fast, to get back upstairs to civilization.

Without permission from my brain, my hand slowly reached for the doorknob. Grabbed. Pushed forward. I listened. Nothing. I stuck my head in. Just a bunch of broken banquet tables and stained chairs. But what was behind the stack of tables? I gripped the skillet tighter.

"Hanna," I whispered.

Nothing.

"Are you in here? I'm a friend of your mom's." I stood frozen, straining to hear the smallest movement.

She wasn't there. I backed out of the room. Jack and the man were still conversing in low tones. I crept toward them. I came to a T intersection and peeked right. Empty.

I peeked left in time to see Jack give the bag to someone in an open doorway. He pulled the door shut and it clicked. He turned my way, and his mouth became thinner and straighter than the blade of a knife. In three strides he was in my face. I didn't even have time to raise the skillet. He stood so close my skin buzzed.

"Charlee." He spoke quietly. "What are you doing down here?"

This time my story bubbled up, unbidden and so speedy I wondered if it was actually true. "I thought I might want to set a scene in my next novel in a place like this. When you brought me down here before, I —"

"What are you doing with that?" He gestured at the pan in my hand.

"Um. Nothing. Just found it by one of the rooms."

He took it from me. "You shouldn't be here." He grabbed my arm and spun me back the way I'd come. "It's not safe."

When I wavered as to which direction to go, he stepped in front of me to lead the way. I had trouble keeping up with him.

"Why isn't it safe?"

He didn't answer right away and I thought maybe he hadn't heard me. But then he said, "Homeless people sometimes find their way in here and camp out in the dark corners." We reached the room with the kitchen storage. He stepped in and placed the skillet on top of one of the boxes, then glanced around the room, studying it like he was taking inventory.

Suddenly he whirled to face me. I could smell the detergent he used to wash his clothes. "People can be violent if they're spooked or cornered."

It sounded more like a threat than a warning. And the rough way he propelled me through the rest of the maze and up the stairs didn't seem like concern for my safety. In fact, he shoved me around a corner, where I ran smack-dab into saRAH coming down the stairs.

Even in the dim light I could tell she was flustered. She didn't look excited to see her boyfriend, like I would expect. Of course, she probably also didn't expect her boyfriend to be with me in the dark basement.

"What are you doing down here?" Jack asked.

"I was . . . looking for you."

I'd heard many lies in my day, and told

316

my share too, so I felt confident this was hogwash. And I'd had enough.

"Were you coming down here to meet Watanabe?" I asked. When saRAH didn't respond, I turned back to Jack. "I think they've got a little hanky-panky going on." Deflecting from any mention of drug dealing seemed prudent in this unnerving passageway.

"How dare you!" saRAH said.

Jack pushed ahead of me on the stairs. "What's she talking about?" he asked saRAH.

"I don't know, Jack."

"You don't know? Really?" I elbowed Jack to the side so I could stand on the same step to confront her. "You don't know why you've been huddled with Michael Watanabe down by the pool area?" I sighed. "Just yank that boyfriend Band-aid off. If Jack's not the right guy for you, then call it quits. Better for both of you."

saRAH took Jack's hand. "Jack, she doesn't know what she's talking about."

"Have you been meeting him in secret?" Jack's voice was low and quiet.

I was surprised when she immediately admitted she had been. The implication dawned on me. "You ARE dealing drugs with him! Did you get Hanna using again?"

"What? What's she saying, saRAH?"

saRAH glared at me. "Why don't you shut up?"

"Why don't you tell us what's going on?" I wished I still had the skillet. It was wobbly, but it was something. Plus it had worked with Billy the PI, although he was a bit of a sissy. saRAH was no sissy.

"Not that it's any of your business, but Michael and I have been trying to find Hanna."

Jack started to speak but she cut him off.

"You and I both know one of us should have heard from her by now. Michael has been checking his contacts and I've been checking with everyone I know."

"Why didn't you say anything?" Jack asked.

"I didn't want to worry you." Even in the bad lighting, I knew she was crying by the way her voice hitched. Jack moved up the stairs to hug her.

I took the opportunity to flee upstairs, mind whirring. Was saRAH that good of an actress? Was she telling the truth? Jack sure seemed to believe her. Had she been on the way downstairs to meet someone? Watanabe?

Reversing my steps, I returned to where they still embraced on the stairs. "saRAH,

318

who were you meeting down here?"

She didn't lift her face from Jack's shoulder so her words were muffled. It sounded like she said, "Trombone Bill." I didn't pursue it because the look Jack shot me felt like it left a mark.

I made my way up the stairs and opened the camouflaged door into the hallway near the Clackamas Room.

"There you are!" Lily squealed when she saw me. "You're late for your dialogue workshop! Hurry!"

All through my presentation about dialogue, my mind wandered to Jack and saRAH, to Clementine and Watanabe, to Brad and Greg Pitt. My workshop notes were not only useful but absolutely necessary. During the question-and-answer time at the end, I had to ask them to repeat every single question. My brain refused to focus. Who was that man with Jack in the basement? What was in that bag Jack carried? Was saRAH telling the truth about Watanabe? Who was Trombone Bill? A real person or the kidnapper's code name?

By the time the workshop ended, I'd convinced myself that the man Jack met, and who saRAH was on her way to meet, must have been Brad Pitt.

As soon as I'd answered last-minute questions from the attendees, I claimed starvation and ditched the hallway for the restaurant, ignoring the fact that the conference lunch was in the opposite direction. Halfway across the lobby, I spied Brad talking to one of the dog handlers and hurried over. I checked the time: 11:35. Brad wasn't supposed to be back until 2:00.

"Hi, Charlee," he said. "Have you met Mr. Sparkles?"

I looked from the terrier to the handler, not sure which one he meant. But I recognized them as the hotel guests from my hallway this morning.

"Mr. Sparkles is my dog," the handler said. "I'm Carl. And Brad here was trying to put a positive spin on the fact that we're already out of the agility contest." He nuzzled the terrier in his arms and spoke in baby talk that insulted every baby, every canine, every dog-lover, and most cats. "Poor widdle Sparkles-poo snapped at the judge during the walk-through before our competition even began."

Brad Pitt turned to me. "I offered to buy them both a drink, but they refused."

"Enough liquor to drown my sorrows would cost you a pretty penny, my fine sir."

"No worries. I foresee a windfall in my

future. Besides, I'd like the company."

Brad Pitt was coming into some money? Like a plastic bag full of cash? But if he did have it, where was it? And if he didn't have the money, then — ohmygosh. He wasn't Trombone Bill. He was the muscle. The hit man. The one getting his hands dirty.

But he looked nothing like a hit man. Not that I knew any, except fictional ones. But still. He wasn't a muscle-bound goon. All that charm would be wasted as a hit man.

If Brad was the kidnapper, he needed the ransom paid soon or he'd make the call to start having people whacked. If he was the kidnapper's hit man, the one doing the whacking, he'd have to receive that call. And if I was completely wrong and he was neither, then I had nothing to worry about. I swallowed hard. Was the business he had to attend to — which supposedly would keep him away until 2:00 — delivering the ransom Jack had given him in the basement? Was it over? Had the ransom been paid and Hanna freed? I checked my phone. Nothing from Viv. I had to know which scenario was real. I couldn't wait much longer if the clock was still ticking.

"I'm afraid I'd be bad company, Brad, and Mr. Sparkles can't be trusted to hold his liquor." Carl nuzzled the dog again. "Isn't that right, Sparky-poo? We came back with the other handlers on lunch break. We might have recovered enough to go back for the rest of the competition later this afternoon." He booped noses with Mr. Sparkles.

The dog, clearly embarrassed by the fuss, growled at him. When that didn't keep Carl out of his face, Mr. Sparkles turned and growled at me. He must have thought as an outsider I'd have special abilities to terminate such outrages.

I took a half-step closer to Brad Pitt. "I'll have a drink with you." Before he could respond, I turned toward Mr. Sparkles and said in a singsong voice, "You shouldn't growl at me. Don't you know who I am? I'm the famous mystery writer, Charlemagne Russo." I figured if this went very, very badly, maybe Carl would remember my name and that he was the last person to see me alive. Just before I went to have a drink with Brad Pitt, kidnapper or hit man.

"You two enjoy yourselves. Mr. Sparkles and I will be revisiting his obedience training." Carl lowered the terrier to the floor.

"We'll be in the bar if you change your mind," Brad Pitt called.

Carl gave a wave and Mr. Sparkles snarled at me as they walked toward the patio area.

Brad Pitt moved in the direction of the

bar, but stopped when he realized I wasn't with him. He circled back to where I stood. "Coming?" he asked.

"I have some nice wine in my minibar."

Seventeen

As Brad Pitt and I walked across the lobby, my stomach churned and my tremor became more pronounced. I was equal parts terror and righteousness. I knew in my gut that Brad held the key to Hanna's disappearance. Unless Jack did. Or Viv. Or Roz. Or Michael Watanabe.

Brad was the only one I could concentrate on right now. I reminded myself that he was either the kidnapper, the muscle, or just a harmless flirt. Regardless, I had a foolproof plan.

Beginning with Clementine. Mr. Sparkles's handler might or might not remember me if all this went sideways, but Clementine would. I saw her leaning against a table sipping from a Hello Kitty thermos. I gestured comically to her to come over to us. She ignored me. I tried again. She puckered up her face and spread her hands, palms up.

"Come here."

Clementine did some loud staring at me. I knew what she was thinking: that if I wanted to talk to her, politeness and protocol dictated I go over there. But I knew if I did, Brad Pitt wouldn't follow. I needed him to hear our conversation. I gestured again.

With body language that would make any recalcitrant teen proud, she heaved herself from the table, made a show of recapping the lid to her thermos, and shuffled over to us.

"Just a sec," I said to Brad Pitt while we waited for her.

When she reached us, I said, "Hey, Clementine. I wanted to tell you that since I don't have anything else on my conference schedule today, I'm going to chill in my room. Upstairs. Maybe do some writing." I desperately hoped she would pick up on the fact that I had to present another workshop that afternoon and deliver my keynote speech tonight. I clenched my fists to control my tremor and hoped she wouldn't call me out on my lie. I purposely avoided mentioning Brad Pitt's name so he wouldn't get suspicious that I was setting him up or leading him into a trap.

"That's why you called me all the way over here," she stated rather than asked.

"Yep. Just wanted you to . . . you know . . . know."

With an eye roll and a tug at her beret, she turned away from us and I was left alone with my plan.

Brad Pitt had been checking his phone while he waited for me, and now he slid it into the pocket of his khakis and smiled at me. "Ready?"

As I'd ever be. "Yeppers." What the hell? Chill, Charlee.

We got to my room and I ushered him inside. I immediately excused myself to the restroom and splashed cold water on my face. When I returned, he was standing behind the loveseat staring out the sliding door. I glanced at the digital clock on the desk: 11:45. Perfect.

"Nice view." He moved toward me. "Nice view in here, too."

His voice was like honey and I had to remind myself of my purpose. And my boyfriend. For a million different reasons, Ozzi would hate this plan. Unless it worked.

I let Brad Pitt grope me long enough to steal his phone and slide it into my back pocket. I couldn't run the risk he'd call for help or make the call to have someone kill Hanna or a conference attendee, since time was almost up. I had to separate him from his phone and keep him sequestered. There was only one place I could do that.

"Slow down, cowboy. We've got all afternoon." I disentangled myself and handed him two hand towels from the bathroom. "The sun's finally out. Go dry off the furniture while I get us some wine."

"Whatever you say. I'm all about the slow and easy."

"And we don't really know each other. Let's talk for a while."

He slid open the patio door and stepped out, one towel in each hand.

I found a demi-bottle of Malbec that looked to hold probably two glasses of wine. I knew I'd be drinking it alone. He glanced at me, grinned, and went back to drying one of the wrought-iron chairs.

As he maneuvered around the patio, the sun played tricks, shooting silvery rays in unnatural directions that made me dizzy and left a sour taste in my mouth.

Now or never.

I placed a plastic cup upside down over the top of the bottle and walked with elaborate nonchalance to the balcony door. As I passed the coffee table in front of the loveseat, I bent my knees to set down the wine. Three seconds later I'd closed and

327

locked the balcony door.

Brad Pitt hadn't noticed. He kept drying the tabletop. The eighth floor was too high for him to jump, and I knew the furniture was bolted down so he couldn't cause mischief out there. We'd both be safe until the police arrived and I could show them the Strength in Numbers website comments.

Sitting on the loveseat with my back to the balcony, I dialed Viv's number over and over until she picked up.

"Good grief, Charlee. What?"

"Is Hanna back yet?"

"No, what —"

"Hang on. We're doing a conference call." Before she could speak, I put her on hold and dialed Detective Kelly. I clicked them both in. "Detective Kelly, it's me, Charlee Russo. I have evidence of that kidnapping I was telling you about. Viv Lundquist is on the line with me. Her daughter, Hanna Lundquist, was the one kidnapped. They want a ransom of $339,000 and said if it's not paid by noon today, they're going to start killing people at the writers' conference at the Pacific Portland Hotel."

"Is that true, Ms. Lundquist?"

Viv didn't miss a beat. "Absolutely not. Charlee is overreacting. She doesn't have kids — do you have kids, Detective?"

"I do."

"Then you know that twenty-five-year-olds have lives of their own and don't have to tell us where they go. Charlee is just overprotective and an imaginative novelist. I'm so sorry she's wasted your time."

Detective Kelly was quiet for a moment, then said, "Ms. Russo, you are this close to being charged with false reporting. Watch yourself." He disconnected.

Viv stayed on the line, though, to shriek at me. "You're going to get Hanna killed! I have this under control. The kidnapper said he'd call me, but not when. That's why I haven't been answering your calls. Time's almost up and if he tried to call just now —" Viv released a strangled cry. "I'm going to offer him all the money from the conference fund. It's not as much as he wanted, but it's all I can get my hands on. Maybe it'll be enough if I promise him the rest later. Besides, he can't expect me to get to the bank on Saturday!"

I heard her take big gulps of air. Quietly I asked, "Viv, has Hanna really been kidnapped, or . . ."

"Or what?"

"Or are you in some sort of financial jam?"

"Oh my god, Charlee. Seriously? How can

you even ask that?"

"Just answer my question, Viv. Because if this is some sort of scam —"

"Scam." The word landed there with a thud.

"Viv, if this is some sort of scam, then I'm in so much trouble." She didn't hear since she'd hung up on me.

Didn't matter, because who was I kidding? I was in so much trouble anyway.

I pulled the phone away from my ear and heard a light tapping on the balcony door.

"Charlee? The door's stuck."

I dropped my phone on the loveseat and turned around. Brad Pitt peered in with his hands cupped around his eyes. When he saw me looking, he quit tapping the glass with his index finger and used it to beckon me over. I reached for the bottle of Malbec on the table, twisted off the screw cap, and tipped a long pull straight from the bottle.

What should I do now? I would have bet my favorite knock-off Ferragamos that Viv would finally have allowed the police to be involved. And that Detective Kelly would have been at least curious when I'd named names. And didn't ransom and a threat of murder rise to the level of professional law enforcement intervention? I hadn't even gotten a chance to talk to them about the

SIN website. Did people really call all the time and bother them like this? Were the police immune to people like me?

I squinched my eyes against Brad Pitt's renewed tapping. It reminded me too much of that poem by Edgar Allen Poe: "Tapping, tapping . . . at my chamber door . . . merely this and nothing more."

So instead of solving Hanna's kidnapping, I'd kidnapped someone of my own.

I picked up the bottle again. Tipped it back. With a sigh, I stood and moved to the sliding door. But instead of unlocking it, I leaned against the back of the loveseat and looked outside. Tipped the bottle again.

Brad Pitt removed his cupped hands from the glass and stepped backward, stumbling over one of the chairs. He tried to move it out of his way a couple of times before squatting to see that it was bolted down. He rested his backside against the wrought-iron table. He smiled at me. "Charlee, it seems you're having second thoughts." He raised his voice so I could hear. "Perfectly understandable. Protecting yourself. I get it. It's hard to be a woman these days. We don't have to do this. I'll leave right away. Please open the door. I'll even let you leave the room first, if that'll make you feel better. Or call housekeeping. Or the concierge. Whatever you need to do to feel safe."

I continued to stare at him and sip from the wine bottle. I had no idea what to do.

Brad Pitt flinched, then looked skyward. Soon, his shirt was spotty with raindrops. He laughed, though. "Hey, it's starting to rain. This might be the funniest thing that's ever happened to me. It'll make a great bar story." He flashed sad puppy eyes as it rained harder.

Had I been wrong about everything? Would a kidnapper be so charming about being locked outside in the rain? Or when he'd been expecting some afternoon delight? I'd really thought that Strength in Numbers information was crucial, but now I wasn't so sure. And I really, really thought Viv would finally see reason and be thankful for the involvement of the police. And I really, really, really thought the police would show at least mild curiosity about my questions and theories.

What about Jack? Were the things I found suspicious about him simply evidence of him doing his job? And Roz could have any number of reasons for being in contact with Hanna's rehab place. And I had nothing but gossip that Michael Watanabe was dealing drugs.

But that didn't mean they couldn't all still

have something to do with Hanna's disappearance.

My head throbbed with indecision and cheap wine.

"Charlee?" Brad Pitt's hands were cupped around his face, pressed to the glass again. "I promise I won't tell anyone about this, if that's what you're worried about. It was all a misunderstanding that we'll laugh about . . . maybe tomorrow. Just a little rendezvous gone cattywampus. C'mon, please?"

I stared at him and drained the bottle. I was already in this much trouble, I might as well take it all the way. I wrapped my palm around the door handle but kept the lock engaged.

"What did you mean when you said you foresaw a windfall in your future?"

Brad Pitt noticed I'd moved and stood directly in front of me. His shirt was soaked through and his hair dripped rain on to his nose. "What?" He cupped his ear.

I raised my voice and repeated myself through the glass.

"When I said what?" He frowned.

I didn't respond this time. Just kept staring. He'd heard me. I could see him thinking.

His face brightened. "Oh. My expense account. I was happy to buy Carl and Mr. Sparkles a drink because I have a high per diem reimbursement."

"What business are you in?"

"I'm a consultant."

"What are you consulting in a hotel full of writers and dog show people? You've been hanging around the hotel but you're not either one."

"Those are the only two choices?"

He had me there. I tried a different line of questioning. "What do you know about an organization called Strength in Numbers?"

Brad Pitt crossed his arms. Stared at his feet. Then met my eyes. "I didn't have anything to do with that lawsuit. It was my brother Greg who was involved in that annexation fiasco." He placed one palm on the glass door.

"Then why was there a comment on the website from B. Pitt?"

"I don't know. It was probably my brother Greg. G. Pitt." He wiped his brow with his arm. "Look at your keyboard. Aren't *G* and *B* next to each other?"

Were they? I moved to my laptop and opened it. Not next to each other, but the *G* was just above the *B*. Oh, fudge. All this because of a typo? My attempt to save Hanna went completely off track because

G. Pitt couldn't type?

My confidence plummeted. Not sure how I'd explain this if he ratted me out to the cops, I flipped the lock to let in this guy who was only guilty of wanting a tryst. I slid the door open to allow the sodden, miserable-looking man back inside.

"Brad, I'm sor—"

He hurled his body at me with a growl.

EIGHTEEN

Brad Pitt pounced on me, but stumbled as he crossed the raised threshold.

I scurried backward, crashing into the loveseat. As I tried to make my way around it, he grabbed my arm and dragged me back. I thrashed and he lost his grip.

I was in front of the loveseat. Brad Pitt leaped over it. I scrambled toward the hallway door. Every time I broke free, he was there to drag me back. I rolled the desk chair between us and thrust it at him like a lion tamer.

Grabbing the room service napkin I'd draped over the armoire cabinet last night, I flung it in his face while dodging under the open cabinet door. He was temporarily blinded and the cabinet smacked him in the face. I was within arm's distance of the suite door and sweet escape when he slammed the rolling chair into me, knocking me off my feet. My shoulder hammered the wall. I sprawled in the alcove, fingernails scrabbling on the tiled floor.

He was between me and my exit. With calm determination he casually reached up and flicked the security bolt across the door.

Nobody was coming in until one of us went out.

I belly-crawled into the bathroom. Heaved myself up using the doorknob, panting, my shoulder screaming for ice. If I could just lock . . . the . . . door. I slammed it but it didn't shut all the way. Brad Pitt had gotten the toe of his boot inside. Rammed it back open. I dove into the tub. He reached for me, grabbing and missing three times as I swam to the opposite end using the craziest non-aquatic stroke ever devised. He grabbed my ankle and held tight, a pit bull on a bone. I thrashed and squirmed, pulling him into the tub. He was a third of the way in at one end while I was a third of the way out at the other, but still he held me tight. I writhed to escape his grasp, pulling on the shower curtain for misguided and ineffective help. The curtain rod crashed down, blanketing us with the Mondrian-designed curtain. Flailing to unwrap himself, he let go of my ankle. Before I oozed over the edge of the tub, I tucked the curtain around him in an attempt to slow him down.

337

There's a reason restraints aren't made from a nylon/polyester blend. It didn't hold him. He lunged for me. I retreated on hands and knees, but I only made it to the alcove outside the bathroom door before he leapt over me and blocked my exit with the six-foot rolling luggage cart.

I shoved it with all my strength, ramming it into him. He crashed into the wall with a loud OOF, then buckled to the floor. I found my feet and pivoted toward the bedroom — where I found my voice, too. I remembered Scout's trick with the luggage cart and how the hotel manager had been adamant about the "No Barking" rule this weekend.

At the top of my lungs I yelled, "Sing, Scout! Sing!" over and over again, banging my fists on the bedroom wall, hoping Scout and Scott were done with their competition and back in their room next door.

I scrambled across the king-sized bed, trying not to disturb the pillows and give away my location. Dropped down to the floor. I landed hard on the collapsed ironing board and clamped a hand over my mouth so I wouldn't cry out in pain. Maybe Brad Pitt would look in the closet first and I could zig the other direction to safety. I held my breath. Listened for the closet door. Silence.

Lack of oxygen made me dizzy and I slowly let out my breath. As I inhaled, I felt movement above me on the bed. Slow. Methodical. Again.

He knew I was down here. Stalking me over the top of the bed.

My shoulder and knee were shrieking at me to move, to get away, but I had nowhere to go. The bed wasn't tall enough for me to go under and I knew I couldn't explode over the top with enough force to knock him out of the way.

I felt for the iron. I was sure it had to be down here somewhere. Every time I reached in a new direction, I felt the bed give with the weight of his crawling. I'd see his face over the edge any second now.

I couldn't find the iron. My only chance was to keep low. If he popped his face over the edge with his Jack Nicholson "Here's Johnny" macabre grin, I could bolt.

Crawling low, looking like a super-slo-mo agility dog, I silently made my way toward the foot of the bed. I twisted my head and saw the comforter fluff with his weight.

Right hand and left knee. Four inches.

Left hand and right knee. Four more.

Ninja-like, four more.

His hand grabbed a fistful of my hair and yanked. I twisted away, flattened on the floor. My hand hit something solid. Fingers slid around the handle. Rising to a kneeling position, I slammed that iron with the full force of my fury into the side of Brad Pitt's face.

He collapsed spread-eagle on the bed. Still gripping the iron, I raced for the doorway shrieking my fool head off. I fumbled with the security bolt, sure he was ready to pounce again despite what I'd done to him.

I finally flung the door open. The *Do Not Disturb* sign flew off the handle and bounced off Scout's snout, causing her to briefly pin her ears back in fear. She then sang like a diva at the crescendo of her operatic debut while I shrieked. Behind her stood Scott, pale, eyes wide, every muscle tensed. The hotel manager and Jack hurried toward us.

Scout bounded into the bedroom, hair raised, ears perked, still singing. Scott followed her.

I quit shrieking but continued to hold the iron in one hand.

The hotel manager wrapped his hands around my biceps. "What's going on? What happened?" When I didn't answer, he shook me, making the water slosh in the steam reservoir of the iron.

I looked at the iron, then at Jack, then back at the manager. Horrified at my tight

340

grip on the weapon, I dropped it at my feet. We watched as it landed with a thud, slowly teetering to one side. I raised a shaky finger and pointed into the bedroom. "Kid . . . napper."

The manager and Jack pushed past me. I hung back at the doorway to the bedroom. Brad Pitt was still knocked out. Growling quietly, Scout stood over him. The manager returned to where I stood.

With halting words, I briefly explained what had happened. "You need to get to Brad Pitt's room. He might have her tied up in there."

The manager looked again at the unconscious man sprawled on the bed, then back to me. The look on his face told me he wasn't sure who or what to believe.

"But he's not checked in under his real name. I don't know which room —" I was flustered. It hadn't occurred to me that I still wouldn't be believed.

"I know which room it is," Jack said. "It's my job." He scurried out.

The manager followed him and I followed the manager. I called over my shoulder to Scott, "Guard him!"

The three of us raced up two flights of stairs to the tenth floor. By the time I made it to the hallway, Jack already had positioned his master key in a door sporting a *Do Not Disturb* sign.

Before he could open it, the manager put his hand on Jack's forearm. "Are you sure?"

Jack looked at me and nodded.

"Wait," the manager said. He reached past Jack and pounded on the door. "Hotel management!" He pounded again. "Hello?" When nobody answered, he stepped back and nodded at Jack.

The door swung open. Cautiously Jack and the manager stepped in. "Hello? Anyone here?"

I tiptoed behind, worried I was wrong and we wouldn't find Hanna. And worried that we would.

Brad Pitt's room looked exactly like mine, but his blackout drapes were pulled and I couldn't see clearly. The manager crept into the living area, Jack to the bedroom. I hit the light panel and flicked every single bulb on, bathing the room in incandescence.

Neither of the men spoke. I broke in half. I'd kidnapped and assaulted an innocent man. He'd attacked me in self-defense. I leaned against the wall and slid to the floor.

As soon as Jack and the manager made a thorough search of this room, I would no doubt be arrested.

A slight rustling of the shower curtain attracted my attention. I glanced toward the others, but they hadn't heard anything. Maybe it was my imagination. Wishful thinking. I crawled across the bathroom to the edge of the tub. When I reached it, I silently counted to three while methodically gathering the shower curtain and my nerves.

When I got to three-and-a-half, three-and-three-quarters . . . four, I yanked my fistful of curtain.

Hanna Lundquist, bound and blindfolded, a room service napkin jammed in her mouth, cowered in the tub. I reached for her. At my touch, she pitched backward, trembling near the faucet.

"It's okay, Hanna. I'm a friend of your mom's. My name's Charlee Russo. I'm here to help."

Jack helped me untie her and get her out of the tub while the manager rattled off apologies to Hanna.

"Call the police," Jack snapped at him, clearly miffed that the manager was worried about potential liability right then rather than Hanna's well-being. He hugged her, and I remembered they were old friends.

At first her arms hung limply at her sides, but then she gripped him tight around the neck.

The manager hurried away, pulling his

phone from his pocket. Jack got Hanna a glass of water, which she drank in one long gulp.

"What else can we get you?" I asked.

"I gotta pee." She shut the bathroom door and Jack and I waited uneasily in the alcove.

She was clearly in shock and I hoped the police would bring paramedics for her. We heard the toilet flush, water in the sink, and then the door flew open.

"Where is that son of a bitch?"

Maybe not shock. Perhaps rage. "He's in my room. Unconscious, last we saw."

In two strides Hanna was in the hallway. "Which way?"

Jack and I exchanged a glance.

"On eight. Let's take the stairs."

I wasn't sure this was a good idea, since the police weren't here and Brad Pitt could be awake now, but it didn't seem like Hanna was stoppable right now.

Jack led the way and I hurried to keep up with them. My shoulder and knee throbbed, but I sure didn't want to miss a minute of whatever was going to happen next.

When we got to my room, the door stood open and Hanna stormed in. I reached the bedroom in time to see her haul off and slug Brad Pitt in the jaw. He'd been sitting on the edge of the bed, Scout snarling at him, and now he flopped backward.

Jack, Scott, and I all exclaimed at the same time.

"Dayum."

"Oh!"

"That's gonna leave a mark."

Scout looked up at Hanna, wagged her tail, and sat at her side.

Hanna rubbed her knuckles and shook some pain from her hand. Seemed she might have some experience with brawls. "Did you call my mom?"

"On it."

When I'd finished talking to Viv, the manager found us and told us the police were on their way.

Jack rubbed Hanna's knuckles.

While we waited for the police and Viv, Scott insisted on getting ice for Hanna's hand and for my shoulder and knee, even though I told him I was fine. It hurt like the dickens, but I didn't want any coddling right now. I needed to focus.

Brad Pitt struggled to sit, then probed his face. I could see discoloration and swelling beginning near his temple. Scout warned him to stay put by growling quietly and shoving her nose into his. Scott called Scout to his side, allowing Brad to sit at the edge of the bed.

I expected a tearful confession to tumble out, but he just sat there.

"Okay, spill. What's all this about? You really were the B. Pitt on that comment on the Strength in Numbers website, weren't you?" I demanded.

He didn't respond.

"So how does that tie in with you whacking writers at Viv's conference?"

He narrowed his eyes. "Whacking?"

"Killing, offing, making them swim with the fishies."

"You watch too many movies. Besides, I told you that was my brother's problem."

We glared at each other. The longer we stared, the angrier I got.

"You have two seconds to tell me why you kidnapped Hanna. She was found tied up in your hotel room —" I gasped. "That first day, you said you had a roommate here at the hotel! And that the roommate was cramping your style. Like your brother cramped your style at home. Hanna was here all along and you weren't the least bit nervous about it! How dare you!"

"How dare me? How dare Viv?"

"What did my mom ever do to you?" Hanna asked.

"I'll tell you what she did . . . just ruined my life, is all." His voice was hard as gravel.

346

"How'd she do that?"

Brad Pitt looked at each one of us in anger. Then his shoulders slumped and he looked at his feet. His voice softened. "I'm sorry, Hanna. I didn't mean to scare you. I wasn't going to hurt you —"

She started to speak but I shook my head to silence her. I didn't want his confession interrupted by an angry outburst from her. Plenty of time for that later.

"What were you trying to do?" I asked.

He sighed. "I wasn't going to hurt her. I only wanted Viv to pay for what she did to my brother . . . and me. When Strength in Numbers helped defeat that annexation proposal my brother was involved in, it ruined him. He lost his law practice, his family, his home. He had to move in with me, which just about ruined me. He couldn't get another job, sunk into a depression. A crowbar wouldn't have pried him off my couch. I needed him out. But the only way to do that was to get him his own place to live. Then he could waste away on his own couch and leave me out of it."

A revelation slowly dawned on me. "The $339,000 ransom. Is that the price of a house?"

He nodded. "A nice one. He'd be happy there. Or as happy as Greg can be. On the

347

other side of Oregon from me."

"You kidnapped me to get my mom to buy your brother a house?" On the last few words, Hanna raised her voice and lunged for Brad Pitt, pushing his shoulders, slamming him flat on the bed.

Jack pulled her away as she drew her fist back to punch him again. When she was safely restrained, Brad Pitt rolled to one elbow.

"Scout." She and I were on the same wavelength and she bounded up on the bed, nose to nose with Brad Pitt. We left Scout to guard him and the rest of us moved to the living room.

Hanna was wobbly and needed to sit. Jack helped her to the loveseat, then got her another glass of water. He reached for something on the floor by the wall. He picked up Brad's phone, which must have landed there in our scuffle.

The manager stood where he could listen for the police. He noticed the armoire cabinet door hanging open and closed it. We all watched while it meandered open again.

I took a deep breath and said to the manager, "I think Jack's involved in this too. I don't think Brad Pitt has told us everything."

Scott moved between Jack and the door, crouching a bit and raising his arms in a karate stance.

Jack didn't move. "What?"

I ignored him and spoke again to the manager. I told him about the duffle bag I saw Jack carry to the hotel van. I told him about Jack pocketing Carl's room key that morning. And I told him how I'd followed Jack as he snuck through the bowels of the hotel and handed a bag to a mystery man in the shadows.

"You mean when I gave a bag of food to Trombone Bill? What does that have to do with anything?"

I turned to Jack. "What about Carl's room key?"

"Who?"

"The guy with Mr. Sparkles."

"You mean the key that didn't work? That one?"

Scott inched away from Jack and looked at me with concern. Neither one of us was sure of what we were doing.

"Okay, then what about that duffle you snuck out for Roz?" I sounded more accusatory than I felt. None of this was going as I'd expected.

The manager groaned. "So it's true. She was stealing from the hotel to start her own restaurant. I didn't want to believe the kitchen staff."

Jack's eyes widened. "She was doing what? I'm so sorry! I didn't know. She told me she was taking that stuff to be cleaned with an ionizer."

"An ionizer?"

"What's that?" I asked.

"Probably nonexistent," Jack said glumly. He slapped his forehead. "I noticed a bunch of kitchen stuff missing from storage the last time I was in the basement." He cut his eyes at me. "I should have realized."

I stared at Jack. So when I'd wondered if he was taking inventory when he'd returned the skillet, that's really what he was doing.

"Did you follow me to Watanabe's in the rain?" I asked him.

"Yes, but not on purpose. It's on my way home."

I stared at him for a bit, then said to the manager, "Maybe he's not involved after all."

There was a commotion in the hallway. Viv rushed in, followed by Lily, Orville, and Clementine. The three of them hung back while Hanna melted into Viv's arms.

saRAH poked her head in the room but hovered in the doorway. Hanna reached out to her and they hugged and cried a bit.

When they moved apart, saRAH stepped over to Jack. He reached for her hand. Hanna raised her eyebrows at their public display of affection. Jack shrugged and Hanna smiled at him.

I asked Viv, "Did you know about Roz's new restaurant?"

She pursed her lips and then turned to the manager, looking him directly in the shoes. "I'm sorry, Dale. I hated what she was doing, but I couldn't convince her to come clean."

"Yeah, I hate when people don't listen to good advice from their friends." I elbowed her.

"I'm sorry about that too," she said. "And some of it we don't really need to discuss ever again, right?"

"Right." I knew she was talking about how she had come this close to embezzling from the conference. Heck, maybe she actually already transferred the funds, but I didn't want to know. "Is that why you were arguing with her in the parking lot?"

"Yeah. Normally it wouldn't have been a big deal, but she wanted me to move the conference to someplace where she could do the food, and she was hounding me for all my other contacts. And for the record, it wasn't a restaurant. She was starting a catering company so she could go all over to set up small satellite companies. She didn't want to have only one place. She wanted to be able to work and play all over Oregon. Go down to Eugene and hang out during the Asian festival, and Ashland for the Shakespeare Festival, and to the mountains and the coast."

I thought back to my search of Roz's office. "Why do you think she wrote 'never again' at the top of the contract for this conference?" My eyes widened at my inadvertent confession that I'd searched Roz's office. In fact, the three items I'd swiped were still in my messenger bag.

My friend raised her eyebrows at me, but she didn't ask the obvious question of how I'd seen the contract. I'm sure she already knew the answer. Luckily, nobody else asked either.

"I know exactly why she wrote that on the contract," Viv said. "When we were hashing out the details, she wanted this to be the last contract between the Pacific Portland Hotel and the Stumptown Writers' Conference. She even showed me some photos of the servers she was interviewing and the kitchens she was looking at renting."

"Of course." I nodded. "The photos I found in her desk." I clamped a hand over my mouth.

"You searched her desk?" the manager asked.

Viv helped deflect his question. "What Roz didn't understand — no matter how many times I told her — was that a conference is so much more than food." She touched the manager on his sleeve. "It's the space here that I like."

I smacked a palm on my forehead. "That's also why she was in touch with the rehab place. She'd have a reason to hang out on the beach for a few days while she set up and serviced their catering contract."

Viv nodded. "When I went there, they gave me the third degree —"

"You went to ReTurn A New Leaf?" Hanna asked.

"I'm sorry, baby." Viv put an arm around her shoulder.

"You thought I was using again." Hanna's voice wasn't much more than a whisper.

"Hanna." I spoke gently. "We just wanted to find you. The important thing is that we did."

"And that you weren't using," Jack said.

"I would have told you if she was using." Garth appeared in the doorway. When he spied Hanna, he rushed to her, brushing Viv aside. "I was so worried when you didn't answer my calls or respond on Symwyf."

Viv's jaw went slack. "You . . . knew?"

I stepped toward Viv to catch her as she wobbled. I eased her into a seat and then turned toward Garth.

"You were the one who posted that photo of me?" I asked.

He scowled at me over the top of Hanna's head. "That" — he paused — "was a photo of *me*. I grabbed a screenshot from a fan's page. I wanted to let Hanna know I was at the conference so she could contact me. I thought maybe she'd lost her phone."

"Since you lied about traveling the world, what's the truth? Where have you been?" I asked him.

"I've been right here. I have an apartment in Beaverton."

Viv gasped and turned toward Hanna, who simply nodded.

I still didn't understand. "How could you not be" — I waved a hand up and down his flowing kaftan — "recognized?"

Garth batted away the excess fabric of his kaftan until he could reach into the back pocket of his matching harem pants. He flipped open his wallet to expose his driver's license photo: clearly his face, but also a tidy man-bun and a buttoned up Oxford shirt with a boring, diagonal-striped tie. Probably khakis and tassled loafers, too.

"You look like you work at a marketing firm."

"Close." He pocketed the wallet. "Attorney's office."

"Viv led me to believe you were a criminal."

"Lots of people think attorneys are criminals."

Nobody laughed at his joke.

"You're an attorney?" I asked.

"Nah. I've had enough run-ins with the law that I don't think they'd take me. I'm a worker's comp investigator for the firm."

"You've been in Oregon all this time?" Viv asked.

"How else could I have breakfast with my daughter every Sunday?"

Incredulous, Viv looked from one to the other. "You knew?"

"That's what fathers and daughters do, Viv," Garth said.

Hanna nodded.

"You knew." The reality slowly settled over Viv's face.

"Of course. But it was clear you didn't want me to know, so Hanna and I decided it was easier on everyone if you thought I was out of the country." Garth crossed the room and touched his forehead to Hanna's, then to Viv's. He held it there. "You should have told me what was going on, Viv. But the important thing is that our daughter is safe."

"She's safe," Viv repeated, hugging Hanna tight as Garth stepped aside.

Garth then touched his forehead to mine. "Thank you for saving Hanna."

"I wish I could take credit, but most of it was dumb luck."

Scott smiled. "I told you stepping in dog poop was lucky."

"It wasn't luck." Clementine pushed away from where she was leaning on the wall, her multitude of plastic beads clattering. She picked up the iron from the floor where I'd dropped it. She used its heft for a few biceps curls. "Seems Charlee *does* know how to use an iron."

Then she did the most remarkable thing. Without prompting, cajoling, begging, or straining any muscles, Clementine smiled. A big, goofy, full-toothed grin. Almost as if she'd known how to do it all along.

Before I could whip out my camera to preserve this remarkable phenomenon, three uniformed police officers arrived, followed by two EMTs and a man wearing a wrinkled shirt and a loosened tie. He flashed a badge and asked, "Which one of you is Charlemagne Russo?"

His authoritative tone made my scalp prickle, but I slowly raised my hand.

He thrust out one hand. "I'm Detective Kelly." Pause. "Gene Kelly." He saw my eyes widen. "My mom was a fan."

NINETEEN

I wiped my mouth after finishing every last bite on my plate at the banquet that night. The people at my table were chattering happily about the conference — who they met, what they learned, gossip they'd heard. Everyone knew the full story of Hanna's kidnapping roughly ten minutes after we rescued her. Something to do with the celebratory haiku Garth had composed about it.

I let the noise from three hundred diners wash over me as I glanced around the room. Garth caught my eye and raised a glass of water in my direction. I wondered if it was artisanal, or at least free-range and cage-free. I raised my glass in return, relieved that everything had worked out.

All the East Coast faculty members had made it to the conference by the time the banquet started. The ones too tardy for their workshops either rescheduled or arranged times to meet with the writers who had requested appointments with them, either here in Portland or by phone the next week.

Even the food managed to be delicious. I spied Jerry standing near the kitchen with his hands behind his back and a self-satisfied grin on his boyish face as the wait staff scurried in and out.

I pushed back from my seat and dropped my napkin over my empty plate before crossing over to him. "You should be proud of yourself. Dinner was delicious."

"Right?" Then he blushed. "I mean, thanks." He leaned toward me. "I had help."

"Clearly." I swept my arm toward a waiter carrying a tray piled high with dirty plates.

"No. I mean, yes. But I want you to meet my Uncle Moe. You made me start thinking differently about my job here. I didn't have to do what Chef did, even if I could. So I called Moe." He held up one finger, and I waited until he returned with an older man wearing a trucker hat emblazoned with the slogan, *Don't make me burn your wiener.* The man also wore a truly magnificent apron.

Uncle Moe noticed me staring at it. "I'm a Tactical Grill Sergeant." He proceeded to give me a tour of the pockets of his camouflage apron. Six cans of beer — four full, two empty — in the ammo belt draped like a bandolier across his chest. Four sauce pockets with colorful bottles peeking out. Spice pockets packed with mysterious shaker tops. Tool pockets holding spatulas, tongs, long forks, and basting brushes. And an easy-to-reach squirt bottle on his hip that he explained was for flare-ups on the grill. His arsenal was easy to deploy as the situation warranted.

I wanted to find out more about Uncle Moe, but I remembered there was one detail I still didn't know. "Why did the chef get fired?"

"Because all those people got food poisoning from him," Jerry explained. "Chef was cutting corners for a long time. That lady in charge" — he indicated Viv in the back of the room — "made a complaint to corporate. She said it was a good thing she didn't eat anything at the meeting or there would have been hell to pay — pardon my French. That won't happen on my watch."

"You mean —"

"Yep," he said proudly. "I got a promotion."

"Good for you, Jerry. Congratulations."

Lily caught my eye and gave me the "okay" sign before climbing the three stairs to the dais.

"That's my cue," I told Jerry, pulling a

nervous face.

"Good luck," he said.

"I'll need it." I returned to my seat while Lily introduced me.

She ran through the list of my credentials and said many complimentary things, politely leaving out how I'd been questioned in the murder of my agent. "Please help me welcome the savior of this conference and all-around good egg, Charlemagne Russo." She gave a gleeful sweep of her arm, and I rose from the table clutching both my phone and my printed notes.

Lily waited until I reached the podium and we shared a brief hug. She whispered, "You're gonna kill 'em!"

I giggled nervously as I organized my notes. While the applause died down, I pushed the button on my phone and proudly noted 98 percent power. I set it to one side, smoothed my papers, and skimmed my title — *ACHIEVE: Seven Things I Know About Writing* — and the notes that reminded me what the acronym stood for.

My hands trembled, so I gripped the sides of the wooden lectern with both hands. The clapping slowly stopped and people shifted in their seats.

I looked at the packed room of writers sitting at banquet tables expectantly awaiting my words of writerly wisdom. Viv and Hanna stood at the back of the room with their arms around each other's waist. Viv gave me an encouraging thumbs-up.

Clementine smiled at me and gave me a good-natured *hurry it up* gesture.

I glanced at my notes again, then lifted my eyes and grinned at the crowd. Shifting my weight, I jutted out my left hip. I let go of the lectern and leaned one elbow on it. "I'm not gonna lie. On Wednesday when I flew in, I was scared to death to give this speech, but a helpful stranger at the airport showed me a simple trick to organize my thoughts. But now, only three days later, that all seems like a lifetime ago. Isn't it fascinating how we humans are capable of compartmentalizing our lives? We expand and contract to allow new information and experiences in. So tonight, after everything that's happened, I want to step back into my writer's box and talk about the seven things I know to be true about writing. I'm using an acronym, ACHIEVE, which you can use too." I slid my notes and phone to the side. I didn't need them. "*A* is for ability, to craft a story. *C* is for courage, to put yourself out there. *H* is for hocus-pocus —"

The audience laughed.

"We all know sometimes you need magic to make it all work right. *I* is for imagination, *E* is for editing, *V* is for voice, and last but definitely important, *E* is for earnings."

A woman whooped her agreement and a man shouted, "That's what I'm talkin' about!"

I explained the seven ideas in more detail and included some helpful hints and funny anecdotes, with a generous dose of encouragement. I ended my speech by reminding them that it wasn't so long ago that I sat where they sat, looking to launch my own career.

"If I can do it, you can do it."

The room erupted in thunderous applause. I wiped a tear before Lily jumped to the stage to present me with a leather notebook tied with a pretty bow.

The next day, I walked through the Portland airport talking to Ozzi on my phone. I'd caught him up on everything after the banquet. Today was a bit more subdued, given my attendance at BarCon last night. People had wanted to buy me drinks. Lots of drinks. How could I refuse them that pleasure?

"So I'm through security and almost to my gate. Looks like the flight will be on time. You'll be at DIA to pick me up?"

"Absolutely. Can't wait to see you. I have a surprise for you." He made some sexy noises in my ear.

"Is it ice cream? You know how I love that salted caramel swirl," I teased.

"Correction. I'll see you in Denver with two surprises. I love you, Charlee. I'm glad you're safe."

"Love you more. See you in three hours and fifty-two minutes."

I dropped my phone into my bag and wandered around, looking for something to eat before I got on the plane. One kiosk looked interesting, but there was a man in line blocking my view of the menu board. He picked up his order and turned around. It was the man who'd helped me with the acronym for my speech.

"Sir Robin of Locksley! Pip, pip, cheerio, and all that rot."

He frowned, then grinned in recognition. "Charlemagne Russo! Fancy meeting you here today."

"What? No accent?"

"Nope. I'm just plain ol' Ricky today. Too exhausted to pretend."

"So I take it the wedding was fun?"

"A little too much fun." Ricky rubbed his head with his free hand. "And it cost me a small fortune." He tipped his head toward some seating nearby. "Care to join me?"

"Yeah, let me grab a sandwich."

When I sat down, he said, "I'm dying to know. How did your speech go?"

"I don't even know where to start." I told him the entire story of the conference while we ate.

When I finished, he stared at me, stunned.

I laughed at the incredulous expression on his face. "The things we do for friends, right?"

ACKNOWLEDGMENTS

I've been haunting writers' conferences since 1999, often as a member of the faculty. While they've never been quite like the fictional Stumptown Conference, they are always filled with characters, laughter, and learning. BarCon, you'll be happy to know, is a real thing. After-hours at the hotel bar is when so much magic happens. If you're a writer, aspiring or otherwise, I encourage you to find a conference to attend. Go hang out with your tribe. And if they've double-booked a dog show, you better send me photos!

If you're strictly a reader, there are conferences for you too! If you've never attended Left Coast Crime, Malice Domestic, or Bouchercon, put them on your bucket list. Enjoy hanging out with your favorite authors, meeting new ones, and attending panels on all facets of crime fiction. Don't forget to add BarCon to your schedule there, too!

Subscribe to Becky Clark's *So-Seldom-It's-Shameful* News for contests, giveaways, sneak peeks, and other behind-the-scenes shenanigans at beckyclarkbooks.com.

Be the first to know when Becky Clark's books are available or on sale.
Follow her at:
BookBub
Goodreads
Amazon
Facebook

ABOUT THE AUTHOR

A highly functioning chocoholic, **Becky Clark** is the seventh of eight kids, which explains both her insatiable need for attention and her atrocious table manners. She likes to read funny books so it felt natural to write them, too. She's a native of Colorado, which is where she lives with her indulgent husband and quirky dog.

Becky loves to present workshops to writing groups and is a founding member of the Colorado Chapter of Sisters in Crime. Visit her on Facebook and at BeckyClarkBooks .com for all sorts of shenanigans.

The employees of Thorndike Press hope you have enjoyed this Large Print book. All our Thorndike, Wheeler, and Kennebec Large Print titles are designed for easy reading, and all our books are made to last. Other Thorndike Press Large Print books are available at your library, through selected bookstores, or directly from us.

For information about titles, please call:
  (800) 223-1244

or visit our website at:
  gale.com/thorndike

To share your comments, please write:
  Publisher
  Thorndike Press
  10 Water St., Suite 310
  Waterville, ME 04901